# ADRIFT

## NEW YORK TIMES BESTSELLING AUTHOR
# JANA DELEON

Still Water

*"The water tells none of its secrets." – Nikos Engonopoulos*

# CHAPTER ONE

KATARINA PETRAS HURRIED out of the university library and down the sidewalk, glancing at the big clock tower as she went. She was going to be late for dinner again, which meant another lecture from her mother and days of disapproving frowns from her father. But once she'd started researching her term paper, she'd gotten wrapped up in the details and had lost track of time. The silver lining was that she had almost everything she needed to get started writing the paper.

Not that it would matter to her parents.

Her parents had immigrated from Czechoslovakia right after their marriage, looking for a better life for themselves and their future children, which had ultimately consisted only of Katarina. But they still clung hard to some of the old ways of the tiny village they were from, and one of those was the belief that their daughter needed a good husband, not a good education. Fortunately, Katarina had been an excellent student and an even better long-distance runner and had gotten scholarship money for college. Her parents wouldn't pay, even though they could afford to, but at least they'd finally agreed to let her live at home while she attended school and worked part-time.

Of course, their 'approval' had come with stipulations. Curfew was still 10:00 p.m. weekdays and midnight on weekends, just like high school. Dinner at home every Sunday night at 6:00 p.m. was her mother's additional stipulation, and it might as well have been carved in stone. Dating Josef Danek, son of her father's boss, was her father's implied request, even though her mother had voiced her disapproval of the idea more than once.

Her father hadn't come straight out and said she was required to date Josef, but when her mother was out of earshot, he'd pushed his boss's son so hard that Katarina realized dating him was probably the key to keeping her father happy. And she needed to keep her father happy. Especially since he was the one who brought home the money that paid for the house she needed to live in and the car she needed for school and work. Two more years, she kept telling herself. Two more years until freedom.

The enormous price of that freedom was dating Josef.

When her father had first started hinting, she'd lucked out as Josef had been seeing another woman. She'd managed almost two years of school before Josef and his girlfriend broke up and her father had managed to get Katarina on Josef's radar. They'd gone out several times now—without her mother's knowledge, per her father's instruction—but Katarina was certain she would never have feelings for Josef. Not positive ones, anyway. If she was being honest, she didn't like him all that much as a person, much less as a romantic interest.

His father, Ivan, was a wealthy businessman who spoiled

2

Josef, giving him plenty of cash and not a lot of responsibility. At least, it appeared to Katarina that Josef had no shortage of money or free time. When she'd asked him about his work, he was so vague that she had to assume he didn't have regular duties, much less a set work schedule. That also meant that he had plenty of time to pursue Katarina, and that was becoming a problem.

So far, she'd managed to avoid the most aggressive of his advances, and given that her father worked for Josef's father, he hadn't pushed as hard as he probably would have if there had been no business connections. But they were fast approaching a crossroads where Katarina was going to have to tell Josef she didn't wish to see him any longer, and she was afraid of what that would do to her college plans.

She worked as much as she could at a local clothes shop and put back every dime she could to prepare for this eventuality, but she didn't have enough to pay rent and living expenses in LA. To add to the pile, Josef's father owned the store where she worked. And since her parents provided her car, that was one more thing she didn't have the funds to replace. Public transportation was an option but not a great one, especially if she wanted to ensure she arrived at work and classes on time. Sometimes the schedules didn't exactly line up with her committed hours. Like now, when her car was in for service, and she was minutes from missing the last bus.

"Katarina!" A woman's voice sounded behind her, and she slowed to look back.

Another student, Amy, was hurrying to catch up, and Katarina held in a sigh. She liked Amy well enough, but the girl always needed help with something and right now, Katarina didn't have time for whatever Amy's latest crisis was.

"You're practically running," Amy said as she half jogged up, completely out of breath.

3

"I'm going to be late for dinner, and you know how my parents are," Katarina said, picking up her pace again.

Amy's face fell as she struggled to keep up. "Oh, then you don't have time to chat."

"Not today. Catch me tomorrow."

"Okay. But I think you're going to be fine on that dinner thing—at least where your father is concerned."

"Huh?"

"I just saw him go into the practice field with another guy."

"*My* father?"

Amy nodded.

"Crap!" Katarina let out a string of cursing as the bus she'd been trying to catch pulled away from the stop.

"Was that your bus?" Amy asked.

"Yeah. I don't suppose you're driving today, are you?"

"No. Mom gave the car to my little sister. Like she has anything worthwhile to do. Probably sitting at the boardwalk with her useless friends. Maybe you can catch your father and get a ride with him. Your mom can't complain if you come in late together, right?"

Katarina considered this and nodded. "That's a good idea. I'll see if I can catch him and if not, I guess I'll be springing for an Uber and apologizing to my mother for a week. Thanks, Amy!"

Katarina shifted directions and jogged toward the practice field, wondering what business her father could possibly have at the college. Not that she really knew much about her father's job. All he ever said was that Ivan had brought him over from the old country when he'd established his business in LA and that he was one of Ivan's right-hand men. Ivan owned a bunch of different businesses—restaurants, bars, retail stores, dry cleaners, pawnshops, and commercial real estate. Including the store Katarina worked in, although she'd

4

never seen him there. But she supposed that's why he had people on payroll, like her father. To help oversee all his investments.

The stadium lights shut off at the practice field, and she cursed. If she didn't catch a ride with her father, she was really going to pay for it. By the time she got an Uber home, she'd be at least thirty minutes late. She turned up her pace and was practically running by the time she slipped through the open gate and into the sports field. The night lights were on, of course, but didn't illuminate much, and the storm brewing overhead had blocked any light that the moon might otherwise provide.

Since she couldn't see well, she stopped to listen. A couple seconds later, voices carried past her with the gusts of wind from the upcoming storm and she headed for the field. She stopped at the edge of the bleachers and looked around. The little bit of moonlight that was coming through the storm clouds was just enough to let her know the field was empty, but the bleachers were too dark to see in most places. She scanned the sidelines, squinting, and finally spotted three shadows moving in a field entrance about fifty feet away.

She put her hand on the bleacher rail to guide her and made her way toward the figures, moving slowly since the moonlight had disappeared completely, and the area she was walking through was pitch-black. When she got closer, she recognized her father's voice yelling about missing money. The other voice sounded like Coach Mayhern, the football coach. But that didn't make any sense. What in the world could Coach Mayhern have to do with Ivan's businesses?

She took a few cautious steps closer, and the moonlight came back just enough that she could finally make out the three figures. One was her father, Gustav, and one was indeed Coach Mayhern. She recognized the other as a man who also worked for Ivan but couldn't remember his name. She'd only met him in person once.

"I just need some time," Coach Mayhern said, his voice pleading.

"Time to what?" Gustav asked. "Put together the money you stole from Ivan? He supplied the product. He expects to be paid for it."

"I swear, it was just to get me out of a pinch," Coach Mayhern said. "It will never happen again."

"No," Gustav said. "It won't."

Everything appeared in slow motion as Katarina watched in horror as her father pulled out a pistol and pointed it directly at the coach. At first, she thought maybe he hadn't fired because there wasn't a loud bang, but Coach Mayhern screamed in pain and clutched his chest, and Katarina could see blood seeping between his fingers. After a couple seconds, he dropped onto the pavement.

Katarina covered her mouth with her hand, choking back a cry. This couldn't be happening. Her father was a businessman. He wore custom-made suits and drove a Mercedes. They lived in a nice house in an upscale neighborhood. Her mother didn't work. This was a scene out of a gangster movie. Not her life. Not her family.

But there her father stood, holding a pistol and staring down at a dying man, with an expression completely devoid of emotion.

"Cleanup should be here soon," Gustav said to the other man. "I'm late for dinner. Take over."

The other man nodded and Gustav started to walk away, but as he did, lightning flashed across the sky and he turned in Katarina's direction. His eyes locked on hers and widened. As thunder ripped through the night sky, Katarina spun around and ran faster than she'd ever run before.

# CHAPTER TWO

EMMA TURNER SMILED as she pulled off the bridge and onto Main Street on Tempest Island. It was everything the advertisements had said—beautiful, quaint, pristine. No row of high-rise hotels blocking the view of the ocean. No parking lots the size of a football field that led to chain retailers. Just a small downtown area with one- and two-story buildings, a cute neighborhood behind the Main Street that extended down the coast to the east, and scattered cottages along the Gulf to the west.

It was peaceful and perfect.

Emma had spent the last two years working her way around Florida, starting on the upper East Coast, then moving down around the Keys, and finally up the Gulf Coast. She'd seen an article on Tempest Island when she was working in an art store in Tampa and had been instantly drawn to the white sand and crystal-clear turquoise water.

Which presented a problem.

For eight years now, Emma had limited her stops to larger cities. It was easier to stay lost in a crowd and to avoid relationships that came with questions she didn't want to answer. Of course, Florida was still the South and she'd always gotten her share of nosy parkers wanting to hear her life story, but she'd never stayed anywhere long enough to develop the kind of friendships that had her wanting to share her secrets. Besides, no one else needed her problems piled onto their lives. Most people were just trying to make their own situation work. They certainly didn't need her baggage added to their own.

Or the threat that came along with it.

So all Tempest Island would be was a short stop on her never-ending journey—a well-deserved vacation. Sometimes, when she was in between cities, she'd take a week or two somewhere, just to think about her next move and try to relax a bit, even though she was fairly certain she'd forgotten how. In the past eight years, she'd seen some pretty amazing things—Yellowstone National Park, Niagara Falls, the Grand Canyon, vineyards in California, mountains in Montana, beaches everywhere there was one—but this pretty little stretch of sand called to her as nothing else had, even though she'd only seen it in pictures until today.

Which probably meant she'd been pushing too hard and needed a break.

She pulled into a parking space at the motel, happy to see several available slots. The island was on the verge of tourist season but with any luck, she'd get in a week before kids got out of school and families flooded the island. Hopefully by then, she'd be refreshed and on to her next adventure. It helped if she put it that way—adventure. It sounded better than 'blending into another city with another dead-end job.'

She hopped out of her car and started toward the motel,

then changed her mind. She could always see about a room later. Right now, the Main Street shops were calling her. It wouldn't hurt to check out the town before she committed to a room. What if the people were all snooty? Then she'd have to move on and would have already hauled her things inside.

She pulled a hair band out of her pocket and tugged her long auburn hair into a loose knot. It wasn't officially summer, but it was already too hot to have her hair clinging to the back of her neck. She pulled out her sunglasses and looked around, deciding on a direction.

The motel was on the west side of Main Street, so she started walking east up the sidewalk, taking in the businesses on both sides. The bookstore on the other side of the middle of Main Street called to her, its weathered brick and pretty striped awning beckoning her to come inside. She would bet anything the interior was full of hardwood bookshelves, had comfortable furniture, and smelled like leather and lemon furniture polish. She'd always loved to read and already knew she'd be stopping inside on her way back to the motel. The ice cream shop next to it was also a real threat.

She looked to her right and took in a pizza joint that had the required red checkered table linens. The smell of tomato sauce and pepperoni drifting out was enough to tempt her inside, especially as she'd skipped breakfast and—she glanced at her watch—apparently lunch. But it could wait a little longer.

The next storefront was for a surf shop, where brightly colored boards stood in stands outside. Hand-painted text on the stands advertised rentals as well as lessons. She glanced at the glass windows and caught sight of a sign next to the door.

*Help Wanted.*

She frowned. It didn't say what kind of help, but did it matter? Tempest Island was a far cry from her normal stops and besides, no job advertised in a storefront window would be paying well enough to cover housing on the island, assuming anything was even available. That meant commuting from the mainland every day, and she knew from other places she'd visited with a similar setup that traffic going over the bridge could get really backed up in tourist season. Plus, she couldn't fade into the background in a small place. Not enough people.

*Tourists are people, and there will be plenty of them soon.*

She frowned and stared at the sign for a bit longer, then before she could change her mind, pushed the door open and went inside. Likely, she wouldn't like the store, the owner, or the job. Maybe even all three. By checking, she wouldn't have to worry that she'd missed an opportunity. She could mark this off her list and continue with her vacation, then worry later about choosing her new location and job.

A man at the counter looked up as she walked in, and she slowed as she assessed him. If this was the owner, he was younger than she'd expected. She put him early to midthirties based on stature and facial lines, although his bleached-blond surfer hairstyle gave him a more youthful appearance. He smiled at her as she approached the counter. His bright blue eyes—the same shade as the T-shirts he was folding—pinned her, and she felt her pulse tick up a notch. This guy was seriously gorgeous.

"Hi, I'm Mark," he said. "Welcome to my shop."

"Emma," she said.

"How can I help you?"

She glanced at the table behind the counter and saw a picture of him with a pretty redheaded woman and a little girl who looked like a combination of both of them. The wedding band he wore reinforced the picture and earned more points in his favor. A married man with a small child and a business to run would be too busy with his own life to take an interest in hers. And now she was also safe recognizing how attractive he was because he wasn't on the market.

"I was wondering about the job," she said. "Is it still available?"

He nodded. "I just put the sign out this morning. No takers yet, but most everyone who passes by is young and inexperienced and looking for only summer employment."

"Can you tell me about it?"

In the past several years, her direct customer retail experience was minimal, as she preferred to stay hidden in the back offices where she had limited contact with people. But there was something about his shop and his smile that made her feel welcome, and she hadn't felt that way in a long time. Surely vacationers looking to take up an activity would be easier to deal with than the impatient and unsatisfied retail clientele she'd briefly worked with years ago.

"Sure," he said. "I'll admit, it's sort of a hodgepodge of things. The truth is, I bit off more than I can chew, and now I'm trying to figure out how to tread water. For starters, I decided to offer lessons last year and it went so well that I'm already filling up this year and the season hasn't even started yet. Then a buddy convinced me that I should have a YouTube channel about surfing and paddleboarding because it would help advertise the shop and maybe even get monetized and be an extra revenue stream. Don't get me wrong, I think it's a great idea, but I don't see how I'll have time for all of that and everything to do with running the shop."

She nodded. "YouTube is an excellent way to have a sideline business, though, especially if it helps push your main one. So the job is...?"

He laughed. "Right, sorry. Sometimes I go off on a tangent. Basically, I'm looking for someone to handle the things I don't like to do. Starting with the accounting. I'm more of an operations guy. Sitting in that office and looking at the beach is not nearly as fun—or as profitable—as being out there with customers."

She smiled. "Well, lucky for you, I love the numbers side of things, and hiding out in offices appeals to me as well as I'm more of a spreadsheet person and less of a people person. But I doubt the accounting is a full-time job. Do you expect the person you hire to work in the shop as well?"

"No. I mean maybe in a pinch, but I have a seasonal salesperson lined up for the summer. In addition to the accounting, I'll need this position to keep up with the inventory. That's probably easier to do when the store is closed, so if you can flex hours for before the shop opens or maybe evenings, then that task would go quicker because we're not closed any days during season. Aside from that, what I guess I really need is a personal assistant. At least, that's what my buddy called it."

"To handle what exactly?"

"Just general stuff that I never seem to have time for—mailing packages, picking up supplies for the shop and sometimes myself, keeping up with my lessons schedule and getting those people the forms and information they'll need to participate. I try to email them so they have them ready when they get here. Make sure ads are running on time and correctly online and in the local newspaper, and if this YouTube thing catches on, then I guess that's a whole other set of books to keep."

He didn't look thrilled with the prospect, and she had to hold back a smile. A lot of people felt that way about the back end of their business. And that's where she shone.

"Daddy! Daddy!"

The door to the shop was flung open, and a redheaded spitfire around five years old ran past Emma and behind the counter. The little girl jumped up, and Mark lifted her up for a kiss. Emma recognized her as the girl from the photo, just a bit older. A young woman—not the woman in the picture—trailed behind her, looking a little harried.

"Hello, Lily," Mark said, smiling at the child as he put her down. "How was school today?"

"Same as always," Lily said. "Daddy, Miss Jane says I can't have an ice cream cone."

Mark raised his eyebrows. "And why do you think Miss Jane said that?"

Lily gave a dramatic sigh. "Because you told her to."

"That's right," Mark said. "Miss Jane is only doing what I've asked her to do, so you'll respect what she says."

"Not even a little bitty cone?" Lily begged.

"Not even the tiniest of tiny ones," he said. "You know the rules—no sweets before dinner. Now, get upstairs and change and you and Miss Jane can have some time on the beach before I close up."

"Okay!" Lily took off for the back of the shop, and Jane gave Mark a thankful look and hurried off behind her.

"My daughter, Lily," Mark said.

Emma smiled. "I gathered as much. She's adorable."

"And knows it. I have to keep on my toes to make sure she doesn't use it to her advantage."

"Well, that's what parents are for. I take it your wife works outside of the home as well?"

Mark frowned and sadness flashed across his face. "My wife passed away about a year ago. Breast cancer."

Emma's heart broke at the thought of that little girl losing her mother and this seemingly nice man losing his wife.

"I am *so* sorry," she said. "I'm sure that was very hard on both of you."

He nodded. "It was. Still is sometimes. I mean, it gets better, but I catch myself wanting to give in to Lily's demands because she lost her mother. It's hard to tell her no, even when it's for her own good."

"Well, it looks like you're doing an excellent job, and Jane seems to have a handle on how you want things done."

"Jane is great. She's a college student majoring in early childhood education, so the perfect sitter for Lily. And she's a local girl, so everyone here knew her, which made me more comfortable hiring her."

"Of course. So you're not from here?"

"A transplant. Bought the business three years ago when I saw it advertised in a surfing magazine. It was a gamble but it's done pretty good. It's just time to elevate it to better, you know?"

"I understand."

He stared out the window for a couple seconds, then seemed to push the sadness away and looked back at her. "So, the job? Did I explain that well enough?"

"I think so," she said. "What's your pay range?"

He named a figure that was higher than she expected but still wouldn't afford her a rental on the island. And the motel rates would go up the deeper into summer they went, pricing her out of that option as well, even if they had a vacancy.

"Do you have a résumé?" he asked, breaking into her thoughts.

"I can email you one."

"I'd love to have one if you're interested. If you have accounting experience, you've probably got the job. I'm kind of in a bind at this point. I really should have started looking months ago."

"I definitely have accounting experience and I'm interested in the job, but I'm not certain how long I'll be sticking around. If everything looks good to you, can we give it a trial—maybe two weeks? That would give me time to get your accounting in order anyway and also to decide if the island is going to be a good fit for me. And for you to decide if I'm a good fit for the job."

It would also give her time to assess the job and the living situation. If she liked the job well enough, then she'd figure out the living situation on the mainland, even if it meant sitting in traffic every day, although having flexible hours some days would help on that end. Her unexpected attraction to Mark was somewhat disconcerting, but ultimately it didn't matter. A grieving widower was just as good as married. Maybe even better, since some of the married men she'd run across had hit on her worse than the single ones.

"I can do a trial," he said and handed her a business card. "Just email me your résumé and as long as everything checks out, you can start next week."

"Great. I'll get it to you this evening."

She headed out of the shop and continued down the sidewalk in a bit of a daze. She glanced back at the surf shop and saw Mark remove the *Help Wanted* sign from the window. What the heck had she done? She'd committed to a job in a small tourist town, for the widowed father of a young girl, who also happened to be one of the best-looking men she'd come across in her entire lifetime. It was as if she'd lined up every rule she'd made for herself and found a way to break all of them at the same time.

She let out a sigh as she walked. It wouldn't work. Her best bet would be to get in her car, drive to New Orleans, and get lost in the crowd again. Don't send the résumé and just disappear. Mark would put the sign back out and find someone else to hire and she wouldn't be compromising the way she preferred to do things. What was the point of a two-week trial? Based on what she'd seen so far, it would just give her more time to get attached to this lovely town. That would only make it harder to go.

She crossed the street and walked into the bookstore. At least she could pick up a paperback to read over lunch and maybe sit on the beach for an hour or two before heading for the mainland to drum up a room for the night. Tomorrow morning, she'd direct her car up Interstate 10 to New Orleans and forget she'd ever set foot on Tempest Island.

# CHAPTER THREE

THE INSTANT EMMA STEPPED INSIDE THE BOOKSTORE, COOL air and the smell of lemons washed over her. She couldn't help smiling. It was exactly as she'd imagined it would be—with the glossy bookcases stretching from floor to ceiling and natural light flowing in from the huge windows in the front of the store. An attractive older woman with short wavy blond hair and a youthful gait headed her direction and smiled.

"Welcome to my store," she said. "I'm Bea. Can I help you find something?"

"Nothing in particular," Emma said. "I just wanted to pick up something new to read."

Bea nodded. "What's your genre?"

"I like a lot of different things, but I think I'm in the mood for a good mystery or thriller."

"We got the latest Kate Coleson in this week."

"Oh, I love her."

"I have a display right over here." Bea walked off and grabbed a book from the display. "You need anything else?"

"No. I think that book will do me."

Bea headed for the register, and Emma trailed behind her.

"I have to say, it's rare to see younger people in here anymore, especially for fiction. Your generation usually does all their reading electronically."

"My Kindle crapped out on me last week. I haven't gotten around to replacing it yet. And sometimes I just like holding a paper book, you know?"

Bea nodded. "You on vacation?"

*Not since I broke my rules and applied for a job with a sexy owner.*

"More like traveling through. I saw advertisements for the island and thought I'd make a quick stop just to stretch my legs. Then I got hungry after walking past the pizza place and figured I'd pick up a book, have a late lunch, and look at the beautiful water before heading on."

"Well, you couldn't pick a better place to relax and take in the beauty. It's a shame you're not staying. You should come back as soon as you get a chance."

"Maybe I will," Emma said. So far, everything about Tempest Island was appealing.

"Damn it, Shakespeare!" a woman's voice yelled from a back room in the bookstore.

As Emma looked in the direction of the yell, a huge gray cat came running out a door, a hot dog wiener in his mouth. A woman probably about the same age as Bea, but with a little larger frame and brown hair piled up on her head, chased the cat into the bookstore and threw her hands in the air when the wiener thief jumped onto a display and launched to the top of a bookcase.

"If that cat doesn't stop stealing my lunch, I might lose weight," the woman said. "Then where would we all be?"

Emma grinned as the woman turned around and caught sight of her at the counter.

"Sorry," she said, looking a tiny bit embarrassed. "I didn't realize we had a customer."

"This is Nelly," Bea said. "My best friend, coworker, and part-time cat wiener supplier."

"I'm Emma. Nice to meet you, Nelly. And you too, Shakespeare."

She looked up at the cat, who was enjoying his wiener and looked entirely too pleased with himself.

"How'd he manage to get it away from you?" Bea asked as she took cash from Emma.

"He opened the microwave and took it right out," Nelly said.

Bea froze and stared. "You've got to be kidding me."

Nelly threw her hands in the air. "I can't make this crap up. That cat is a menace. Next thing you know, he'll be drinking our wine stash in the refrigerator."

Bea wagged a finger at the cat. "You stay out of our wine stash, or you'll be relocating to a place where they only serve dry cat food."

Shakespeare stared at Bea for a moment, then flicked his tail and turned away, not even remotely bothered.

Emma laughed. "I get the impression he knows you're lying."

"My nine-millimeter will leave an impression," Bea muttered, then handed Emma a bag with her book. "If you change your mind about staying for a bit, the motel has some nice rooms with great beach views. There are little balconies off the back. Can't fit more than a couple chairs on them, but what more do you need? Anyway, it was nice meeting you, Emma. Enjoy your book."

"It was nice meeting you as well," Emma said. "I really love your store. It's just perfect."

Bea beamed. "I think so too."

Emma headed out as Nelly and Bea started up a discussion about what to do with the thieving Shakespeare and how the whole store was going to smell like hot dogs and she couldn't help smiling. The two women and the cat were hilarious—the perfect characters for the perfect small-town setting. It was like everything on Tempest Island had been written into the script of a TV movie.

She crossed the street and made her way to the pizza place, already inhaling the incredible smell of tomato sauce and garlic before she even pulled the door open. Inside was even better. A young man at the counter greeted her and asked if she had a to-go order. When she indicated she'd be dining in, he waved her to the dining room and told her to take her pick of tables and someone would be over in a bit.

It was too early for the dinner rush and past the lunch one, so only two other tables were occupied. Emma picked a two-top in the corner at the back of the dining area located in front of a huge window that looked out over the beach. She gazed out at the ocean and let out a contented sigh. The sands were so white and the water so turquoise that it looked tropical and not at all like the other beaches she'd seen. At least, not the ones she'd seen in person.

"Welcome to Island Pizza. Can I get you something to drink?"

Emma turned to see a teen girl smiling at her and holding a pad.

"Ginger ale, please," Emma said.

The girl made a note. "Do you know what you'd like to eat or do you need some more time?"

Emma shook her head. She'd known what she wanted to eat since she'd walked by the first time. "I'll have a small supreme with traditional crust."

"Perfect," the girl said. "I'll grab your drink and the pizza will be out soon. Would you like a side salad?"

"No, thanks."

The girl nodded and headed for the kitchen. Emma pulled her newly bought book out and turned to the first chapter. By the time her pizza arrived, she was already invested in the story. Kate Coleson knew how to draw you in right from the beginning, and Emma appreciated the diversion. She made it through another couple chapters while she ate, then thanked the girl and left her a nice tip before heading out.

She walked slowly toward her car, debating her next move. It was late afternoon, so she really should find a place for the night. The mainland was going to be cheaper than the island, and if she was leaving for New Orleans tomorrow, there was no point in spending the extra just for one night. But she was already here, and it wasn't as if one night would kill her. She never made a lot of money, but she knew how to manage what she had and had become quite adept at turning less into more.

When she reached her car, she stood beside it, trying to make up her mind. Then the door to the motel swung open and an older gentleman with silver hair stepped out. He caught sight of her and smiled.

"Are you checking in?" he asked.

"I...well, I was trying to decide," she said.

"I just had a ladies' church group cancel," he said. "Apparently they felt the need to share a cold and had to reschedule. I can offer you a great rate for a week if you're interested. And that's a room with a Gulf view."

He named a price that was well below what she would have expected to pay, even before tourist season. It was a sign. Emma wasn't one for fanciful thoughts, but ever since she'd stepped on the island, things had been prompting her to stay. Her instincts hadn't steered her wrong so far. Maybe she needed to listen to them again, even though this wasn't her usual fare.

"That sounds great," she said. "Let me grab my bag."

"I'm Gary," the man said as she stepped up to the counter inside. "I own the motel."

Emma glanced around the lobby with its pale blue walls, white porcelain tile floors, beach paintings, and tropical plants, and she smiled.

"I'm Emma. Your motel is really pretty. The whole town is, actually. At least what I've seen so far."

"You been here all day?"

"No. Just a couple hours, but I've been to the surf shop, bought a book, and had some pizza."

Gary nodded and patted his slightly rounded stomach. "I can attest to the fact that it's really good pizza."

She laughed. "It is."

"I can offer you a corner room on the second floor for the price I gave. The best view and the quietest."

"That would be great." She pulled out her one and only credit card—prepaid—and passed it to Gary.

"Straight up the stairs and to the right," he said after she signed the slip. "If you need extra towels or pillows, just hit zero on the phone in the room and it will ring down here. I'll get your bag."

"Don't worry about it. I'm just bringing up this one for now. Thanks, Gary."

Emma grabbed her overnight bag and headed for her room. When she pushed the door open, she stopped for a moment to sigh. Huge patio doors were on the back wall. The blinds were completely open and the view of the Gulf was incredible. She noted that the bed was on the wall opposite the patio doors and couldn't wait to wake up tomorrow to that view. A small desk was on the end wall and had a window right over the top of the desk that provided a side view of the beach as it stretched down the west side of the island.

She tossed her bag on the bed and hurried over to slide

open the doors and step out onto the small balcony. The smell of salt water rushed over her, and she closed her eyes and drew in a deep breath, the evening sun beating down on her face. This was a small slice of heaven.

Finally, she released the railing and headed back inside and dug the business card out of her purse. Her mind was made up. She was going to send Mark—she looked at the card—Mark Phillips her résumé. And if he hired her, she was going to take the job. Maybe it wouldn't work out and she'd be gone in a week. Or maybe it would go well, and she could spend the summer here and then move on after tourist season when Mark wasn't likely to need full-time help any longer.

Either way, she was making a stop on Tempest Island.

She was safe here, she reminded herself.

*Emma Turner* was safe. Katarina Petras was no more.

————

MARK TAPPED ON THE KEYBOARD, his frustration increasing every second he tried to wrangle the new accounting software into submission. It was days like this when he missed his wife in so many ways—as his romantic partner, his daughter's mother, and his office manager. His CPA had insisted that he do a better job tracking income and expenses, hence the new software. Since Mark's idea of submitting records for his tax return had consisted of tossing a year's worth of receipts and invoices into a storage container, he respected the man's point. And he'd had to pay extra for his lack of dedication to administrative tasks.

His CPA had also pointed out that it was impossible for Mark to make decisions about the future of his business or his personal life when he didn't have a handle on how much money was coming in and going out. Another valid but annoying point, but also the one that had ultimately sent him by the office store for the *Help Wanted* sign. The business had always made money. Not a lot, but enough for him and Lily, especially now since they lived above the store. Housing costs were minimal and commuting costs were nonexistent.

But he'd been lax about the financial end of things ever since Beth passed. They'd taken out life insurance policies as soon as they'd had Lily, knowing that if something happened to one of them, the other would benefit from that cushion of less financial worry while trying to figure out how to restructure their lives. So he wasn't worried about paying the bills, and the shop had always made a decent profit. But he couldn't continue to coast along, tossing paperwork into a plastic container, and expect that it wouldn't become a problem at some point.

Costs were always going up—utilities, products, payroll—and without knowing the profit margin for the individual items in his store, he had no idea if he needed to change up inventory, increase prices, or simply discontinue certain things. Not only was the income Beth had made doing bookkeeping for other businesses additional revenue lost, but now he also had to pay someone to do the work she'd been doing. He definitely had to get a handle on business profit so that he could do a better job planning for his and Lily's future. He couldn't put it off any longer.

Lily would be starting first grade soon, and that would fly by. Then there would be activities or sports, then the needs of a teen to contend with, then college. He'd had a year to get used to the idea that he was a widower and make sure Lily was as adjusted as a young girl who'd lost her mother could be. It was time to focus on his business responsibilities again so he could continue to do a good job taking care of his family.

He pushed the keyboard back and rose from the chair. But

not today. He'd reached his limit with the software. Despite having a couple hours of lessons and making a million phone calls to support, he just wasn't getting the hang of it. And this was the software his CPA had recommended as user friendly for non-accountants. He'd hate to see the one his CPA used.

He double-checked the front door to make sure it was locked, then he shut off all the downstairs lights and headed upstairs. It had been a huge advantage that the previous owner had converted the top floor of the building into two apartments. The one he and Lily lived in had two bedrooms, two baths, and an open kitchen and living room that had huge patio doors that led onto a large deck that faced the Gulf. The other apartment was a small one-bedroom, one bath, with patio doors in the living room that led onto the same deck.

Both had been vacation rentals before Beth died, and his CPA had suggested he offer up the smaller one again. But so far, he'd resisted, not wanting anyone to share walls with him and his very young daughter. It was probably silly as there was a side staircase that provided rear access to the deck entries, and the interior door to the rental could be locked from the inside to prevent access to the shared interior landing and stairwell. The interior stairwell also had a locked door at the bottom in the office area, which meant no one could even get up to the door of his and Lily's apartment. And with separate access, he didn't have to interact with renters unless something broke and he needed to address it. Or unless they were all on the porch at the same time.

But still, he couldn't pull the trigger.

Maybe it was something he would do some more thinking on, especially if he ever got his numbers figured out and didn't like how they looked. He already knew he wasn't interested in doing vacation rentals because he didn't want the mess or the noise that came with it, but there were mainlanders who worked on the island and might be interested in a place there so that they didn't have to commute over the bridge every morning.

He heard Lily giggling before he opened the door to their apartment and felt his heart soar. For a long time after her mother passed, she never so much as cracked a smile. Mark had tried everything to coax his daughter into happiness, even for a couple seconds, but he'd remained frustrated and felt inept when all his attempts failed. The therapist had assured him over and over that he was doing everything right—that these things took time and there was nothing anyone could do to hasten it. Lily would deal with her mother's death in her own way and her own time. Since she'd never regressed with regard to speech or bathroom training or had any behavioral issues that were reason for concern, the therapist had declared her as handling things very well and quite frankly, better than most at her age.

When he walked inside, he saw Lily and Jane dancing in the living room. Jane had Lily by the arms and was helping her twirl round and round. Lily was wearing a frilly pink ballet skirt. Lately ballet had been her obsession, and Mark figured he should start looking for a place for her to take lessons. It would be easier to accommodate that interest than her previous one to become a mermaid.

Jane looked up as he walked in and smiled. She was such a great nanny for Lily, and Mark was grateful that Bea had recommended her. She never turned on the television and deposited Lily in front of it so that she could chat on her phone, which is exactly what he heard other parents complaining about. By the time he got home at night, Lily was ready to tell him about her exciting afternoon but always tired enough to be in bed asleep by eight o'clock.

"Sorry I'm running a little late," Mark said as Jane gave Lily a hug then grabbed her purse from the counter.

"No worries," Jane said. "I didn't have plans."

"Still, I'm adding some extra to your pay tomorrow."

Jane grinned. "I'm certainly not going to turn you down. The university is raising tuition for the fall. Again."

"That sucks," Mark said.

Jane had told him when she interviewed that she had an academic scholarship, but it didn't cover everything. She wanted to work so that she could pay the balance and not have to take out loans. Starting out in your career after graduation was hard enough, but entering adulthood with debt made it even harder. Jane's parents were good people, but they didn't have a lot.

Jane shrugged. "That's life, right? No sense going into it without being prepared for anything that might happen."

He clapped a hand on her shoulder as he walked her to the door. "I wish I'd had your clarity that young. Heck, I wish I had it now."

"You're doing all right," Jane said and grinned as she walked out. "See you tomorrow, Lily!"

"Bye!" Lily called out and hurried to give Mark a hug.

He grabbed her and swung her up, then twirled her around once before putting her down. "You hungry?"

"Starved. Can we have pancakes?"

"For dinner?"

Lily gave him a serious look. "Daddy, pancakes are good *any* time."

"You're right. What was I thinking?"

"You were thinking that whipped cream on top would make them even better."

"Okay, but tomorrow night, we have to have some vegetables."

Lily let out a dramatic sigh. "If that's what it takes."

After he and Lily enjoyed pancakes, he read three stories to her. Then he took a shower, dropped onto the couch with a beer, and turned on the TV. He was exhausted but knew if he tried to go to sleep now, he'd just toss and turn, his mind racing with the long list of things he needed to do. Maybe if he could get someone hired for the numbers stuff, his stress level would drop.

That thought made him think about Emma, the woman he'd talked to in the store today, so he grabbed his laptop to check email. He didn't really expect to hear from her. She didn't appear to be local, and the job was only sort of defined, and he wasn't exactly paying a fortune. Still, there was always hope.

He accessed his business email and was surprised to see 'Résumé' in a subject line. Delighted, he clicked on the email and prayed that the woman checked out. He'd gotten a good feeling about her and if she had the skill set for the work and was happy with the pay, then she might be the answer to his prayers. At least for however long he could keep her interested. When things slowed down in the fall, she might decide to move on to something with more responsibility and some room for advancement. But even if she only stayed the summer, that would be enough to get him caught up and free up his time for the sideline pursuits during the tourist season. He could reassess his needs in the fall if she decided to move on.

As he scanned the résumé, he smiled. She hadn't hedged on her experience with the bookkeeping end of things, which was great. Even better, she'd only worked for independent stores— no chains or big-box stores. And the accounting software he'd purchased was one of those listed in her experience section. Perfect. She'd changed jobs a lot, but she definitely had that free spirit vibe, so that wasn't surprising. Still, she'd included letters of recommendation from previous employers along with contact information to verify, and just scanning them let him know that everyone had been happy with her work and sad to see her go.

He tapped his fingers on his laptop. It was probably best to call those references tomorrow and verify them, but he was itching to have this settled. He blew out a breath. This wasn't like him at all—to make a decision so quickly and without overthinking everything the way he had been doing since Beth passed.

But maybe it was time to try a different approach. His instincts had always been solid, which is what had gotten him through two tours overseas and saved his butt countless numbers of times on the surfing circuit. He checked his watch and saw it was just a few minutes past nine. Before he could change his mind, he grabbed his cell phone and dialed.

"Hello?" Emma answered, sounding a bit hesitant.

"Hi, this is Mark Phillips from the surf shop. I just finished looking over your résumé, and if you're still interested in the job, it's yours."

"Oh," she said, clearly surprised. "Don't you want to call my references?"

"Are they going to tell me anything that's not in these letters?"

She laughed. "Well, no."

"Then let's give it that trial run you mentioned. If at the end of a week or two, it's not working out for either one of us, we part ways with no hard feelings."

"That sounds perfect. What's the dress code?"

"The island is super casual. Anything you would wear in public will do."

"Great. When do you want me there?"

"Yesterday," he said. "But I'll settle for Monday morning around nine. You should get to enjoy at least one weekend here without thinking about work."

"Then I'll see you Monday morning."

Mark hung up and smiled. One thing handled.

Only a hundred more to go.

# CHAPTER FOUR

KATARINA DUCKED INTO AN EMPTY DORM ROOM AND LEANED *over to catch her breath. She was an excellent runner but sprinting for long distances wasn't something she was trained to do, and she'd basically sprinted across the entire campus. As her breathing normalized, she pulled up the security camera app on her phone. She checked the different screens and saw her mother and father in the kitchen. It looked as though they were arguing. She accessed the live feed and turned up the volume.*

"*How could you make such a mistake?*" *her mother yelled.*

"*She shouldn't have been there,*" *her father said.* "*No one should have been there but me, Tomas, and that idiot Mayhern.*"

"*But she* was *there,*" *her mother said.* "*Did you tell Ivan?*"

"*Of course,*" *her father said.* "*I had no choice.*"

*Her mother cursed.* "*That's our daughter.*"

"*You think I don't know that?*" *her father said.* "*But what happens if she goes to the police? If the police investigate me, they'll move straight up the ladder to Danek. I'm supposed to prevent him from being under investigation, not produce a witness that can send trouble his way.*"

*He mother blew out a breath.* "*What does he want done?*"

*"What do you think?"*

*Her mother gasped. "You don't have to..."*

*"No. Someone else will take care of it."*

*"But not here. Not in this house. Assuming she even comes home."*

*"I've given them everything. They'll find her at the university or at a friend's house, and there are more men watching the bus station."*

Katarina clutched the phone and sank onto the floor, dissolving into sobs. She'd been trying to convince herself that what she'd seen was a waking nightmare—that it wasn't real. But it was beyond real. Her father might be Ivan's right-hand man, but it was clear that Ivan's enterprises stretched beyond the ones documented. Her father had killed a man. A man who sold 'product' for Ivan and didn't kick the profit back up as he was supposed to. And if that profit was worth killing over, then there was no way the product was legal.

What was she going to do? She couldn't go home, that was clear. And with her car in the shop and the bus station being watched, she had no way to get out of town. There were probably men searching the campus right now. It wasn't as though she could stroll out and hail a cab.

Noise in the hallway caused her to freeze, not even taking a breath, but then the sounds of cheerful students echoed and she relaxed. She rose from the floor and opened the door just a crack. It was a group of students dressed in costumes and who must be headed to a party.

"Come on," one of the girls was saying. "Someone has to go as the nun."

"You can't pick up hot guys dressed as a nun," another girl said.

Before she could change her mind, she stepped out of the room and caught up with the group.

"Excuse me," she said. "Did I hear you say you have a nun costume?"

A blond girl dressed as Catwoman turned around. "Yeah, and it's really great. See?"

*She held up the habit and smiled. Her watery eyes gave away her already-tipsy state.*

*"I don't suppose I could buy it from you?" Katarina asked. "I thought I was going to stay in and study, but it's been one of those weeks."*

*"You can have it," the girl said. "We're going to a party. This school is hard. Everyone deserves a night off. You can walk over with us if you want. It's not that far off campus."*

*"Great," Katarina said and took the outfit. "Just let me pull this on."*

*She stuck her phone back in her jeans pocket, then yanked the habit over her head and pulled it down. It was all one piece with the head part connected to the robe part with the giant cross necklace to finish it off. Cheaply made, but all that mattered was that no one would recognize her. Especially walking with a bunch of other costumed students.*

*She had no idea where they were going, but all she needed to know was 'off campus.' She'd figure out the rest from there.*

EMMA BOLTED STRAIGHT UP in bed, sweat pouring down her face, her heart pounding so hard in her chest that it hurt. She clutched the blanket against her and forced herself to breathe slowly in and out until her racing heart began to slow. When the worst was past, she reached for the bottled water on the nightstand and took a big drink. She'd left the patio doors open when she'd gotten into bed to read so that the ocean breeze could blow through the room and she could hear the sound of the waves crashing on the beach. She must have dozed off while she was reading.

But now, the curtains whipped around the sides of the doors in a frantic dance. Cool wind gusted in, and lightning flashed over the stormy seas. She got up to close the patio doors and no sooner had she pulled them shut when a sheet of rain enveloped the tiny balcony, peppering the glass with huge drops.

That was it. The incoming storm had triggered the dream.

It had been a long time since she'd had one. More than a year, and that one hadn't been as vivid as this one. This time, she'd been cast back to that evening as if it were happening all over again. Everything was so clear, so detailed, even down to the inebriated girl's glassy eyes.

*It's not just the storm.*

She flopped down on the bed and sighed. No use glossing over her recent decisions. Breaking her well-established employment rules, combined with the storm and her current suspenseful fiction material, had stressed her system enough to kick it into overdrive, and the dream was the result. Maybe she should call Mark in the morning and tell him she'd changed her mind. But despite the horrible way she'd awakened, everything else she'd experienced on the island had tugged at her to stay. After all these years, could her instincts be that far off?

Lightning flashed again and this time, thunder rolled across the sky, so loud that she was sure the entire motel shook. Tempest Island, she remembered. Probably named for a good reason, and she was witnessing that good reason firsthand. Storms like this were common near the coast. In all her stays near the ocean, she'd seen hundreds of them. This was just one more. And the next would be one more after this one.

It had been eight years. Her parents were both dead. Katarina Petras had disappeared and was presumed dead.

Surely no one was looking for her anymore.

She propped up her pillow and leaned back against the headboard, watching the storm as it raged outside. And then said a quick prayer that she was right.

# CHAPTER FIVE

ALAYNA SCOTT INCHED BACKWARD ON THE STAIRS, clutching the bottom of the cardboard box. Her boyfriend, Luke Ryan, was below her, holding the other end. His focus on her, the box, the steps, and constant direction was one of many reasons he'd been the commander of a SEAL team. If not for the bullet that had rendered his knee less than perfect, that's where he'd probably be right now—off somewhere saving the world. But if not for that injury, Alayna would never have met him, and more importantly, she might not even be alive.

When Warren, her former boyfriend, was arrested for money laundering for a drug cartel, it had cost Alayna her restaurant in New York City. So she'd fled to Tempest Island and her Aunt Bea to attempt to salvage her fractured future. Although she'd been assured by the FBI that she was in no danger from her former boyfriend or the cartel, that had turned out to be inaccurate. She'd met Luke just weeks ago, and the feelings that had started developing from the moment they locked eyes had intensified along with the life-threatening situation, until all of it had come to a deadly conclusion for the man trying to harm her.

Since then, she and Luke had been inseparable.

Luke, who had been forced to leave his team due to the injury, had taken a SEAL instructor position with the Navy at the base on the mainland. But at this moment, all his energy was going toward helping her get this heavy and delicate box onto the second floor of her aunt's bookstore and into the space that would house Alayna's future restaurant.

"One more step," Luke said. "Please be careful. Are you okay?"

"I'm good," she said, concentrating on placing her foot just the right distance up and back, then carefully lifting the box.

After another couple minutes of getting the box across the deck, angling it in the door, and sliding it across the floor, they finally deposited it in the walk-in freezer. It wasn't fired up yet and was the safest place to store something delicate while the rest of the space was being finished out.

"Thank God," Alayna said as she stood upright and stretched her arms over her head.

"And this was the light box?" Luke asked.

"Yeah. The other one is twice as heavy, but the company will deliver that one tomorrow."

"Why couldn't they deliver this one?"

"I didn't buy them at the same place. The chandelier that's coming tomorrow was current merchandise at a custom lighting store. The pendant lights came from a smaller home furnishing vendor with no delivery service."

"I thought you said they matched."

She nodded. "They were both made by the same artist. Do you have a knife?"

"I'm a SEAL."

He pulled a knife out of his pocket and opened the top on the box. Alayna reached in and pulled out a foam block, and he cut the tape wrapped around it. She placed the bottom of the foam on the box and pulled off the top, then she picked up the pendant light to show him. It was hanging pieces of glass in different lengths, and the individual pieces were the different shades of blue that you saw in the ocean just across the street.

"That's really pretty," he said. "I can see why you wanted it."

"The big one that will go in the center of the dining area is a rectangle and the glass hangs so that it looks like waves. It's simply gorgeous. The minute I saw it, I completely ditched my traditional decorating plans in favor of the high-end coastal look with a lot of white and blues."

"I think it would be beautiful either way, but I can see where ocean colors could be both calming and elegant. I think people are going to love it."

"I really hope so. I found some glasses with just a hint of blue in them and the most beautiful white dishes with a thin turquoise ring around the outside. I've got my eye on some linens that would be perfect, but I've heard some gossip about an upcoming sale, so I'm going to wait a few days, and..."

She trailed off, then laughed. "I'm going to bore you to death with all these details."

He smiled and gathered her in his arms for a kiss. "You could never bore me. It makes *me* happy to see *you* this happy."

She smiled. "When I think of where I was just weeks ago, I can't believe it. I never thought I'd have anything worthwhile again—didn't even think I deserved to—and now I've got the best life I've ever had. I'm on Tempest Island again with Aunt Bea, I'm opening a new restaurant, and I have the hottest guy on the island to spend my time with."

"And I have the most beautiful and talented woman to spend my time with."

"Get a room, you two."

Bea's voice sounded behind them and they looked over and laughed.

"We're in a room," Alayna said. "Sort of."

"I don't think what you two have in mind is something the health inspector would approve of in a space made for food storage," Bea said. "Besides, cold makes some things difficult and less impressive."

Luke started laughing as Alayna stared at her aunt in dismay.

"Good Lord, Aunt Bea," she said as she walked out of the freezer. "The walk-in isn't even plugged in yet. And the things you say..."

Bea grinned. "So how are things coming? I heard you guys tromping up here and figured I'd come see what's new."

Luke glanced at his watch and gave Alayna a quick kiss. "I've got to run. I have class in an hour and have to change clothes."

"You train SEALs," Bea said. "All you need to do is take off some clothes, get in the water, and off you go."

"I'm afraid you need more than a swimsuit," he said. "Weapon chafing is a real thing."

He grinned at them and left. Alayna watched him go and then looked over at Bea and realized she was watching him as well.

"That man is a prime specimen," Bea said. "Aren't you glad you wised up and took him up on his offer?"

"You're awful! And yes."

"You have any problems with the storm last night?"

"No, but we flipped all the patio furniture over beforehand so we didn't have to go chasing it down. Now, let me show you the new lighting."

"I can't wait to see it."

Bea's phone rang and she pulled it out of her pocket and answered.

"What's up, Nelly?" she asked, then sighed. "Be right there."

"What's wrong?" Alayna asked.

"Apparently Veronica Whitmore is downstairs demanding my presence."

A wave of apprehension coursed through Alayna. The Whitmores were one of the oldest and wealthiest island families. Carlson Whitmore, Veronica's husband, ran the local bank and the city council. Those two things gave them the ability to make demands on some of the businesses and residents, and they took full advantage.

Bea had never needed their money and not being able to control her was the bane of Veronica's existence. Alayna had attended high school with their daughter, Melody, and the girl had gone out of her way to try and make Alayna miserable. Alayna had already had one run-in with her since she'd been back on the island, and it appeared her attitude hadn't improved. The fact that Melody had set eyes on Luke and then Alayna had landed him probably didn't help matters.

"You don't think it's about the restaurant, do you?" Alayna asked.

"Who knows with Veronica," Bea said. "But don't you worry about it. Just slip out the back door and go about your day. I've been handling Veronica for longer than you've been on earth. I'm sure today is not going to be any better or worse than any other time she's gotten a stick up her butt."

Alayna hesitated, not wanting to leave Bea to deal with the dragon lady, but her aunt was also right—Bea knew how to handle Veronica. Alayna's being there might just make things worse.

"Okay," Alayna said. "I'll call you later."

She headed out the back door and went down the stairs to the parking lot. Then she stood there for a moment, hands on her hips.

"Well, crap," she said out loud.

They'd hauled the lights to the bookstore in Luke's truck. Alayna had intended to get Bea to take a quick break and give her a ride home, but now she was going to have to wait out Veronica or walk the couple miles to her cottage. It was only May, but the sun was already beating down on the island, and because they were going to be carrying the box, she'd worn jeans rather than her usual shorts. She really wasn't feeling a long walk wearing denim.

The smell of freshly baked waffle cones drifted by and she set out between the buildings. She'd grab a cone and send Bea a text, asking her to call when she could give Alayna a ride. The ice cream shop was next to the bookstore, and she could see Veronica arguing with Bea through the plate glass window as she hurried inside.

Birdie Armstrong, one of Bea's longtime friends and the co-owner of the ice cream shop with her husband, Tom, smiled as she approached the counter. Then her smile wavered as she studied Alayna.

"Is everything all right?" Birdie asked.

"I'm not sure," Alayna said. "Veronica Whitmore was demanding to speak to Bea, so she told me to get scarce before Veronica spotted me. Now Veronica's in the bookstore with Bea and it doesn't look good."

Birdie frowned. "You think it's about your restaurant?"

"Probably. Maybe. I don't know."

Birdie nodded. "Veronica seems to get ruffled over a lot these days. The rest of us aged and got hot flashes. Veronica just got meaner. Bea says it's because she rose from hell and the heat only gives her energy."

"Ha." Alayna let out a single laugh. "That sounds about right."

"Don't you let that bother you. Bea can handle her. I'll grab you a cone and I'll bet Bea's sent her packing before you're done."

"Thanks, Birdie."

Alayna sat at a stool as far away from the windows as she could get and prayed that everyone was right about Bea handling Veronica. Her life was finally getting back on track and for the first time in a long time, she could see a future again. The last thing she wanted was her dream to cause Bea problems.

———

BEA STARED at Veronica as she proceeded to list all her grievances with Bea and Alayna. It wasn't the first time the woman had taken a shot at her niece and it wouldn't be the last. Bea had never figured out what her problem was with them exactly, but figured it started with Bea not bowing down to her like the queen she thought she was. Then Alayna came to live with Bea and she was prettier, more talented, and far nicer than Veronica's daughter Melody, so that probably sealed the deal. Veronica's glee at Alayna's situation in New York had been obvious and clearly, she'd expected the girl to tuck her tail between her legs and disappear from society. Then it all unraveled, leaving Alayna free of any suspicion and with the hottest man on the island at her side, and Bea figured that was straw and camel.

"It's unconscionable," Veronica said. "That girl brought a killer to our island."

"It's not like she loaded him up in her car and ushered him down here," Bea said. "And blaming victims isn't a good look for anyone, especially with city council elections coming up."

"This island is the victim. And as long as Alayna stays here, we're all at risk."

"At risk of what?" Bea asked. "Having more tax revenue from her restaurant?"

"This island doesn't need another restaurant. We have plenty to eat here."

"Glad you feel that way. You won't be taking up a table then."

Veronica pointed her finger at Bea. "That niece of yours is not going to ruin this island."

"This island has managed to get by with you on it all these years. I'm sure it can handle a chef."

"We'll see about that." Veronica whirled around and stomped out of the store.

Bea looked over at Nelly and shook her head.

"Is it too early to start drinking?" Bea asked.

"Drinking doesn't count when you've had to talk to Veronica," Nelly said. "Kinda like calories don't count on holidays."

"That sounds both equitable and prudent."

"You want me to pour you a shot of whiskey?"

"Better wait on that," she said as she checked her text message. "I need to pop out as soon as I send in that book order and give Alayna a ride home. Besides, if I get started on the bottle with you now, your husband will have to haul us both home in a wheelbarrow."

Nelly grinned. "Wouldn't be the first time."

Bea laughed. "Guess not."

"You think she's going to try to cause trouble with the restaurant?"

"I'm sure she would if she could, but she knows what the zoning says. Hasn't changed in years and would take a majority vote of the council to get it changed now. Since most of the council members own businesses on the island, I don't see them being interested in dishing out something that could be done to them later on. And it's a bad precedent to set."

Nelly nodded but didn't look convinced. "And by the time they got anything passed, the restaurant would already be open, right? If the business is existing, aren't there laws to prevent the council from shutting them down?"

"It's still possible to, but the reasons have to stand up in court because the business owner can sue for valuation and loss of revenue, even future revenue. Cities don't want to have those sorts of payouts, so you rarely see that kind of thing unless the business is one that's clearly harming the town."

"How soon could the council be put to vote?"

"The request has to be introduced at one meeting and then they have until the next to research the issues. They'd vote at the next month's meeting."

"And they meet this Thursday, right?" Nelly asked, now looking a little worried.

"Yeah."

"Can Alayna get it open in a month?"

"I think so."

But with the necessary construction, inspections, and the hiring process, Bea wasn't sure.

# CHAPTER SIX

Emma crossed the street, her mind set on a single goal—eating ice cream. The smell of the waffle cones permeated the air downtown and as soon as she'd stepped out of the motel, her stomach had sent her on a quest. The motel had bagels and pastries available in the lobby every morning and she'd popped down earlier to grab a bagel. She'd enjoyed it with coffee sitting on her tiny balcony and taking in the sight, sound, and smell of the ocean. Then she'd cracked open her book and was well on her way to needing to buy another by the time she realized she probably needed to get out and move around. It had been so relaxing that she'd felt all the tension leaving her body as she'd sat there.

She didn't have anything planned for the day...for the whole weekend, for that matter. Last night, when she'd been startled by the storm and the nightmare, she'd wanted to pack up and leave at daybreak and forget she'd ever heard of Tempest Island. But when the sun broke through this morning and lit up her room, she opened the patio doors and took in the smell of salt air and the beauty of the sunlight across the turquoise water, and she just couldn't bring herself to do it. Maybe she'd regret staying, but she knew for certain she'd regret leaving without even giving it a try.

She walked into the ice cream shop, relishing the cool air as she stepped inside. It wasn't a long walk from the motel, but the temperature and humidity made everything seem warmer, even wearing shorts, a tank top, and sandals. An older lady was behind the counter, and a young woman, probably about her age, was seated on a barstool. They'd been in conversation when Emma walked in, but both turned and gave her a smile as she approached.

"Hello," the older woman said. "I'm Birdie. What are you in the mood for today?"

"From the smell wafting down the street, everything," Emma said.

The woman sitting at the counter laughed. "That smell is what had me headed this way. Well, that and needing to kill some time while waiting on my aunt. I'm Alayna."

"I'm Emma. It's nice to meet you both." Emma looked up at the list of ice creams. "I think I'll have a mint chocolate chip cup with waffle cone pieces."

"Good choice," Alayna said and motioned Emma to a stool next to her. "That way you get the waffle cone but don't have to worry about dripping. Are you visiting the island?"

"Yes. Well, sort of. Actually no," Emma said, then shook her head as she sat. "Sorry. That was confusing. I came to the island for a short vacation but have somehow ended up taking a job at the surf shop."

Alayna brightened. "Oh, that's a great shop. And Mark is so nice. He set me up with a paddleboard. I'm still only okay at it, but he was so helpful and patient with all my questions."

Birdie nodded in agreement and set the ice cream in front of Emma. "I didn't know Mark was hiring but he's needed help for a while, I think. With the back-end stuff especially. He's not much of one to complain about things, but I've heard him call that bookkeeping software the devil a time or two."

"Well, I'm going to start exorcising the devil first thing Monday morning," Emma said.

"That's great," Birdie said. "I know he'll be relieved."

Emma took a bite of the ice cream and sighed. It was just the right blend of sweet and minty and was so creamy. The waffle cone pieces were crisp and had just enough sugar to complement the ice cream but not override the taste.

"Sorry," Emma said and grinned. "I needed a moment."

Birdie looked pleased. "All the recipes in here are mine and my husband's. I'm glad you like it."

"All of them are terrific," Alayna said.

"You haven't had all of them," Birdie teased.

"Yes, but now that I've moved back, I intend to," Alayna said and looked at Emma. "Life goals."

Emma nodded. It was a goal she could get behind.

"So I assume you're both locals?" Emma asked.

"My husband and I came here over three decades ago so might as well be," Birdie said.

"I sorta am," Alayna said. "I moved here when I was fifteen to live with my aunt. She owns the bookstore. My parents died in a car crash."

"Oh, I'm so sorry!" Emma said. "That's horrible, especially for you to be so young. I'm glad you had your aunt. I met her yesterday when I bought a book. She seems like a cool lady."

"Aunt Bea is something else," Alayna said.

Birdie snorted. "That's selling it short by a mile at least."

Alayna laughed. "Birdie is one of Aunt Bea's besties, so she knows where all the bodies are buried."

"I should," Birdie said. "I helped dig the holes."

They all laughed, and Emma found herself surprisingly relaxed in the company of these women even though she'd barely met them. It was just the sort of atmosphere you'd hope to find in a place like this, but usually didn't. So far, Tempest Island was exceeding expectations by a mile.

"Anyway," Alayna continued, "after high school, I moved to Austin for a while to attend culinary school and then to New York City to work. But I moved back a few weeks ago and am opening a restaurant in the space above the bookstore."

"You're a chef?" Emma asked, fascinated by this well-put-together but completely approachable woman. She'd always admired people who could cook, especially at a professional level.

"She's not just a chef," Birdie said. "She was a star in the big city. Tempest Island is lucky to have her. This girl can make toast taste like a five-star meal."

Alayna blushed a little, and Emma could tell she was pleased by the compliment.

"I do all right," Alayna said. "But it's because I love being in the kitchen. There couldn't be a more perfect job for me. Do you like to cook, Emma?"

"Lord, no!" Emma said and laughed. "But I love good food, so I'll happily be a customer."

"Where are you moving here from?" Birdie asked.

"The Tampa area," Emma said.

"Is that where your family is?" Birdie asked.

Emma shook her head.

Here it was, the inevitable background check that always happened in small places where everyone knew everyone else and everything about them. This was exactly why she'd never taken a job anywhere but large cities. But if she had any intention of staying on Tempest Island, she needed to decide what she was going to tell people and keep it consistent. Because this wouldn't be the last time someone asked.

"I... My family is all gone," Emma said. "It's just been me since I was twenty."

Birdie and Alayna gave her sympathetic looks and Birdie reached over and patted her hand. "I'm so sorry, dear," she said. "Surely a nice girl like you has got a friend or two to count on."

"I'm afraid not," Emma said. "I've never stayed long enough to make that sort of friend. I guess you could say I've never found my place. I get restless and then need to move on. That's how I wound up on Tempest Island. I cut ties with Tampa, tossed my belongings into my car, and was moving on to the next thing. This was supposed to be a vacation stop, but since I'm starting my job on Monday, I guess that's all changed."

Alayna studied her with a fascinated expression.

"So you just drive until you find somewhere you want to stay for a while?" she asked.

Emma nodded. "Not very scientific, but I've found it's harder for things to go wrong when you don't make plans or have expectations."

"Lord, isn't that the truth," Alayna said. "Well, I'll be your friend while you're here. However long that may be. I'm new here myself, in a way, and could use a girlfriend. Mine from high school are long gone."

Emma felt a warmth in her belly that hadn't been there in so many years that she was surprised when it came. Alayna seemed nice and she'd lost her parents, too. Granted, completely different circumstances and Alayna had her aunt who'd rescued her, but they both knew loss. And there was something about the way Alayna put things—something about her expression when she mentioned New York—that had Emma wondering if there was more behind her return to the island than she was saying. Alayna seemed lovely and happy, but there was that flicker in her eyes of someone who'd been through hardships.

A kindred spirit.

"Only a crazy person would turn down being friends with a chef," Emma said.

Birdie nodded. "Mark hired himself a smart one, I see."

Alayna's phone went off and she checked her texts and frowned.

"What's wrong?" Birdie asked.

"Nothing really," Alayna said. "Bea's got a problem with a delivery and said it might be another hour before she can give me a ride home."

"Well, crap," Birdie said. "If Tom were here, I'd take you myself, but he's off at the boat store again. I have no idea what that man does at the boat store for hours on end. We only have one small bass boat. It's not like we're equipping the *Titanic.*"

"I'm pretty sure it's a man thing," Alayna said.

Birdie sighed and nodded.

"Could I give you a ride?" Emma asked.

"Oh no!" Alayna said. "I don't want to bother you. You only have a couple days of vacation now that you took a job. You don't need to waste it playing Uber driver for me."

"Unless you live in Alabama, I can't imagine it's going to take much of my day," Emma said. "Besides, I don't have anything planned, and what are friends for, right?"

"If you really don't mind," Alayna said, "that would be great. If I sit here another hour, I'm going to eat more ice cream. And as much as I love that idea, my thighs hate it."

"I don't mind," Emma said. "Are you ready now? I've polished off this ice cream way faster than should be allowed and sitting here longer is going to be dangerous."

"Ready when you are," Alayna said and hopped off the stool. "What do I owe you, Birdie?"

Birdie waved a hand in dismissal. "On the house for both of you. Now get out and enjoy the day."

"Thanks!" Alayna said.

"Thank you," Emma said. "I'm going to have to up my daily run, but I'm definitely going to be back."

Birdie gave them both a smile and a wave as they left.

---

HE LEFT the shop in Miami smiling. He was getting closer.

For eight years now, he'd been tracking Katarina Petras, and finally, he was closing in. People didn't talk the way they used to, especially when a strange man was asking questions about a single woman, but he still managed to get enough from the occasional exchanged looks and facial expressions to know that Katarina had stopped in a location for a bit.

He presumed she changed her appearance and often, people didn't even recognize her from the old photo he had. But when they looked long enough, he figured it was because they saw some similarities to someone they knew but couldn't quite place her. And based on those reactions, he was fairly certain Katarina had been in Miami, working at this store. Of course, none of the employees would verify that, but the new girl told him she'd been hired seven months earlier and everyone else had been working there for over a year.

He was getting closer.

Seven months seemed like a long time, but with every city he managed to track her to, he was narrowing the gap. Years had become months. Eventually, he'd narrow it to zero.

And then Katarina would pay for all the damage she'd caused.

# CHAPTER SEVEN

As Emma and Alayna left the ice cream shop, Emma pointed to her car parked in front of the motel.

"So you said you don't have plans, right?" Alayna asked.

"Nope."

"How about you grab a swimsuit and go paddleboarding with me?"

"Oh! I don't know. I've never done it."

"It's not hard. I mean, it's definitely some effort, but not impossible. It's such a beautiful day and I'd really like to go out in the Gulf. But if I go by myself, Aunt Bea or Luke will have my hide."

"Who's Luke?"

Alayna blushed. "My boyfriend."

"Boyfriend? And you've only been back a few weeks? Either you brought him with you or that's some seriously fast work."

"It was fast work and when you see him, you'll know why. So will you please come out on the board with me? Pretty please?"

Emma laughed. "Okay, I'll go."

"I knew you wouldn't be able to resist."

"Of course not. I'm hoping to see this Luke up close."

Alayna grinned and Emma headed into the motel. She waved at Gary and hurried upstairs to put on her swimsuit and grab some sunscreen. She couldn't remember the last time she'd done something with a girlfriend. There had been one girl in Charleston who had been the closest thing to a friend that she'd had, but she'd moved back to California, and Emma had decided it was time to move on. And there was a coworker in Tampa that she'd done a few after-work things with, but they'd kept everything very surface level.

Usually, Emma limited her social outings to groups or the random coworker who was as private as she was, like the girl in Tampa. That way, no one really pressed her for intimate details of her life, and since she'd always pretended disdain for social media, no one could stay in touch when she pulled up stakes and left. A choice few people had her email and her previous employers had her cell phone number, but it was a prepaid one and she changed it out every few years.

When she got back downstairs, she saw that Alayna had stepped inside and was chatting happily with Gary. Emma looked at them and wondered what it would have been like to grow up in a place where everyone knew everyone, especially a place like Tempest Island, where so far, people were friendly.

"Ready?" Alayna asked when she spotted Emma.

"As ready as I'm getting," Emma said.

"I'm going to take Emma out paddleboarding with me," Alayna said.

Gary smiled. "It's a good day for it. You girls be careful and have fun."

"Thanks!" Alayna said as they headed out.

Alayna directed Emma west on the main road, and Emma

took in the area as she drove. "This side is a lot less populated," she said.

Alayna nodded. "This side of the island is a lot skinnier than the east side of downtown, so there's really only room for houses on the Gulf side. The Sound side is so narrow in some spots that water comes over the road during big storms. It's the perfect location as far as I'm concerned. Close enough to the bookstore and ice cream shop, but no one is staring at you when you sit on your back deck."

"That does sound perfect," Emma said, and before she could change her mind, she violated yet another of her personal rules. "I know New York is the place for food, so I get why you'd go there after culinary school, but can I ask why you returned? I mean, everything I've seen of the island is great, but I know it can't compare to the restaurants in the big city."

Alayna frowned. "That's a long story. Tell you what—let's take the board out, then when we're exhausted, we'll sit on the deck, have some drinks, and I'll tell you the mostly unbelievable story of the past year of my life."

"Now you have me all interested. I was expecting the usual things."

"There's nothing usual about my return to Tempest Island."

Emma nodded. The tension in Alayna's mouth and jaw when she spoke was apparent. Whatever had happened in New York was so unpleasant that even though Alayna seemed to have established a good life on the island with an upcoming restaurant opening and a new boyfriend, the stress of it still showed on her face.

"My house is the next one," Alayna said.

Emma pulled in the drive of the pretty white cottage with turquoise trim and smiled. Palm trees and tropical flowers adorned the sand-filled front lawn, and sea oats ran down both sides of the cottage, blocking it from view of the cottage on the right side. The nearest cottage on the left side was a good fifty yards away with high dunes in between, creating a ton of privacy one wouldn't normally expect in a tourist area.

"This is so pretty," Emma said as they headed for the front door.

"Wait until you see the view," Alayna said and opened the door. She stepped inside and turned off the alarm system and Emma followed.

It was small but efficiently laid out, and the turquoise walls and white cabinets and trim made the entire place feel fresh and calm. Emma took in the bevy of high-end kitchen appliances that lined the limited countertop space and smiled. If she had her own place, it would probably only have a toaster oven, a microwave, and a coffeepot.

Past the open kitchen and living room area was where the real show began. The back wall of the living room consisted of two huge patio doors, the glass bringing the sand and sea from the outside to the inside. She gazed out at the water and sighed.

"You're right," Emma said. "It *is* perfect."

"I'm really lucky. Bea bought this cottage and the one next door back years and years ago before the island got popular with the tourists. The empty land on the other side is turtle and bird nesting ground and is protected so nothing will ever be built there. She rents the other cottage but has kept this one for personal use only for years now. Luke is renting the one next door."

"Which is how you met," Emma said.

Alayna nodded. "And all part of the story I'll tell you later. I'll put on my suit and meet you on the back patio. You can leave your cover-up in the living room. It will blow away on the deck."

Seconds later, Emma stepped onto the patio and took in the sounds and smells of the ocean along with the view. In all her travels, she'd never been to a place where she felt such an instant connection. The sea here brought a sense a peace to her that she hadn't felt since she was a child.

*If only it wasn't temporary.*

Alayna walked outside, breaking Emma from her thoughts, and handed her two beach towels. Then she grabbed a big turquoise paddleboard from brackets on the side of the cottage.

"Do you need help?" Emma asked. The board was significantly bigger than Alayna.

"I'm good," Alayna said. "It's lighter than it looks. Just bulky. But trust me, you'll be thankful for all that space when you stand up on it."

She tucked the board under one arm and grabbed a paddle, and they headed down to the beach.

"When it's really calm, I love to paddleboard in the Gulf," Alayna said. "Days like today, where there's hardly any surf, don't come along very often. I usually end up boarding in the Sound."

"But the board can take the waves, right?"

"Oh, the board would be fine. *I* would be a disaster."

Emma laughed. "I'm sure I would be as well. But I can't wait to try it. I've seen people doing it and always wondered. I really appreciate you inviting me out."

Alayna smiled. "I told you, I could use a friend. And I think you're going to be a good one."

"I'd like that. It's been a long time since I've had a friend. A real one if you know what I mean."

Alayna nodded. "Me too. I lost track of high school friends after we all scattered to enter adulthood. I was too busy in culinary school and while working my way up to New York.

And that city definitely wasn't the easiest place to meet people. So many don't make it and leave, and the ones who stay are working so hard to keep their heads above water or move up that they have little time for anything else."

"I can see that. It's been the same with me moving around. I guess I didn't see the point of getting invested because I knew I wouldn't stick around. But maybe I should make a bigger effort. I'm probably missing out on a lot of fun. Like this."

"I wouldn't say you've been wrong to do it. It's worked for you, and I don't blame you for not wanting to form an attachment that you know won't last and will make leaving hard. But I do think that if you click with someone, maybe it's worth it, even if it's only for a couple months or a year or whatever. I have a good feeling about you, and I think we'll click just fine."

Emma warmed at the thought. She hadn't had a real friend since college. And even then, the relationships lacked depth since most of her energy went toward school and fending off her parents' antiquated desires for her future.

"I have a good feeling about you too," Emma said.

A flash of something passed over Alayna's expression—pain, uncertainty, regret? Emma couldn't pin it exactly, but it made her wonder all over again what had happened to Alayna that caused those momentary lapses from her normal sunny personality.

"Okay," Alayna said as they reached the shoreline. "Just toss the towels back there somewhere and we'll head into the water."

"You aren't going to give me instructions on land?"

"I asked Luke the same thing when he taught me, but it's not necessary. You'll see. We won't even get in water over your head."

Even though she was a strong swimmer, that made Emma

feel a little better. That and the fact that the water was so clear she could see her toes.

When they'd gotten waist-deep, Alayna explained to Emma how to position herself when she got on the board and gave her two different ways of getting from kneeling to standing. Emma had always been athletic and had continued running and training at the gym no matter where she'd lived, so she knew she was in decent shape. But every sport worked some muscles harder than others, and Emma had no doubt that tomorrow some parts would be telling her just how much more she needed to add to her routine.

She jumped on the board and positioned herself sitting back on her feet where Alayna indicated. Alayna clutched the board to steady it, and Emma took a deep breath and pushed herself up into a standing position. She wobbled at first, and Alayna told her to space her feet out farther. When she inched them out, it stabilized her a bit more and she let out the breath she'd been holding. This wasn't so bad.

"You're doing great!" Alayna said. "Okay, now here's the paddle."

Alayna handed her the paddle and explained how to use it, and Emma took her first strokes toward the bank. She was smiling the entire time, unable to recall the last time she'd tried something new, much less something this fun.

"The view from up here is incredible," Emma said. "It's amazing how just a few feet give you an entirely different perspective."

Alayna, who'd been walking along with her as she paddled, nodded. "I love kayaking as well, but the view is much better from the board. Okay, we're getting pretty shallow, so now you're going to turn."

Emma followed Alayna's instructions and had just about made it all the way around when she paddled a little too forcefully and sent herself off-balance. She pitched off the board and hit the water, then popped up immediately, laughing at herself.

"I got in too much of a hurry," Emma said.

"I do the same thing. Do you want to go again?"

"Absolutely!"

They spent almost two hours in the water, trading the board off so one could rest while the other paddled. By that time, they were both ready to call it quits and headed to the bank.

"I'm glad we got out here when we did," Alayna said. "The wind's starting to pick up, and I can already see the waves forming."

They headed back to Alayna's cottage and rinsed off under an outdoor shower, then Emma sat in a patio chair—as instructed per her host—while Alayna said she was going inside to get them something to drink. Emma was so lost in the view and rehashing the paddleboarding in her mind that it seemed like no time until Alayna popped back out with a pitcher of margaritas, glasses, and a tray of crackers, cheese, and dips.

Emma took the tray from her and placed it on the table. "I would have helped if I'd known you were hauling half the kitchen out here."

"Professional chef, remember? This was nothing."

"Well, it looks fantastic. Did you make the dips?"

Alayna nodded. "Try the one in the blue tray. It's a crab dip I'm thinking about offering at the restaurant."

Emma scooped up a generous serving of the dip onto a cracker and popped the whole thing in her mouth. It was an explosion of cream cheese, chives, and crab with just a hint of spicy.

"I would eat there just for this," Emma said and scooped

another serving.

Alayna smiled, clearly pleased. "Well, now that I've worn you out and given you alcohol and good food, I'll tell you the story of why I returned to Tempest Island. Then you can decide if you still want to be friends."

Emma stared. Where had that comment come from? What in the world could Alayna have possibly done that would make Emma not want to be her friend?

"Unless you're a serial killer, I'm not giving up another shot at this dip," Emma said.

Alayna gave her a rueful smile. "Nothing so glamorous. Just a woman who picked the wrong man and paid dearly for it. I was dating Warren Patterson III."

Emma sucked in a breath. "Oh my God! I don't ever watch the news. It depresses me. But my coworkers talked about the whole thing for weeks. They said his girlfriend was stalked and almost killed after he'd been arrested, then escaped. That was you?"

Alayna nodded. "My life flashed before my eyes right behind you in the cottage."

Emma shook her head. "I can't believe it. And I don't know why I didn't make the connection with that story and Tempest Island, especially when I decided to veer this direction."

"If you don't watch the news, you might never have caught the location, much less my name or even the whole story surrounding it. Most reporters spent their time calling attention to New York City and the Pattersons. I can tell you what happened if you'd like, or you can google it."

"No. I don't trust the media to get things right. And why would I want to read third-party reporting when the person who knows exactly what happened is sitting right next to me? If you don't mind, that is. I don't want to bring all that up if it's going to upset you."

"Actually, I think it might help. I mean, I've told the story to a ton of cops, and FBI, and the DA and of course, Aunt Bea, but I've never really covered it with someone who wasn't invested in some way, you know? I think it might do me some good to lay it out."

"Cathartic?"

"Maybe. Anyway, if you're willing to listen, I'd like to try."

"Of course."

"So the whole nightmare started the night of a December party," Alayna began.

For the next hour, Alayna told Emma about everything that had transpired with Warren. Periodically, Alayna got a bit choked up, but she refused to stop, saying she needed to finish. She told Emma about how she fled New York for Tempest Island and how everyone had assured her she was safe. How she'd met Luke and they'd had an instant connection. And how working together, they'd saved each other's lives.

By the time she was done, Emma was teary-eyed and clutching Alayna's hand. She knew—so much better than most people—just how terrorized Alayna had been. How foolish she'd felt, finding out that people she trusted and cared about were nothing like the front they wore. How she'd known that something was still wrong—that she wasn't safe—despite all the reassurances to the contrary.

Emma and Alayna had more in common than Alayna would ever know.

"I am so sorry you went through all of that," Emma said when she finally found her voice. "It all seems so fantastic, and yet, it's your life."

Alayna squeezed her hand. "There are moments that it's still surreal. I'll wake up sometimes and for a split second, I think I'm back in New York. And then it all comes rushing back in and I'm overwhelmed all over again. But already, it's happening less. And Luke and Aunt Bea ride me hard about being so tough on myself."

"Why are you tough on yourself? Nothing that happened is even remotely your fault. You got caught in the middle of something you didn't create and definitely didn't ask for. You lost your restaurant and almost lost your life. There are plenty of people who should have a guilty conscience about what happened, but you're not one of them."

Emma choked up a little as she delivered the last words. She'd meant everything she said, and yet she was spouting this advice at Alayna that she had never quite been able to take herself.

"I don't feel responsible," Alayna said. "I think what I still have trouble reconciling is that Warren completely fooled me. It made me question my judgment. Earlier, when I said I had a good feeling about you, I meant that, but it's something I struggle with. I have to force myself to accept that my instincts aren't wrong—it's that Warren was so good at deception. Intellectually, I get it, but that doesn't stop those moments of doubt."

Suddenly, Alayna's shifts in expression that Emma had seen earlier made perfect sense, especially as it was something Emma lived with herself. "I can see that, and I wish I had some words of wisdom for you. I know it's got to be incredibly hard to process all of that, even now."

Alayna nodded. "Everyone wants me to forget and move on, and I'm working on it, I swear. But it doesn't just go away because I'm safe now."

"Time will help. Unfortunately, you can't speed that up."

"At the rate my skin is aging in this sun, I don't think I want to."

Emma smiled. "At least you have Luke. You proved that you *can* trust the right person."

"Luke is my real-life hero. He was a Navy SEAL before his injury forced him to step back from that role. I'm only one of many lives he's saved."

"But the most important one as far as he is concerned."

Alayna sniffed. "I can't wait for you to meet him. And thank you so much for listening to me. I've taken up a good chunk of the day with my depressing story. I hope the paddle-boarding and the food make up for it a little."

"I'm glad you shared it with me, and I don't find your story depressing at all. I think it's inspiring, and I believe you're going to have the most successful restaurant in the area and come home to a sexy war hero every night. You might have had an extreme rough patch, but you're on your way to living the dream now."

Alayna smiled. "I'm so glad you came into the ice cream shop. And that I forced you to come home with me. I hope the job works out well for you and you stay a long, long time."

Emma caught herself right as she frowned and tried to adjust quickly enough that Alayna wouldn't notice, but she didn't make it.

"I know, staying in one place isn't your thing," Alayna said. "But you have to stop someday, right? Maybe it will be here."

Emma felt her chest tighten as she took in Alayna's hopeful expression. It had been so long since she'd felt that tug of kinship, of wanting to matter to someone. She'd blocked herself off from emotional involvement for so long that she'd forgotten what it felt like to care about someone else. But Alayna's story had moved her in a way that nothing else had since that night. Still, when the time came, Emma knew she'd disappear from Alayna's life as quickly as she'd entered it.

Tempest Island, no matter how attractive, was just another stop in the road.

# CHAPTER EIGHT

MARK TURNED ON THE LIGHTS IN THE SURF SHOP AND FIRED up the computer at the register. The store didn't officially open until 10:00 a.m., but his new employee was due in a half hour. Assuming she showed. He hated to admit it, but he had his doubts. Emma's résumé had shown solid experience that could be parlayed into a good-paying position at a bigger store, and she could have a desk job only. Not this hodgepodge of stuff that he needed done. She was more than qualified to handle the bookkeeping and completely overqualified to run his errands.

Probably, she'd rethought the entire thing over the weekend and at 9:00 a.m., he'd get a phone call letting him know she'd come to her senses and decided to pursue something more defined and with better pay. Either way, his original plan of getting here early and trying to force some form of organization in the office was likely a waste of time. Which was the perfect excuse to scroll through the new T-shirt offerings rather than attempt to focus on random piles of paper on the desk.

He was so involved with his perusal of the catalog that a

knock on the front door of the shop surprised him. He glanced down at his watch—8:55. Unless it was a customer with the wrong opening time or a really ambitious delivery driver, Emma had shown up. He jumped up from the desk and hurried into the store, his pulse ticking up a notch when he saw Emma standing at the door.

She smiled as he approached and he felt a jolt that hadn't coursed through him in a long time. Attraction. Shocked at the unfamiliar feeling, he slowed but managed to keep from stopping abruptly, which would have looked odd. Where the heck had that come from? Granted, he was a normal guy, but those kind of normal-guy feelings hadn't happened since Beth passed.

Immediately, guilt coursed through him, and he tried to talk himself off the edge as he took the remaining couple steps to the door. The attraction didn't have to mean anything. He'd loved Beth with every inch of himself and still did. But he wasn't blind and Emma was an attractive woman. Even more attractive this morning with her mass of auburn hair flowing down her back, setting off her green eyes. Her face and arms had a glow that indicated she'd spent some time in the sun this weekend, and it stood out perfectly against the pale yellow tank she was wearing.

He forced a smile and silently yelled at his mind to stop spinning. Why the hell hadn't he noticed all of this before he offered her a job?

*Because you were too worried about the accounting and Lily's future and were so desperate for salvation, you weren't paying attention.*

Well, he was paying attention now.

He took a deep breath and forced his troubled mind into silence. His feelings were perfectly normal, especially given how long it had been since he'd been in the company of a woman. Romantically, that is. But they didn't have to mean anything. Emma was his employee and that was all she'd ever be. He'd just focus on the business and everything would be fine.

He unlocked the door and pushed it open, waving Emma inside.

"I had convinced myself you'd changed your mind and wouldn't show," he said.

A flicker of doubt crossed her face, and he knew that she was also questioning her decision.

"I booked a week at the motel, so you've got me for that at least," she said. "And if things go well for both of us, then I'll find a more permanent living situation."

He nodded and locked the door behind them.

"Come with me and I'll show you your office," he said. "It's not fancy or big and the drawer sticks on the right side of the desk. I've also been meaning to get a new chair. The current one leans a little to one side, but I figured when I hired someone, they could take a look and pick out something they liked."

She gave him a shy smile. "I'm sure it will be fine."

He motioned her into a tiny office. "This is it."

She glanced around—it didn't take more than a glance to see everything—then waved at the stacks of paper covering the desk.

"I assume that's the accounting?" she asked.

"I'm embarrassed to say that it is."

"How many weeks are you behind?"

"Um...how many in this year?"

"Oh Lord. You really do need help." She dropped her purse on top of a file cabinet. "Tell me where to find the bathroom and coffee, then get me a log-in and I'll get started."

He blinked. "Just like that? You don't want me to go over the new accounting software?"

She raised one eyebrow. "I'm going to assume that if you knew how to use the new accounting software, it wouldn't look like the file cabinets blew up."

He laughed. "That's true enough. The instructions are in that binder under the stack next to the keyboard if you need them. Break room is next door to the office and there's a bathroom in there. I keep coffee, water, sports drinks, and the random soda in the fridge. If you like anything in particular, let me know and I'll stock it."

She nodded. "What about the upstairs? Do you keep any inventory there?"

"No. It's all been remodeled into living space, which is where Lily and I live. The first door we passed on the left is the room that serves as storage. I try to keep inventory on the low side since most of my suppliers fulfill orders in a week or two."

"Perfect. That keeps costs down and less inventory means less to track."

He stood there watching her as she looked down at the messy desk then back up at him with a smile, which shook him out of his stupor. What was he doing standing there like an idiot? She'd asked for information. He'd given it. Now he needed to get out and let her do the job she seemed perfectly capable of doing, assuming her résumé was the gospel.

"Well, I'll get out of here and let you get to it," he said. "My office is across the hall from yours. I'll be in there until the store opens, then I'll be up front. If you need anything or have any questions, let me know."

She nodded and took a seat in the chair. "Thanks. I'm sure I'll have lots of questions once I get everything organized and start on the accounting."

He headed across the hall to his office, shaking his head as he walked. She'd looked almost excited when he left. As though she was actually looking forward to delving into that nightmare on the desk. He couldn't understand the sentiment at all, but he appreciated the fact that she felt that way.

This might work out after all.

———

It was after noon when Emma leaned back in the crooked chair and turned around to look outside the window. As soon as she'd entered the office, she'd wondered why the desk had been placed in the center of the room and facing the wall when the view directly behind it was better than a painting. Of course, as she watched the gentle turquoise surf roll in, she figured it was probably self-defense. It might be harder to concentrate on work with all that temptation just inches away.

Still, she planned on asking Mark if she could rearrange everything. The file cabinets along the side wall that made the office entirely too narrow could move to the back wall. The folding table against the back wall—which currently housed more stacks of paper and boxes of accounting records from years past—could probably be relocated into the storage area, which she'd peeked in on before she'd gotten started and verified it had some available space. That would leave only the printer on a rolling cart on the side wall and should significantly reduce the claustrophobic feeling of the small room.

That and getting the tons of paperwork organized and filed.

But she'd made a credible dent so far. At least she'd separated the paperwork on the desk into stacks of paid and unpaid invoices, receipts, and random documentation that belonged in files. She'd take a quick break to stretch her legs and back—something she should have done hours ago—eat the bagel and banana she'd snagged from breakfast this morning at the motel, and then tackle the accounting software.

She rose from her chair and stretched her arms over her head, leaning back. Since he'd given her instructions, Emma hadn't seen hide nor hair of Mark, but she'd heard him greeting and talking to customers as his laugh trickled down the hall. He sounded upbeat and enthusiastic, and she wondered what it would feel like to wake up every day in paradise and then head downstairs to a job you loved.

*After getting his motherless daughter off to school.*

She saddened at the thought of that heartache. That was the definite downside. But Lily seemed like a great kid, and Mark had Jane and his friends on Tempest Island to help. He appeared to be doing a good job handling everything. Well, except the accounting, but she couldn't really fault him for that. Not everyone was cut out for the numbers game. In fact, her experience had been that most people weren't. Even those who managed to gain some competence at it often relegated the tasks right up there with exercise and root canal.

She snagged a bottled water from the break room and headed for the back door at the end of the hall. When she stepped onto the deck, the heat hit her first, then the smell of salt water and suntan lotion. She drew in a deep breath and slowly blew it out. Perfection. If someone could bottle it up into a room deodorizer, she'd buy it.

The patio was large and had a picnic table on one side and Adirondack chairs lining the other side. The deck above provided shade for the seating area. She slid onto the picnic table bench and put her lunch on the table. Of all the places she'd worked, this was her absolute favorite. It didn't take more than a half day to make up her mind. Her office might be small and cramped—something she'd work on fixing—but lunch and breaks were definitely going to be the highlight of her day. Even when it got super hot and humid, she knew she'd still be sitting here on the deck, watching Mother Nature at her finest. It helped that shorts and a tank were within the dress code.

She unwrapped her bagel and took a big bite. She'd skipped breakfast and hadn't noticed she was getting hungry while she was working. But now that she'd caught sight of food, she was starving. If she wanted to make the most of her lunch hour, rather than spend the majority of it acquiring food from one of the local restaurants, she was going to have to pick up some easy-to-fix meals. There was plenty of room in the break room cabinets and refrigerator to put some sandwich stuff, fruit, and some crackers. She'd make sure Mark didn't mind and then do a shopping trip this evening at the grocery store downtown. She had a mini fridge in her motel room, so she'd get some stuff for there as well.

She'd just taken her second bite when Mark walked outside. He saw her at the table and strolled over with a sandwich and a sports drink and sat on the other end of the bench facing the water.

"I see you found my favorite lunch spot," he said.

She nodded. "I might have to negotiate a longer lunch hour."

He smiled. "It's unlike anything else, isn't it? The ocean, I mean. No matter how many times I see it, I'm still caught up in its strength and beauty."

She nodded, completely sharing his sentiment. "Have you always lived close to the water?"

"Always. I've been really lucky. My parents were hippies who lived in a shack near the beach in Southern California. They cleaned office buildings at night so they could surf during the day, and probably because it was a job they could do without shoes on because no one was around to see. They never put them on unless they had to. My dad got me up on a board as soon as I could walk. No waves, of course. I worked up to that. We didn't have much, but we had the ocean."

Emma pictured Mark's less affluent but simpler childhood compared to hers and decided he'd gotten the better deal. "That sounds wonderful," she said. "Are your parents still in California?"

He shook his head, his expression sad. "My dad died surfing eight years ago. One of those freak things, but they happen. I know that he went out doing something he loved and that's some comfort, but I wish he would have gotten a chance to see me on the circuit."

"Circuit? Like, pro surfing?"

"Yeah. But I got a late start compared to most. I went into the Navy after high school."

"Seems perfect for an ocean lover."

He smiled. "It was. I was on an aircraft carrier and cruised the world. Put in eight years, getting an opportunity to surf at some of the best beaches in the world. Then I got an offer to go pro. A shop owner had seen me in a contest in Hawaii and got a clothes sponsor, board sponsor, and some others. I knew it was a long shot to make a career with, but I also knew I wouldn't get another opportunity. So I left the Navy when my time was up and moved to Hawaii. That's where I met Beth, my wife. She was a sales rep for one of my sponsors."

Emma knew she should stop asking questions because it inevitably led to her being asked questions. But she couldn't seem to help herself. Mark had led a life different from most, and she was interested in how he'd landed on Tempest Island.

"So how did you do on the circuit?" she asked.

"Pretty good. I finished in the top ten of every event for a couple years, then won a few and stayed in the top five. I was thinking my next year was going to be my best and it started off great. Then I had a bad wipeout and hurt my back. It's fine for amateur level but not where it needs to be for me to be competitive in the pros. And if I had another bad wipeout, I could have ended up disabled. I couldn't do that to Beth and Lily, so I retired from surfing, bought this shop, and we moved to Tempest Island. My surfing buddies thought I was crazy, leaving the big surf for the calmer waters in Florida."

"Looks like it worked out for you."

"Best decision I've ever made. I love the beach, the town, the people—everything about it, really."

"You said your father passed away... Is your mother still in California?"

He shook his head. "She's here on the mainland in a memory care facility. Early-onset dementia. I managed to cover in-house care for her at her home until it was dangerous. Then I figured if she was going to have to be in a skilled nursing facility, she might as well be in Florida where I could visit regularly. She doesn't know where she is anyway, so it doesn't matter. Doesn't know me very often, either."

"I'm so sorry."

"Hey, that's life, right? Sometimes it throws you a curveball and you just have to swing at it and hope for the best. At least my mother is generally happy even if her memory is sketchy. It could be a lot worse."

"I love your attitude," Emma said. "Lily is lucky to have you. A lot of parents wouldn't have handled all this as well as you have."

A faint blush crept through his tan. "I think I'm the lucky one. Lily has put me to shame with her resilience, especially given her age."

"You know, I think younger might be better for big

changes. Every day, just about, kids experience something new. I think it's when we're older and more set in our ways that change is harder to assimilate. Especially when it's change we don't want or that doesn't fall within the natural order or timing of things. And even ten times more when it's painful."

He nodded. "I suppose adaptation is easier when you haven't already decided how the rest of your life should be. What about you? You got any family here in Florida?"

"No family in Florida or anywhere else."

He gave her a surprised look. "None at all?"

She shook her head. "My parents were immigrants and fell out with their respective families long before they left Europe. I lost them both when I was twenty, but it's not something I like to talk about in detail."

Mark's expression was so sympathetic that she felt almost guilty lying to him. But she wasn't lying so much as she was simply avoiding telling him the truth.

"I'm so sorry," he said. "That must have been incredibly hard. Is that why you don't stay anywhere too long?"

"Probably. It's easier to move around when you don't have roots holding you in one place, and I'll admit that I enjoy seeing new places and the challenge of tackling a new job. It keeps things interesting and avoids routine."

He smiled. "After the Navy, I was all about interesting and avoiding routine until Lily came along. Now if I have a break in my routine, it's a cause for panic."

"Well, I'm going to get your accounting squared away, so at least if life throws you another curveball, you've got some bandwidth to stretch for it. But I'm really hoping you catch a break and this gives you some time off from work and worry."

"I can feel my shoulders relaxing already. So I assume it's going okay? When I never heard anything, I thought maybe you'd slipped out the back and run away. I was really glad to see you out here."

She laughed. "Trust me, this is not even the biggest mess I've seen. I spent the morning organizing the paperwork on the desk. I'm going to tackle the accounting software after lunch, so you'll probably get a ton of questions then until I learn the expense line items and all that. And I was going to ask you—do you mind if I rearrange the office?"

"No. Why would I?"

"Well, I probably won't be here long term, and I thought there had to be a reason it's arranged with my back to the window..."

"Ah, that was because Beth said it was too distracting to work when she could see outside. She was great with numbers and did all the office stuff, but she also picked up some other local clients and wanted to get in and out as quickly as possible so she didn't have to work late."

"I figured it was something like that, but if it's all the same to you, I think I'd prefer the beautiful view. Relaxation helps my concentration, and it's impossible to look out at all of this and be upset."

"It is, which is why my desk is under the window, although I will admit to doing a lot of sighing when I was stuck with paperwork and wanted to be in the water. Did you figure out something with the office chair?"

"What's my budget?"

He shrugged. "I can afford something good if you have anything particular in mind."

"There was a chair at one of my jobs that was fantastic. Not the cheapest but a long warranty, so a better deal in the long run."

"Send me a link and I'll get two of them. Mine is shot as well. One of these days, I'm afraid it's going to dump me right out in the floor. I inherited them with the store. I'm thinking they were purchased about the time the building went up."

She laughed. "No problem."

He rose from the bench. "I better get the sign turned back to *Open*. I need the summer trade, but it's nice when it's just the locals and they respect an *Out to Lunch* sign. Do you want to move that furniture now?"

"If you have the time, that would be great."

"Let me grab the dolly. It will be easier to move those file cabinets. I have sliders we can use for the desk and the tables."

"Great!" Emma grabbed her wrapper and the uneaten banana and headed inside. Using the dolly and the sliders, they were able to move everything into place without incident or strain, and when they were done, Mark looked around the space and nodded.

"This looks so much better," he said. "Way more open with this layout and that table gone. And that table will come in handy in the other room unpacking inventory."

"Maybe all that paperwork doesn't look so claustrophobic anymore?" she teased.

"It still looks awful to me, so I'm going to head up front and fold T-shirts. Maybe polish the clothes racks and dust the fake plant."

"That bad, huh?"

"You have no idea. Holler if you have any questions."

As he started to leave, he reached for the dolly beside her and for a split second, she thought he was reaching for her. Something in her expression must have shifted because a puzzled look flashed over his face, then he quickly grabbed the dolly and left the room.

She watched as he walked away and blew out a breath. Good Lord, what was wrong with her? She'd completely tensed when he'd reached for the dolly. But why? For a long time after seeing her father murder someone, she'd had dreams about Danek's men catching up with her. It had left her wary about having men too close, and sudden movement usually had her taking a step back. But this didn't feel like that. It was almost as if she was afraid he was going to touch her and also afraid he wasn't.

Which really wouldn't do.

She turned to face her new desk view and sighed. The office, the town, the people, and the work couldn't have been better if she'd ordered it up herself.

Except for her unwanted attraction to her boss.

# CHAPTER NINE

BEA STOOD IN THE BREAK ROOM AT THE BOOKSTORE, HANDS on her hips and locked in a rare moment of having no idea what to say. Her friend Birdie sat at the break room table, her eyes puffy and red from recently crying, and her shoulders hunched as though she'd given up on life. If someone had a broken pipe, a leaky roof, or an investment question, Bea was their girl. Relationships, however, were not in her wheelhouse, which explained why she'd never married.

But Birdie was clearly suffering, and Bea had to fix that.

Fixing things was what Bea did.

"I just don't know what to do," Birdie said. "I know something is up with Tom, and I'm tired of getting the runaround. He's supposedly been to the boat store four times in the last two weeks, but I have yet to see a charge come through for it. Now, what man is in a marine store the size of Walmart and never buys anything?"

Bea shook her head. She couldn't argue with Birdie's logic. And every time she saw her friend, guilt coursed through her because she had been keeping something from Birdie. Something that might explain Tom's lack of retail therapy. When Bea had taken a recent overnight jaunt to New Orleans with Nelly, she'd seen Tom entering an apartment building. The woman who'd let him in was considerably younger than Birdie and had hugged him after she'd opened the door.

Ever since that day, Bea had been struggling to find a way to tell Birdie what she'd seen, but as soon as she'd set her mind on it, she'd have second thoughts and wonder if she shouldn't approach Tom instead and give him an opportunity to fess up. More than anything, she wanted her longtime friends to work out whatever the problem was and get on with their marriage, but so many men fell into this mindset of wanting younger. She had zero idea why. Pop psychologists claimed it was a fear of death, but that made no sense to Bea. When she was around younger people, she was *more* aware of her advancing age, not less so.

"What do I do?" Birdie asked, and the pain in her voice made Bea's heart clench.

She had to fix this. Had to do something. It wasn't fair for Tom to leave her friend in a state of flux. If he wanted something different for the rest of his days, then he needed to man up and tell his wife. He owed her respect at minimum.

"Have you come right out and asked him what was wrong?" Bea asked.

"Over and over. He just makes excuses like he didn't sleep well, or his arthritis is acting up because it's raining, or he must have eaten something that didn't agree, or his allergies have given him a headache. Honestly, if all of those things were wrong with me in a span of a few months, I'd have been to the doctor."

"But he won't go?"

"Not a chance, and I've pushed probably more than I should have in that direction. He just digs his heels in and refuses. Tom has always been stubborn, but I never thought him stubborn beyond common sense."

"So you don't think anything's wrong with him? Medically, I mean?"

Birdie shrugged. "He does seem to get tired quickly lately, but I figure all his energy is spent on another woman. We're not exactly spring chickens. He might have been able to handle two women in his twenties, but he's well past that now."

Bea nodded. She'd been short on male companionship for a while now but even when she was seeing someone, she'd found their time together was more coffee and talks over the sunset these days than kayaking or sexy time. Bea found that unfortunate because she had no intention of slowing down until they covered her with dirt. She often wondered if retirement for some people was like foreplay to death. Too many people quit working but had nothing to quit for. Then they just seemed to stop living.

But that wasn't the case with Tom and Birdie, which was why she was so confused. They were still working their ice cream shop, and she didn't figure they were looking to stop any more than she was looking to stop working at her bookstore. They loved their shop and chatting with all the locals and the vacationers. Thankfully, the money earned from it was no longer a necessity, so finances weren't the problem, either.

"I wish I knew what to do," Bea said. "Have you given any thought to my suggestion of hiring someone to follow him?"

"I wouldn't even know where to start. It's not like I know when he's going to go out on one of his jaunts, unless he claims he's visiting that incorrigible buddy of his."

"What do you mean 'claims'?"

"Because I don't think that's where he was the last time he said he was going to visit. That guy called the other day, and I answered the phone. Even though he'd try the patience of a saint, I'm always pleasant, so I asked if he'd enjoyed their visit. He went dead quiet for a moment, then stuttered around with platitudes like 'always great to see a friend' and 'good conversation is the best medicine.' But I'd bet money Tom never went there."

"And obviously didn't think to ask his friend to cover for him, either," Bea said. "Which means whatever he's up to, he's keeping the secret from everyone, not just you."

Birdie nodded, clearly miserable. "So how do you hire a detective? Do they charge by the hour? Because they might have to watch him for days before he went anywhere. We both have our own play money, so I could afford a bit without taking it from our joint account, but I probably can't cover a lot of time."

Guilt coursed through Bea once more. She already knew where Tom had gone the day he was supposed to be at his buddy's house, so it would be a waste of money and more stress that Birdie didn't need if she hired a detective. This had gone on for too long.

"Let me think on it some," Bea said, although she'd already made up her mind about what she would do. "I'm sure I can come up with something."

Birdie looked at her, a tiny bit of hope flickering in her eyes.

Bea prayed she wasn't about to make things worse.

———

MARK SWITCHED the *Open* sign to *Closed* and locked the front door, then headed to the back and stopped in Emma's office. She was so focused on the computer screen that she didn't even hear him come in. With her back to the door, he didn't want to startle her, so he rapped lightly. She jumped and whirled around, her eyes big.

"I'm sorry," he said. "I knocked because I didn't want to startle you by just walking up behind you, but it looks like that didn't work either."

She'd relaxed as soon as she saw him, but he could still see some tension in her shoulders and jaw.

"That's not your fault," she said. "I've always been really cautious—single woman traveling the country and all—and honestly, I didn't even think about having my back to the door when I asked to rearrange the office. I guess I need to turn the desk back around so that you don't have to text me from ten feet away before you come in. It is your business after all."

An idea occurred to him and he raised up one finger. "Hold that thought."

He headed into the storeroom and dug through a box in the back, smiling triumphantly at his stellar memory as he pulled the mirror from a dusty old box. He wiped it down in the break room, grabbed a picture hanger, and headed back into Emma's office.

"I used to have this on the wall next to the counter so people could see to try on sunglasses and hats, but then I got those stand mirrors."

He stepped up beside her and attached the hanger to the wall to the right of the window, then bent the hook a bit and hung the mirror on it.

"How's that?" he asked.

She looked in the mirror and had a clear view of her office behind her, including the door.

She smiled. "That's perfect. And smart."

"I just didn't want to move the desk again."

She laughed. "We could have hung a bell on you. My mom

did that to our cat because he used to try to steal her hair ribbons."

"Sounds normal for a cat."

"While the ribbons were in her hair."

He grinned. "I can see how that wouldn't be appreciated. Anyway, I'm knocking off for the night. I have to cook Lily some vegetables since I caved and made pancakes for dinner last night."

"That seems a fair trade-off."

"Not to Lily."

"Oh, to be a kid again and have broccoli be your biggest worry." She smiled. "I didn't even realize it had gotten so late. Let me close this down."

He nodded. "So how's it going with the software?"

"Great," she said as she typed. "I know I asked a ton of questions this afternoon, but I have the receipts input and all of the new payables. I can cut checks whenever you're ready. Tomorrow, I'll start getting the inventory items loaded from the shipping orders, then I can take a physical inventory and we'll be all set. I might not get to that point until the end of the week, though."

He blinked. "End of the...*this* week?"

She turned around and grinned. "I told you this was my jam."

"Do you have magic elves in your pocket?"

"Ha! I wish. If I did, I'd have them do the cooking. I'm afraid the domestic side of things is where I fall down in life. Seriously, though, I know you're open on weekends once the season starts, so if I could get in this Sunday to take inventory, that would get everything in line."

"That's no problem." He shook his head. "You walked into my store at exactly the right moment. This weekend is our last Sunday that we're closed. I might need to play the lottery."

She blushed a little and he could tell that his compliments pleased her.

"I don't know how to repay you for all of this," he said.

"That's easy—when you do payroll."

He laughed. "I'll never be able to pay enough for the stress relief you've provided. Seriously. Thank you. From the bottom of my software- and paperwork-challenged heart."

"You're very welcome."

They started walking to the front of the store so Emma could leave.

"I don't suppose you know anything about video editing, do you?" he asked.

"You're on your own with that one. But I'm guessing you could ask anyone under the age of twenty and they could help."

"God, isn't that the truth." He unlocked the door and pushed it open. "I'll see you tomorrow. Thanks again."

She gave him a parting smile that had his pulse ticking up a notch and turned to walk off down the sidewalk. He stood there several seconds, watching her go.

"She's a pretty one, isn't she?"

A woman's voice sounded behind him and he turned to see Nelly standing there, grinning.

"Uh, yeah, I suppose she is."

"Supposing isn't what has you standing there smiling like you won an Oscar."

Inwardly, he groaned. The last thing he needed was the local women trying to fix him and Emma up. His new employee was already jumpy enough, and he had no doubt if pushed the wrong way, she would be happy to toss her things into her car and head out for the next location.

"I'm smiling because she's an accounting magician," he

said. "In a single day, she's gotten more paperwork done than I have all year."

Nelly nodded and patted his arm. "We all need help sometimes. You've done a good job holding things together after your Beth passed, and that little one of yours is an absolute delight. But it's in our best interest to know the things we're talented at and the things we should hire out for."

He gave the older woman's shoulder a quick squeeze. Despite the occasional interfering, Nelly, Bea, and the other ladies on Tempest Island were all fantastic women. They'd helped him so much because they cared and wanted him and Lily to be all right. He was extremely lucky to have found this community before his life fell apart.

"So what talent does Bea lack that she's hired you for?" he joked.

"Well, let's see—she hasn't figured out how to clone herself but still needs time off for the doctors and the occasional descent into debauchery with an eligible gentleman."

"Oh, um..."

Nelly laughed. "It's always amusing how squeamish you young people are about romance. Good Lord, you're supposed to be leading the charge."

"We prefer to lead quietly and without knowledge of anyone else's...uh, charge."

"Well, if you decide to spend some time with that pretty accountant of yours on something besides invoices, you let me know. I'll be happy to watch sweet Lily for you."

"Thanks, Nelly. I don't think you'll be called into service, though, so don't sit around waiting."

"I could tell you the same thing."

Mark watched as she walked off, then sighed and headed back inside the store, locking it up behind him. It was a beautiful day, so Jane and Lily were probably still at the beach.

When the weather allowed, he collected Lily right there on the sand more than he did in their apartment, which was fine by him. It was healthier for Lily, mentally and physically, to be outside doing something, and Jane loved being outside as well.

He headed to his office and exchanged his regular shorts for swimming trunks, tossed his T-shirt on his desk, and hurried out the back door. The surf wasn't high enough to tempt him, but there was time to get in a good swim and build a sandcastle with Lily before he had to tackle vegetables.

He spotted them about twenty yards into the surf where Jane was hoisting a life-jacketed Lily onto her boogie board for a slow, easy ride in on a wave. Lily pulled herself up on her knees halfway to the shore and Mark knew she'd be bugging him to surf before too long. That notion sent him off into bouts of pride and fear, but it wasn't a surprise. He and Beth had both lived for being in the water. Beth had even had a water birth with Lily, so she'd been born into it in every way possible.

He lifted a hand to wave as he jogged down to the water's edge. Lily let out a cry of delight when she spotted him and jumped off her board in the shallows.

"Did you see my ride, Daddy?" she shouted.

"I did," he said as he headed into the water. "You were amazing."

"Good enough to try a surfboard?" she asked.

Jane, who was walking up behind Lily, laughed.

"You knew it was coming," Jane said.

He nodded and smiled at his daughter. "Tell you what. This Sunday, if it's easy waves, I'll take out a beginner board and we'll start working on it."

Lily clapped her hands and started squealing with delight.

"But—" he said and Lily sighed.

"You can only use the board when I'm with you," he

continued. "Jane is not a surfing instructor, and that job is not part of her pay grade. So you won't bug her, understand?"

Lily nodded. "But you'll teach me every day, right?"

"Every day when the surf is good and I have the time. Remember, it's almost vacation season, so after this Sunday, the store will be open every day."

"That's the worst part about summer," Lily said and put on her pouty look. "All those strangers get more time with you than I do."

"All those strangers keep you in bathing suits and pancake mix," he said.

"I know," Lily said with a dramatic flair. "At least I have Miss Jane!"

She whirled around and jumped back on her board, then paddled off into the surf. Jane laughed and shook her head.

"She was born for the water," Jane said. "It makes for pleasant afternoons for me. So much better than sitting inside and staring at the television like most kids do these days. But unless you need anything else, I'm going to head out. I have a psychology paper due tomorrow and want to review it one last time."

"You go ahead," Mark said. "And thanks again for the wonderful job you're doing with Lily."

Jane smiled. "She makes it easy. Most of the time."

"Daddy, look!"

Lily yelled and Mark smiled at his daughter, who'd never left his sight. She was balanced on her knees and riding in a small wave, instinctively shifting her body weight forward when she was about to lose the ride. Yeah, she was definitely born for this.

As she cruised by him onto the sand, she let out a squeal then popped up and pointed behind him.

"Look, Daddy!" Lily said. "That's the lady from the store the other day. Is she going to take lessons? Can I watch?"

Mark turned around and saw Emma approaching them, scanning the sand for shells as she went. She clutched a small bag in her left hand. When she heard Lily's voice, she looked up at them and smiled.

"Seashell hunting?" he asked as she walked up.

She nodded. "I couldn't think of a better way to spend the evening."

Lily looked disappointed. "Oh. I thought you were coming for a surfing lesson."

"Lily, this is Emma," Mark said. "Emma is working at the store, doing the accounting."

Lily nodded and a flash of sadness passed across her face. "Mommy was a 'countant. She's in heaven. Ms. Nelly says God must have needed help with numbers too."

"I'm sure Ms. Nelly is right," Emma said and stuck out her hand. "It's a pleasure to meet you, Lily."

Lily perked right up at the handshake offering, apparently thrilled to be treated like an adult.

"Mommy did numbers, but she surfed, too," Lily said.

Emma raised one eyebrow at Mark. "I sense I walked into the middle of something."

Mark nodded and looked down at Lily. "Sunday. We'll have a lesson Sunday."

"All right," Lily said, in her best overburdened voice. "But Sunday is ten forevers from now."

"Probably only five," Mark said.

"Can I go out again?" Lily asked.

"You have thirty more minutes, then it's time for a bath and dinner," Mark said.

Lily cheered and ran into the water with her board.

"She is so cute," Emma said. "I don't know how you manage not to spoil her."

"Oh, she's spoiled," Mark said. "Just not rotten. The thing is, everything you let them get away with now will come back on you tenfold when they're teens."

"Sounds like the voice of experience. You got friends with rotten teens?"

He laughed. "No. *I* was a rotten teen. I mean, my parents didn't have a lot of rules to begin with, so that didn't help, but I managed to push the issue on the few they did have."

"Seems like you turned out okay. I'm sure Lily will too. Well, I best get on with my walk. I have to balance out all that sitting."

"See you tomorrow," Mark said and watched, once again, as she walked away before turning his attention back to his daughter.

But Emma Turner's beautiful smile kept flashing through his mind.

———

HE LEFT the art store in Tampa and pulled his cell phone out of his pocket.

"I'm getting closer," he said. "She was here, and recently."

"But not now?" the other man asked.

"I doubt it. Once she quits a job, she always leaves the area. But I'm catching up with her."

"You think she'll stop somewhere else in Florida?"

"It looks like she's working her way up the panhandle, but there's nothing as big as Tampa left along the coastline in Florida. I'll check the biggest places along the way, but my guess is she's headed to New Orleans."

"Probably so. Still, it doesn't hurt to stop and see if you find anything."

"Definitely. Listen, I want to stick around here for a bit before heading out. There was one coworker here that I want to follow up on. I think she might know something, but she stayed tight-lipped. Still, I got a feeling."

"We can't afford for Katarina to know we're tracking her."

"I was thinking of taking a harder look at the coworker without her knowing. Then if by chance she's in touch with Katarina, she won't have anything to report."

"Ah. Be careful with that. I don't have connections in Florida to get you off charges like I did in South Carolina."

"Got it. I'll let you know as soon as I have more information."

"Perfect. And remember, when you find her, do not approach. Call me and I'll handle the rest."

"Of course," he said.

But he had no intention of letting someone else settle the score.

# CHAPTER TEN

BEA HURRIED INTO THE ICE CREAM SHOP JUST AS TOM WAS about to flip over the *Closed* sign. He looked up in surprise when she bolted inside and was even more startled when she locked the door and grabbed the sign from his hands and dropped it in the window. He stared at her, slack-jawed, as she drew the blinds. Then she turned to him, hands on her hips.

"You and I need to talk," she said.

"What the heck is going on?" Tom said. "Is something wrong with Alayna?"

"No. Something is wrong with you."

"Me?" Tom stared at her.

Bea studied his expression. His confusion seemed genuine, but that just meant she'd have to be direct. She'd been dreading this conversation ever since she'd talked to Birdie, so there was no point dragging it out with small talk and subtlety. Besides, subtlety was one of those things she'd never really mastered.

"Are you having an affair?" Bea asked.

"What!?" Tom's eyes widened and his entire body went stiff. "No! Good Lord, why would you think that?"

"Your *wife* thinks that. All this claiming to go to the boat shop but never buying anything, checking out of conversations, not *being* present when you *are* present. I know Birdie isn't imagining the changes in your behavior because she's just not that whimsical. But I didn't want to believe it was an affair until I saw you in New Orleans the other day when you were supposed to be visiting that surly friend of yours."

She narrowed her eyes at him. "In New Orleans...hugging another woman in the entry to her apartment building."

Tom stared at her in silence for several seconds, then let out a sigh and dropped into a chair.

"It's not what you think," he said finally.

"Then what is it?"

He shook his head. "I didn't want her to know."

Bea struggled to contain her frustration. "Your wife and partner of thirty-plus years thinks you're having an affair. What could be worse than that?"

"I have cancer."

"What?" It was Bea's turn to be surprised, and she sank into a chair next to him. "You're healthy as a horse. Always have been. The hell you say you've got cancer."

"Trust me, it hit me like a ton of bricks. I just went in for my usual round of stuff and when I got that call back, I sat in that doctor's office a good hour after he told me. I think I was waiting to wake up from a bad dream."

"What kind and what's the prognosis?"

"Prostate, and I'm going to need surgery and probably chemo."

"But you'll be fine after surgery, right?"

"I just don't know. If they can get it all then it's not a death sentence—not an upcoming one, anyway—but there's other things that can happen after."

"Like what? You lose your hair? You're already halfway

there. And you're always complaining about needing to lose weight. Let's look at the positives."

"I was thinking more about losing romantic things."

He stared directly at her, and finally it hit Bea what he was referring to.

"Oh!" she said. "Well, there's options and such, I'm sure. And while I know how you gentlemen tend to think, that's not the part of you that Birdie's concerned with losing. At least, it's not the only part."

Tom blushed a little and stared down at his feet. "I know, but it takes the wind out of a man's sails."

"Okay, well, let's skip the full-sail part of the issue and move on to the pertinent stuff. Starting with how the hell did you think you could keep this a secret? You thought you could have surgery and chemo and Birdie wouldn't notice?"

"Of course not. I was just trying to get as much information as I could and then figure out what all was involved and how I could tell her. That woman you saw me with in New Orleans is a therapist. She helps people work through this sort of thing and has an office in that building. My doctor recommended her."

Bea sat back in her chair, completely surprised. "You actually drove to New Orleans to talk to a therapist?"

He gave her a sheepish nod. "I know. Us men—especially of a certain generation—tend to call that a bunch of hooey, but she's a specialist at medical plans and conversations and she's really been helpful. It didn't feel like it was something I could do on one of those computer video things, you know, and there's no one in the area who does this sort of thing. So I've had to make up these stupid stories in order to get away to see my doctors and that one time to the therapist. I talk to her by phone now."

"Okay, I get it. But none of that will be an issue after today, right? Because you're going to go home and tell Birdie the truth."

He sighed. "I was hoping to put it off a bit longer, but I suppose that's just me being a coward. And if she's already imagining things and is concerned enough to talk to you about them, then I best put her out of the one misery and offer up another."

Bea reached out and took Tom's hand. "This is going to be fine. *You're* going to be fine. We'll all make sure of that."

He gave her a small smile. "Birdie and I are lucky to have a friend like you."

Bea grinned. "Darn right you are. Now get home and give that wife of yours some peace of mind."

She jumped up and headed outside and set off down the sidewalk to the small alley that led to the parking lot behind the buildings. She'd already locked up the store and had sent Nelly home a little early so that she could be certain of catching Tom alone. The situation had nagged at her all afternoon. Nelly had known something was wrong but also knew Bea well enough to know that she wasn't ready to talk about it yet. So her best friend had wisely kept quiet, but that wasn't going to last.

But it was no longer important. Now Birdie would know the truth and at the next get-together of the poker club, Birdie would tell everyone else. Then Bea could tell Nelly what had been troubling her and the best part was, they weren't going to be under any obligation to plan revenge against a man they'd been friends with for decades. She shook her head as she walked, thinking about how strange it was that cancer was a relief. Not that she was relieved, exactly. Cancer was certainly scary, but she had zero doubt that Tom was going to have his surgery, do chemo or whatever else the doctors called on him to do, and he was going to be just fine.

Still, it was yet one more reminder that Bea and her friends were getting older. Not that younger people didn't suffer from the same maladies, but they usually didn't at the rate that the older generations did. It was as if you hit a certain date in time and the warranty on your body parts expired. And everyone knew an expired warranty meant things started to break.

"Bea!" A man's voice called from behind her, and she turned around to see Gary hurrying across the street.

He stepped into the alley next to her and took in a deep breath, then blew it out. "Good Lord, I'm out of shape. I walk-jogged all of half a block to catch up with you and I might need a doctor."

Bea smiled. "I was just thinking about how we're all aging and how it sucks rocks."

"That's one way of putting it. And far more polite than what I was thinking."

"Trust me. Anything you were thinking is far more polite than what I was thinking. I just said something publicly acceptable."

"Well, since you're already thinking along the not-suitable-for-public lines, I need to tell you something."

Bea stiffened. She wasn't in the mood for more crap, but there was no way Gary would have almost run or yelled in the middle of the street unless it was important. He had far better manners than that.

"Is this the kind of thing I need to sit down to hear or load my nine-millimeter for?"

"Probably the latter, but if you could wait until I get back to the motel, that would be great. Collateral damage and all."

"Spit it out then. This day has already gone to hell. Can't get much worse."

Gary didn't look convinced, but he took another breath, then started. "You heard my grandson, Seth, is going to come work with me, right? Well, he was in one of the kitchen shops over on the mainland yesterday, getting some things for his apartment, and he overheard Veronica Whitmore talking to another woman, whom he didn't recognize."

Bea shook her head. She hadn't thought it possible, but her day was about to get worse.

"She's convinced Carlson to try to get the council to keep Alayna from opening her restaurant. If he pushes this to a vote and Alayna can't get the restaurant open before next month's meeting..."

Bea blew out a breath. "I know. I had a run-in with her myself on Saturday and was worried that was the play she'd make next."

"I don't think he can get the votes to rezone if the restaurant is already open. It looks bad to the other island business people, and anyone taking those steps can be voted out. But if the restaurant isn't open yet, that might sway enough of them to keep the peace with the Whitmores. Over half the council has loans with Carlson's bank."

Bea frowned and nodded. She'd already been over all of this in her head.

Gary gave her a worried look. "So what do you think? Can she get it open in time?"

"I would love to say don't worry, but I'd be lying. It's not a small remodel. There's nothing structural, but there's not an inch of the place that won't be touched in some way. With the installation of a commercial kitchen, plus expanding bathrooms and meeting all the codes that didn't apply to an attorney's office, I just don't know how quickly it can happen."

"Yeah, I know. I was ready to sell the motel and move the last time we did a remodel. It was one delay after another. I barely got it open in time for season. So what can we do? You want me to talk to the council members I know—make sure they understand how much Alayna's restaurant will benefit the island?"

"It won't matter. People aren't going to vote the issue. If that restaurant isn't open before the vote, they're going to side with the person who holds their loans. Damn the Whitmores! If they disappeared, this island would be perfect. Instead, we've had to deal with that blot on humanity all our lives."

"I wish I could disagree with you. You know me—I like everyone. And I've really tried to find some aspect of good in them, but I keep coming up short."

"That's because they only serve self-interest. Not the community they're supposed to be taking care of."

"I don't see that changing, and it's no secret that Veronica has always had a problem with you and definitely with Alayna."

Bea blew out a breath. "I was hoping it wouldn't come to this, but I guess I better let Alayna know and see if anything can be done to move the remodeling along faster. Maybe we just need to get the necessary things in place and change the floors and paint and stuff in the off-season. If we can just get her past the inspections, we're good."

Gary nodded. "At least the inspector is from the mainland. Maybe he's not indebted to the Whitmores."

"Might be the only thing in our favor," Bea agreed.

"And it might not be a permanent one. I heard a rumor that Carlson was going to run for mayor."

"God save us all if he's elected. No way anyone will get a fair shake."

"Maybe you should consider running against him."

"Ha! I don't think so. I don't have the discretion for the job. You know how my mouth works."

"Exactly. What politics has been lacking for far too long is honesty. You love this island and the people. Think about it.

Voting for mayor is private. Not like having to raise your hand against Carlson in a council meeting."

"I can't see myself with the patience for the job. Maybe you should run. You said it—you get along with most everyone."

"I don't have the leadership ability. You know good and well that when mountains need to be moved around here, you're the person they give the megaphone to. Just think about it."

Bea watched Gary and shook her head as he headed back across the street. Mayor. That might be the worst idea she'd heard lately, and she'd heard some doozies.

---

EMMA SAT on the balcony of her room and watched as the sun set over the ocean. It was just as spectacular tonight as it had been the night before. She could get used to this—the view, the work, the people. And that worried her. She didn't have the luxury of a normal life. Of forming attachments. Yet in a very short amount of time, she felt a pull from this tiny island and its people that she'd never felt even after months of living in other places.

She sighed.

She was exhausted. That was it. She'd been running for so long and she was simply tired of the way she had to live and yearned for a life that was more than what she'd been given. Of course, yearning didn't mean she could have it, but sometimes she couldn't stop herself from daydreaming about being normal. Like when she'd sat at her desk this afternoon, staring out at the ocean while waiting on vendors to upload. She couldn't imagine a better job in a better place. No people to deal with—only her numbers and that extraordinary view.

And then after work, she'd walked on the beach collecting

seashells. Literally took a step out of the motel and onto sand. She'd chatted with Mark and the super-cute Lily as if it were the way she lived every day. When she'd returned to the motel, her heart had clenched when she'd double-checked the door locks, and it forced her to remember that everything here was temporary.

Just like the past eight years.

Still, she could make it work for the summer, which was better than nothing. Then when the vacationers cleared out, she'd go along with them. Hit up the next city. Maybe a stop in Mobile, or maybe just straight to New Orleans. She had time to decide. In the meantime, she'd enjoy the summer and try not to think about what would happen when it was over.

But tomorrow, she needed to start looking for a more permanent living situation. Even if the motel had vacancies all summer, she couldn't afford it. Most likely, she couldn't afford anything on the island and would have to commute from the mainland. Some places she'd lived before hadn't even had short-term rentals available. She'd been forced to sign six-month leases instead, knowing she'd end up canceling early and paying the associated fees. Now it was something she factored into her budget, just in case.

Mark probably wouldn't know of any places to rent as he lived above the store and had likely never had to think about it. But Bea might know. She'd lived here forever, had her own rental properties, and from what Alayna said, seemed to have her pulse on everything on the island and the surrounding areas. At minimum, she could probably tell Emma where to avoid. On her lunch break tomorrow, she'd step across the street to the bookstore and chat with her.

Alayna had sent her a text that evening asking how her first day had gone. Emma had smiled when she'd seen it and had been amazed how such a small thing had meant so much. She hadn't had a real friend since high school. And looking back, even those relationships seemed problematic now, filled with teen drama. It had been a long time since someone had thought about her without her being in front of them. It was a good feeling that someone had taken an interest in her life enough to ask. And Alayna was an accomplished woman with a boyfriend, friends, and family. She didn't need to collect more people. The fact that she appeared to want Emma to stay tugged at her even more.

And would make it harder to leave.

She sighed again and picked up her water before heading inside, willing her negative thoughts out of her mind. First, she'd shower, and then she was going to fix a sandwich and eat it in bed while watching mindless television. The weather had called for a potential thunderstorm again that night, but Emma was hoping the storm fizzled out or moved in a different direction. Her nightmare the other night had unsettled her, and she still felt that pinpricking on the back of her neck that she got the first few years after she'd run. At first, it had worried her, then she'd decided that it was a result of her breaking rules and taking the job here. Her hyper anxiety would probably level back down to her normal suspicious mode soon.

She fired up the hot water, shed her clothes, then stepped under the steaming stream.

It was just another night. Another storm.

And tomorrow would be another day on Tempest Island.

One less day than she had the day before.

# CHAPTER ELEVEN

THE MORNING WENT BY SO QUICKLY THAT LUNCH WAS UPON her before Emma even realized it. And if she hadn't heard Mark in the break room and then exit through the back door, she might not have even checked her watch. She'd made excellent strides with the accounting software and was certain she'd have everything caught up by the end of the week. Then she could present some ideas she had to Mark about streamlining processes and generate some reports so that they could review pricing. She'd already noticed he was missing out on revenue in a couple of key areas, and it would be best to address price changes before the season really got under way.

She poked her head outside and told Mark she was stepping out for lunch and would be back shortly. There was a flicker of something that crossed his otherwise happy expression—maybe disappointment—and for a moment, she wondered if he'd been hoping she'd eat outside with him again.

She shook her head as she left the store. That was just loneliness talking. Mark Phillips had no shortage of friends and, she would bet, eligible women who would love to spend their lunch hour chatting him up. He barely knew her, and what he did know was that regardless of how well things went, she was ultimately going to leave. More likely, seeing her triggered thoughts about the accounting, something he definitely didn't have a love affair with.

Bea was talking to a woman at the counter when she entered the bookstore, and Emma could tell Bea was less than thrilled with the conversation.

"Agnes," Bea said, her exasperation clear. "How many times are we going to have this discussion? I'm not removing the true crime section. They are not how-to books. The only person who believes that is you. And if you keep insisting on it, I'm going to assume it's because you're using them that way yourself, and I'll need to call the sheriff and fill him in."

The woman in question went board-stiff and glared at Bea. "You have crossed a line! Questioning my character?"

"It's not your character I'm questioning," Bea said. "It's your sanity."

"You can't talk to me like that," Agnes said.

"My store. My words. Open your own store and sell whatever the hell you want. Now, if you don't mind, I've got a customer. You keep pushing me, and I'm going to have that conversation with the sheriff and follow it up with a restraining order."

Agnes whirled around and stomped out, giving Emma a dirty look as she passed, as if Emma's arrival to the store was somehow to blame for Bea refusing to bow down to her unreasonable demands.

"I didn't mean to interrupt," Emma said as she stepped up to the counter.

"But we're all thrilled that you did," Nelly said as she walked out of a back room.

"Ha!" Bea said, shooting her friend a dirty look. "Says the coward who suddenly had indigestion when Agnes walked in."

"It wasn't a lie," Nelly said. "That woman *gives* me indigestion."

"That's valid," Bea said. "So what can I do for you, Emma? You looking for another book?"

"Not quite yet, although maybe I should pick up another. I'll probably finish the one I bought last weekend this evening. My room at the motel overlooks the beach, and evenings have been perfect for reading on that little deck—when it's not raining, of course."

Bea nodded. "The weather has been great during the day. Not so much late nights, but that's the norm. We're happier when things stay that way. Keeps the locals and the tourists out and spending during the day and all the plants get their watering at night. So what else can I help you with?"

"It seems like you know most everything that goes on around here," Emma said.

Nelly snorted, and Bea raised one eyebrow at her friend.

"I didn't mean in a bad way," Emma rushed on to say. "It's just that I've only got a room at the motel for a week and the job is working out well, so I need to find something better than temporary but less than permanent, if that makes sense."

"Sure," Bea said. "All of the businesses on the island have seasonal workers. College kids, mostly. They come in for the summer and then head back out to college in the fall. A lot are from around the area, so they live with family, but there's an old apartment building on the mainland near the airport where those without family nearby stay. It's not fancy, but it's safe, the rent's fair, and they'll do month-to-month with a little higher security deposit."

"That sounds perfect," Emma said.

Bea gave her the name of the apartments. "I wish I could think of something on the island, but everyone books up for the summer. And since my niece and her man have decided to maintain separate quarters, I don't have anything myself."

"They just started dating," Nelly said. "You could try giving them a couple months before you start pushing living in sin."

"I'm pretty sure they're past the sinning part of things," Bea said. "They're just dragging feet on a permanent location for it."

Emma grinned.

"The girl had a rough enough time with that ass—" Nelly glanced over at Emma and cut herself off.

"It's okay," Emma said. "Alayna told me what happened when we went paddleboarding on Saturday."

"That was a horrible, horrible time," Bea said.

Emma nodded. "I can imagine it was. It's like something you'd see in a movie, really. Not something you think about people actually living through, especially not people like Alayna. She's so nice and put together."

"It just goes to show that bad things can happen to any of us," Nelly said. "And we all need to remember that things can go wrong that are out of our control."

Emma felt her heartbeat tick up a bit and tried to swallow down the lump that had developed in her throat. "That's good advice."

"But not always the easiest to take," Bea said. "You let me know if that apartment doesn't work and I'll ask around. We'll find you something. Don't you worry about that. Mark has been needing some help for a while now. You're not getting away that easy."

Emma smiled as her heart clenched.

She already knew it wasn't going to be easy.

———

MARK HAD ALREADY LOCKED the front door after Emma left and put up the *Closed* sign when he heard a knock on the door. He looked up from the counter, where he'd been checking stock on sunglasses, and saw Nelly standing at his front door. What now?

He couldn't duck out the back because she'd already seen him, so he headed over to let her in. Might as well find out what she wanted. If he didn't talk to her now, she'd probably just appear on the beach. And with Nelly and Bea, one never knew what might be in the pipeline. He preferred no audience until he knew what they were up to.

"I won't take much time," Nelly said as she rushed in. "I just needed to ask what's wrong with you?"

The question was so nonspecific, he didn't know where to start.

"So many things," he said.

She nodded. "Yes, well, you're a man and all, so I get that. But I mean why is that lovely Emma looking for a place to rent on the mainland when you have a perfectly good apartment right above the store? It would save her time and the cost of gas, which is nothing to be sneezed at these days. And Lord knows, none of us are paying a king's ransom in salary out here, so it wouldn't kill you to help the girl out, especially as we all know your approach to accounting would scare demons away."

Mark blinked. Of all the things that had crossed his mind when he'd seen Nelly at his door, that one hadn't entered it at all.

"I, uh, didn't know she was looking," he said.

Nelly rolled her eyes. "Did you expect her to pay seasonal rates at the motel all summer? Even if Gary had a room free for that long, she couldn't afford it. And Gary can't afford to give a deep enough discount for her to stay."

"Of course not... I never thought."

He blew out a breath. Of course Emma would have to find a more permanent situation, and had even mentioned it. But he had to admit that lately, his mind had been so cluttered, he hadn't given it any real thought.

"I'm sorry," he said, "but I've been so busy I hadn't considered... I mean, usually the kids have their place to stay before they arrive..."

Nelly frowned. "This is no kid selling T-shirts or ice cream cones. This young lady is whipping your accounting back into shape. She deserves better than an old apartment and an hour or better commute every day."

He stared at Nelly, feeling guilty, but not wanting to state the truth—that he hadn't even considered renting the apartment out since Beth died. If he told Nelly his reasons, she'd accuse him of being silly, and he could sort of see her point. Emma wasn't a tourist who would change faces and habits a week later the way vacationers did. She was his employee. He was trusting her with his bank information. Why couldn't he trust her to live in the same building? It wasn't as though the apartments didn't have locks and dead bolts.

"Wouldn't it be...inappropriate?" he asked.

Maybe that was his out. Old-fashioned values. Because now that the elephant was in the room, he wasn't about to admit that his bigger concern in having Emma live upstairs was his unexpected attraction to her.

Nelly sighed. "You young people really need to check a calendar. Good Lord, I'm not suggesting you move in with her or start a cult or anything. It's just renting a room. To your employee. Do it right and it makes you some money and saves her some. You're happy with her work so far?"

"Thrilled, actually. I can't believe how quickly she's making headway with my mess."

"So you'd like her to stay...maybe even when the summer's over?"

"I...uh, well, I don't know about how business would be..."

"That's a yes. So if you want her to stay, then make it worthwhile. Having a nice, safe, convenient place to live goes a long way toward worthwhile."

"I'll think about it."

"Don't think too long, or she'll sign a lease somewhere not nearly as nice or convenient. It's just not that hard, Mark. Now, I better run. Harold is cooking tonight, and last time that happened I ended up replacing my good pot holder and the garbage disposal."

She hurried out the door, waving over her shoulder as she went. Mark locked up for the second time that evening and headed upstairs. It wouldn't hurt to look at the other apartment—see what kind of shape it was in. He didn't even know if the plumbing and electricity were still in working order. Or the appliances. And there were the random boxes he'd tossed over there to deal with later. Then later had moved to much later, which had become never.

But Nelly was right.

Emma needed a place to live, and he had a place that would probably suit her much better than anything she could find. If everything checked out, he couldn't see any reason not to offer it to her. Not any reason he'd state to other people, anyway.

Maybe she'd refuse.

Then he'd be off the hook.

———

BIRDIE COVERED the remaining casserole and left it on the counter to cool before starting on the dishes. Tom hadn't eaten more than a couple bites, despite her making the effort, yet again, to cook up one of his favorites. She'd tried several times that night to begin a conversation but the two sentences he'd contributed about finding a new vendor for napkins was the most she'd gotten out of him at any one time.

Even worse, when she was staring down at her plate, she could feel him studying her. As if he were gauging something—her mood? Her potential for stabbing him with a dinner knife? The tension was so thick and uncomfortable that she could practically feel it draped over her like a wet blanket.

She reached for a dish towel and Tom placed his hand on her arm.

"Can we talk?" he asked.

She turned around and looked at him. "I've been trying to talk for months now. We just spent a painful hour at the dinner table—over one of your favorite dishes—with me trying to get you to talk. Conversation is not a problem from this side of the marriage."

He hung his head and nodded. "I know. But I'd like to explain. Can we sit?"

Finally. The moment that Birdie had been begging for had come. But now the fear rushed in. Because she was certain she already knew what had caused Tom to check out of their marriage. Hearing him say it would put an end to her not knowing but would also put an end to life as she knew it. And thinking about a future without Tom was something she still hadn't managed.

She sat at the kitchen table and he pulled a chair over and sat in front of her. He stared at his hands for a while as if trying to figure out how to say what he needed to. Finally, he sighed.

"I'm just going to come right out with it," he said. "I haven't been going to the boat store—well, not every time I said I was. And I haven't been visiting my friend. And I think you'd already figured that out well enough."

Birdie nodded.

"The truth is, I've been seeing doctors. Birdie, I have cancer."

Birdie's hand flew up to her mouth as she sucked in a breath so hard it felt as if her chest would explode. She hadn't been prepared for that statement. Not even remotely prepared, and the shock of it made her dizzy.

"Birdie? Are you all right?"

She realized she'd been staring at him, not blinking or even breathing, and her breath came out in a big whoosh.

"Cancer?" she finally managed. "But when? How bad?"

"Prostate, and I've been seeing to things for a couple months now."

"What do we need to do?"

"I'm going to need surgery and chemotherapy."

Birdie let out a cry of relief. "You're not dying! Oh my God, when you said cancer, all I could think of was losing you. But surgery and chemo... I'm not saying they'll be easy, but you'll still be here. Right?"

He nodded. "My doctor says you're probably going to have to put off your plans to take over the world with Bea for a lot more years."

"Bea doesn't need or want my help unless she needs bail money. Nelly's the one who will be sitting in jail with her."

Tom laughed and took her hands in his. "I know you've been worried, and I'm so sorry I did that to you. I was trying to keep everything a secret until I knew for sure what I was up against. I'm afraid I made a mess of everything."

"But Tom, I could have been there with you—for the tests, for the results. I'm your wife. I'm not just supposed to be there for the hard stuff, I *want* to be."

"I was just trying to protect you in case things were bad. Give you a chance for a few more happy days before the worry had to start. I was planning on telling you as soon as I was cleared for surgery, but then Bea got a hold of me and read me the riot act."

Birdie's eyes widened. "Bea? I'm surprised you don't have scars."

"My ears were pretty done in, and she heaped a right good amount of guilt on me. But she was right on all of it."

"She's a good friend...to both of us."

"The best. But now it's time for me to handle things with my wife. I have an appointment on Thursday with my oncologist. We can get Nelly to cover the store for a couple hours if you want to go."

She stared at him. "If I want... Just you try to keep me away."

She leaned over and kissed him hard on the mouth. "I'm not done being annoyed by you yet, Thomas Armstrong. Or charmed by you either."

# Ripple

*"There is no secret to balance. You just have to feel the waves." – Frank Herbert*

# CHAPTER TWELVE

I<small>N THE SURF SHOP STOREROOM</small>, E<small>MMA STOOD UP FROM THE</small> squatting position she'd been in for the last couple minutes and stretched her arms over her head. She'd spent most of the morning entering purchase orders and needed a break from all the sitting, especially as the new office chair wasn't due in for a couple more days. She couldn't take physical inventory in the store until Sunday when it was closed, so she decided she'd start here. Now her legs were protesting instead of her back, and she made a mental note to break out her running shoes after work and make sure she did her stretches before work and before bed. Aside from her paddleboarding session with Alayna and a couple short swims, she'd been lax on exercising and was paying for it.

Mark had been in and out most of the day and at one point that morning, she'd heard a lot of noise overhead. Lily was still in school for another week, so she assumed it was Mark upstairs. It sounded as though he was moving furniture. She started to ask if he needed help with something, but figured it wasn't her business. And the more she inserted herself into other people's business, the more they felt they could insert themselves into hers.

"It's hell getting older." Mark's voice sounded behind her and she jumped, feeling guilty. As if he could read her thoughts.

She turned around and smiled. "I was just thinking I've been letting my running and stretching slide. I've swapped a bit of running with swimming but I'm not doing enough. And the stretching is really something I shouldn't miss."

He nodded. "Can you take a break?"

She glanced at her watch and was surprised to see she'd been at it for three hours.

"Wow," she said. "I wanted to finish counting the T-shirts today but didn't even realize how late it had gotten. Let me just put these tallies on my desk."

He followed her into her office and waited while she placed the inventory lists in her inbox.

"Do you need me to help up front?" she asked as she turned to face him.

"No," he said. "I put up the Be Right Back sign. There's something I need to run by you."

His tone was casual but sounded a little forced, and instantly her guard went up. Had he called her references? Had someone given her a bad review? She was extremely careful with the people she provided—both to ensure they would be positive with their referrals but also discreet enough to never pass information along that didn't have to do with the job. Still, slights could be imagined at any time, and things could change. She'd hate to have to leave the island before her time was up, but if it happened, she would move on, just as she always did.

"I want to show you something upstairs," he said as he headed for the staircase access in the hallway.

She followed him up, relieved that her job didn't appear to be in jeopardy. Maybe he had more records stored upstairs and was hesitant to pile them on her. That's probably what all the shuffling she'd heard up here had been. She stepped out of the stairs onto a landing with two doors, both with dead bolts. He unlocked one of the doors and pushed it open, then motioned for her to step inside.

It was a small room with pale blue walls and French doors at one end that led to a deck overlooking the beach. She realized that deck was the one that partially covered the patio downstairs where she'd eaten her lunch. The room was open to a tiny kitchen with white cabinets and countertops and a sea-glass backsplash with turquoise and blue tiles. The kitchen was a U-shape and one of the sides formed a two-person bar that separated the kitchen from the living area. A gray leather sofa stood against one wall and a flat-screen TV was mounted on the opposite wall. A pretty blue-striped rug lay in front of the sofa on top of hardwood floors that looked like something that had come off an old ship. The coffee table in front of the sofa matched the floors.

Boxes were stacked against the wall under the television and lined a lot of the kitchen counter. There was a door at the back of the kitchen and she assumed it led to another room. Maybe a bedroom, as this appeared to have served as a living quarters before Mark started using it as storage. The entire place was dusty but appeared to be in otherwise good repair.

"There's a small bedroom and a bath through the kitchen," Mark said. "So what do you think?"

She scanned the size and number of the boxes again. "Well, are the big boxes more inventory or is all of it paperwork? I can try to load historical data from the old system and use these documents to fill in the gaps. But if those larger boxes are filled with paper, they're going to be hard to get downstairs without the boxes splitting."

He stared at her for a moment, then blinked. "Oh no. I wasn't talking about... The boxes aren't more work for you. I meant the apartment. I know you have to find a place, and this one is just sitting so I thought I'd offer it up. There's nothing available on the island for longer-term rental, and this would save you the drive to and from the mainland."

Emma's jaw dropped. It hadn't crossed her mind that he'd offer to rent her the apartment, not even when she'd been standing there.

"You want to rent this to me?" she asked. "But you could probably make ten times what I could pay by leasing it to vacationers."

"I could and I used to. But that was back when we lived in a house on the mainland. There's a separate staircase on the side of the building that leads to the second-floor deck, and the two apartments have their own entrances with dead bolts and such. But I just didn't want random people living under the same roof as my daughter. I know it seems stupid to give up the revenue. It's not like I'm rich, but..."

She shook her head. "It doesn't seem stupid at all. It seems responsible. But are you comfortable having me live here? You've only known me a couple of days. At this point, I'm just as random as a tourist."

"But I know who you are. You have a history with references. You're not just a name on a VRBO booking, and you're not going to change every week."

Guilt coursed through her. She was far worse than a random name on a rental booking. Her name wasn't even her own. Except for her jobs, the past she'd given wasn't her own. Nothing about Emma was real except her physical body and her finance skills. Everything else was a fraud.

*It's only for the summer, and his concern is his daughter's safety, to which you're no threat.*

That was true. It wasn't as if she'd be on the island long enough for anyone to discover her real identity. No one had in the eight years she'd been running, and Tempest Island wouldn't be any different. Before suspicion could ever rise, she'd be gone, and shortly after, no one would remember the nice accountant who worked one summer and then moved on. It was both sad and necessary.

"If you're really okay with it, I'd love to," she said finally.

He looked both relieved and a little uneasy, and she knew this decision hadn't been a simple one for him.

"You'll want to see the bedroom first," he said. "It barely holds more than the bed and a nightstand, and the closet is no better than what you have at the motel. The bath is shower stall only, but it was all remodeled before we started doing the vacation rentals."

She followed him to the bedroom and took in the queen-size bed with blue-and-white-striped comforter and pillows. The single distressed white nightstand matched the headboard and was perfect against the same blue walls as in the other rooms. The bathroom contained a sink with a cabinet vanity and mirror, toilet, and a walk-in shower with a solid panel of glass forming the outside wall. The shower surround was floor-to-ceiling white marble that matched the floor. A single bench was built into one side and there were marbled shelves built into the wall to hold bath products.

"This is all so pretty," she said as they made their way back into the living room. "The colors and the distressed floors and furniture are perfect for the location and the size."

He nodded. "My wife—Beth—she picked everything out. She was really good that way. We had a historical home over on the mainland, and she oversaw the rehab after we bought it. It took her a long time because she wanted everything restored correctly. I sold it for double what we paid for it. It was beautiful but more than Lily and I needed, and living here simplified a lot of things when I really needed them to be."

"She definitely had an eye for color and the space."

"She was one of those people who did everything well. It made everyone around her try harder."

Emma's heart clenched. When Mark talked about his late wife, she could hear how much he loved her. It made her sad for him that he'd lost someone he'd loved so much, and sad for herself that she'd never experienced someone loving her that way and probably never would.

"I can't imagine how much you miss her. I know it doesn't help, but I'm truly sorry—for you and Lily."

He managed a small smile. "Actually, it always helps when it's sincere, so thank you. This community was awesome. They rallied around Lily and me and made sure everything was held together until I could manage it again on my own. And we're doing fine, really. But there are days when I look out the store window and think everyone has just moved on with life and only Lily and I are still struggling with her loss."

"Your loss was the biggest."

"There you go, making sense again. Next time I'm feeling like I'm losing my grip, I'm going to come talk to you. You're probably cheaper than that therapist I saw."

She smiled. "For a friend, my ear is always open and free. Although I will admit that I've never turned down a glass of wine or baked goods."

"Duly noted. So do you want to rent the place?"

He named a rate that was equivalent to what she would have paid at the apartments Bea had told her about, but the perks were worth double the cost.

"I would absolutely love to!" she said. "It's beautiful and the view is incredible, and I won't be wasting any time commuting, not to mention the savings on gas."

"Great. My CPA said he had a month-to-month lease form we could use. Since it was a vacation rental, the kitchen and bathroom are stocked with the basics in small appliances, dishes, towels, and so forth, but the one thing it doesn't have is a laundry room. I'll get you a key to the interior stairwell, and you can use the washer and dryer downstairs after hours. Saves you hauling your things to the Laundromat and going outside to go back and forth from the apartment to the store, especially when it's raining."

"That would be great. Thanks!"

"Oh, there's no parking right next to the building, and we try to keep the street parking available for the tourists, but there's a lot across the street behind the bookstore that the retail owners and workers use."

"I don't anticipate much driving anyway, so that's perfect."

"Then it's settled," he said. "I'll get these boxes moved out and get a cleaning crew in. How long is your deal at the motel?"

"I have to be out Friday. They're full up for the foreseeable future starting then, but you don't need to hire someone. I can help move the boxes, and I can definitely clean. It's just a layer of dust, and I'm guessing all the cleaning crews are prepping rentals for season opening."

"More like a couple layers of dust, but you're right about the cleaning crews. It might be hard to find someone on short notice."

"And the boxes? Are they inventory? Old paperwork?"

A pained expression crossed his face and he sighed. "Neither. They're Beth's things—clothes and books and some other things that I was going to donate to the women's shelter."

"Oh Mark." She placed her hand on his arm and squeezed.

"I'll take care of it. If you're ready. If not, I can make some room in the storeroom downstairs."

He shook his head. "It's something I have to do myself. Something I've needed to do for a while now. But with them closed up in here, I didn't have to face it. It's time."

"Let me know if you change your mind."

He forced a smile. "Well, I don't want to hold you up any longer. It's beautiful outside and it's only thirty minutes until closing time. Why don't you head out for the day? You still have time for your run and to sit out and enjoy this sunshine. I'll shut down your computer."

She smiled. "That sounds wonderful. I'll finish up the T-shirts tomorrow."

"Great," he said and motioned to the patio door. "You can take the back staircase out, if you'd like, so you don't have to wind through the store."

She stepped out onto the deck that served both of the apartments, then gave Mark a wave as she headed for the stairs. She fairly skipped down the sidewalk between the buildings, unable to believe her good fortune. She had a job that challenged her, on a beautiful island full of nice people, and now had a place to live right on the sands of paradise.

The hot boss and landlord was the icing on top.

The thought flashed through her mind unbidden and without warning, and her step faltered a bit. Where had that come from?

She shook her head. Who was she trying to fool? Every minute she'd spent with Mark had only served to make him more attractive, and that was a problem. She'd already broken so many of her long-standing and good serving rules—no small towns, only surface-level relationships, and absolutely, positively no falling for a man.

Any man, but especially her boss.

But the thought of packing up her car and driving away was so depressing she couldn't even consider it. Didn't she deserve to be happy? All these years of running or living life on hold. Surely she could afford to relax three short months. To live in a way she wished she could every day. Even if someone was looking for her, they wouldn't be looking at this tiny spot of sand in the big ocean. She'd been so careful to cover her tracks, and Mark hadn't even called her references. No one knew she was here.

And her attraction to her sexy boss didn't matter because he was still deeply mourning his wife.

He was temporary, just like her job. And months from now, he'd be a nice memory.

----

He FROWNED at the security system sticker on the apartment door and walked around to peer in the window. The drawn blinds prevented him from seeing inside, but he couldn't risk breaking into the apartment on the off chance that the woman only had the stickers and no real alarm. He'd need to verify before he risked entry.

The woman was very careful. When she left the art store, she never failed to check her surroundings and her car was always parked on the street, where she had to pay a premium, rather than in one of the cheaper lots. But the lots were in a less populated area, and the lighting was dim—not bright like the area the art store was located in. He also noticed she walked with her hand in her purse, a clear indicator that she was clutching Mace, at best, or a gun, at worst. She was either paranoid or she'd taken on some necessary precautions due to things in her past. He was betting on the latter.

All of which made his job harder.

He'd wanted to search her apartment while she was at work —see if she had anything that might reference Katarina's new identity. So far, he'd come up empty there. He was certain by reaction to the photo he showed around that he was on her trail. But no one was going to hand out a woman's name to a strange man, no matter how nice his business card and how plausible his story. It just wasn't the kind of thing that people volunteered these days, especially employers. He'd tried breaking into a couple of the businesses he suspected Katarina had worked for, but opportunities were limited with good security systems so affordable. And in every case, he'd found all the records were digital and password-protected, so he didn't bother with that avenue any longer. It wasn't worth the risk.

But coworkers couldn't afford the high security like businesses, and even though personal items were often password-protected these days, some people still made notes with a pen and paper or had failed to enter a password on a device. So far, he hadn't seen the same name twice on a calendar, but he'd keep looking. Eventually, he'd find that one person who let the information slip without even knowing it—maybe with a name on a calendar or a post on social media.

So far, everything about the woman he was currently watching indicated she was beyond the average careful, and he'd probably learned everything he could in Tampa. If he couldn't get into her apartment, the only other option was confronting her. But if she had a way to contact Katarina, that would tip his hand. He'd stick around another day or two to try to find a way into the apartment and to make sure Katarina wasn't still in the area, but so far, all indications were that she'd moved on once more. She never stayed anywhere for very long, but this time, he couldn't be more than a week or two behind her. Which meant he had plenty of time to catch up to her at her next stop.

He'd always liked New Orleans. It wouldn't be a hardship to spend a couple weeks in the city, scouting the area for Katarina, taking in the excellent food, picking up the random college girl vacationing. He smiled as he hopped into his car. Yes. He was definitely looking forward to New Orleans. Finding Katarina would be the icing on the cake.

# CHAPTER THIRTEEN

ALAYNA LOOKED FROM CHANCE BARRETT, HER REMODELING contractor, to Bea, unable to control her anxiety. She'd spent her entire Wednesday morning and afternoon fretting over the construction schedule and trying to come up with ways to speed up the process before she met with Chance that evening. But ultimately, it all came down to the man in front of her. The job was on schedule—which was already remarkable —but now they needed more than remarkable. The contractor, young and ambitious, ran his hand over his hair and blew out a breath. He looked around the future restaurant space and shook his head.

"I'm sorry, but there's no way it can happen without hiring on more people," he said.

"So do it," Bea said. "The additional cost isn't a problem."

He gave her a pained look. "I get that, but finding quality people is. The materials and equipment in this remodel require better than the average guy slinging a hammer. The deadline is already tight, and we can't risk someone too inexperienced costing us material or worse, damaging existing structure that's already set to go."

Bea put her hands on her hips. "You're telling me there's no one to hire in the entire state of Florida? Or nearby?"

"I'm sure if I put out feelers, plenty would respond," he said. "But the truth is, the people who have availability to come right away probably aren't the people you want working in here. Last hurricane season caused so much damage along the coast that everyone with any kind of decent skill or reputation is booked out for the rest of the year. Most of those left are the drifters and the people who can't hold a regular job."

Waves of frustration and disappointment rushed through Alayna, and she struggled to keep tears from forming.

"This restaurant is going to close before it ever gets going," she said. "The Whitmores will have the whole thing shut down with the city council before I can get the *Open* sign in the window. They'll win again."

Chance raised one eyebrow. "The Whitmores? As in Carlson Whitmore?"

Bea nodded. "The Whitmores dislike me and Alayna even more than they do everyone else they consider beneath them."

"Which *is* everyone," Alayna grumbled. "Even Jesus. Maybe even God."

"Veronica is pretty sure she *is* God," Bea said. "At least that's what she'd like the rest of us little people to think."

"So bow down or be turned into a pillar of salt?" Chance asked.

"If she could..." Bea said. "But since she has no actual power, she just uses her husband to ruin lives."

"Yeah, I've heard my dad complain about them for years," Chance said. "My parents divorced when I was in high school, and I moved out of state with my mom. I was in private school before that, so I never had to endure much time around their daughter Melody except local parties. But I saw plenty. And I heard enough stories to know to stay far away. I

128

imagine her parents are even worse. I mean, she got it somewhere."

"Your father?" Bea asked.

Chance nodded. "Shane Barrett."

"As in Barrett Development?" Bea asked. "No wonder you're so good at your job so young. Your father is one of the best commercial developers in the state. I'm surprised you're not working for him."

Chance shuffled a bit. "My dad and I manage okay but distance makes that easier. We butt heads too much to get through dinner without arguing over something. There's no way I could work for him. Don't get me wrong, I love him, and he's always done what's best for me, but he's a hard man to be around. That's why I chose to go with my mom when she left."

"Sometimes we need to make our own way," Alayna said. "I respect that."

He nodded. "And because of that, I don't like asking for help—especially from him—but I also can't stand around and watch the Whitmores take you down. I'll talk to him and see if he has any ideas on this. And I'll keep looking for more help and other ways to speed things up. I've already asked my people to work as much overtime as they can, but I have to follow the laws about construction hours as well, so more limitations."

"Yes," Bea said. "The last thing we want to do is give them an easy reason to shut down the remodel, and Veronica is probably watching the crews come and go, just looking for a violation to hang us with."

"What about the plumbing and electrical items?" Alayna asked. "I know you said some things need to be replaced before we can move forward."

"Yeah, some of the wiring was nicked when they did the build-out for the law office, and it needs to be replaced," he said. "That's why you're getting intermittent current in some places. And there's plumbing that needs resealing, maybe some new fittings. I don't want your kitchen dropping into the bookstore."

"Just some of the food from it," Bea said.

He smiled. "I have to admit, the best part of this project is that table Alayna has saved for me opening night. I'm pretty sure I could sell my plus-one slot for enough to pay for the dinner."

Alayna warmed at his comment, but the overwhelming amount of work left weighed so heavily on her that she couldn't manage more than a tiny hint of a smile along with the 'thank you.'

He stared at her for a moment, then brightened. "I just had an idea. Commercial construction has set legal hours, but safety-related repairs don't. My electrician and plumber will both work after hours. It's a bit of an upcharge, but a way to get some of the work done sooner. And my crew would be out of their way and not trying to work around them."

"You're a genius!" Alayna threw her arms around the young man and gave him a hug. A blush crept up his cheeks as she released him.

"Let's save the praise for when the job is done," he said. "I really appreciate the opportunity you've given me here. This job could lead to a lot more, so I have a vested interest in this restaurant opening."

"You let us know if you have any more thoughts on time saving—and if there's anything we can pitch in to do," Bea said. "We're no construction experts but things have to be cleaned, and I do quite a bit of the updates and repairs at my rentals. I'm not the worst painter you could hire, and I can help your carpenters and plumber with hardware and fixtures as well."

Alayna nodded. "You don't want to give me tools or a paintbrush, but anyone who has owned a restaurant is a professional cleaner. Lord knows I have more time than Bea. I just wish I had all her talents."

Bea waved a hand in dismissal. "We all have our own things we're best at. I'm already on my second toaster oven of the year."

Alayna stared. "Second?"

"Which we're not going to talk about since I won't be using your kitchen," Bea said. "But you're perfectly capable of running the bookstore so I can sneak up here and help."

Alayna brightened. "You're right. Oh my God, I'm so frazzled by this that I can't even think straight."

"Don't worry," Chance said. "We're going to make this happen. One way or another."

Alayna said a silent prayer he was right.

————

EMMA PUSHED her cart down the aisle of the island market, loading it with the cleaning supplies she'd need to tackle the apartment. The items would be cheaper over on the mainland, but she believed in supporting the community that was supporting her, so she didn't mind paying the markup. She'd gone through the move-in process so many times before, but this was the first time she was excited about it. Tempest Island had really gotten to her—the place and the people—which is why she'd left the store and gone straight to the market for cleaning supplies rather than heading to the beach.

Logic said she should have turned down Mark's apartment offer, gotten his accounting sorted, and then moved on before she got even more attached. There had been places she'd lived before that she'd really liked, but none that had her mourning their loss when she left. But this was different. She'd felt it the moment she stepped on the island and should have turned around then. Now she was neck-deep in it.

*You deserve to be happy. Even if only for a little while.*

She shook her head as she placed glass cleaner in her cart. Why was she struggling so much with this? She did deserve happiness and she'd found it here. She knew it was only temporary and accepted that. So why the angst? Why was this time so different from other places she'd liked?

*Because you're attracted to your boss.*

Okay, so she was. What woman wouldn't be? He was smart, nice, and superhot. But none of that mattered because he was still in love with his wife. The only person who needed to avoid a romantic entanglement as much as she did was Mark. And that was assuming he was even attracted to her, which he'd given absolutely no indications of and probably never would. Which meant she was safe. Granted, there was some misplaced disappointment to deal with, but safe.

"You're frowning at that cleaner like it owes you money," Alayna said.

Emma turned and saw her new friend coming up the aisle with a basket of fresh vegetables and fruit.

"I guess I spaced out for a minute," Emma said, pushing all thoughts of Mark from her mind.

Alayna gestured to her basket. "Is housekeeping on the blink over at the motel?"

"No. I've found a place to rent, but it's been sitting unoccupied for a while. Nothing bad, but it all needs a good swipe."

"Bea told me she'd given you the name of an apartment on the mainland that does short-term leases. So they had something that will work for you?"

"Actually, Mark offered me the one-bedroom apartment above the store. He and Lily live in the larger one. Apparently, both used to be vacation rentals, but he stopped after his wife..."

Alayna nodded. "It's all so sad. I never met Beth but Bea said she was just lovely, which is high praise coming from Bea. She doesn't hedge, even when someone's passed. Mark is such a nice guy, and every time I think about Lily growing up without a mother, my heart clenches. At least I had fifteen years with mine."

"It *is* heartbreaking, but he seems like such a good father."

"Oh, absolutely! Bea and Nelly can't say enough good things about him. I didn't even realize he had another apartment upstairs, but they bought the store and did the remodeling while I was off trying to conquer the restaurant world. How great is that for you, though? Talk about a perfect situation."

Emma nodded. "It really is. He's charging me the same as an apartment on the mainland would have been, but I save all the money and time of commuting. And you can't beat the view. I keep wanting to pinch myself."

"He must be very happy with your work. And I am thrilled you'll be living here. It gives us an opportunity to hang out more."

Emma warmed at the thought. She'd really enjoyed paddleboarding with Alayna. And she was looking forward to meeting Luke, who'd been conducting an overnight training that day.

"Definitely," Emma said. "I really love it here. I know I have my job and we'll be busy with the season before too long, but it feels more like a vacation."

Alayna smiled. "You wake up every day looking out at paradise, then get dressed and go do a job you enjoy all day, then take in that same gorgeous view at sunset every night. It's hard to be unhappy about any of that."

Alayna pointed to her cart. "If you need to do some more shopping—linens, dishes, and the like—I'm happy to hop over to the mainland with you and show you where to find the best deals."

"Thanks. I carry linens with me and some cookware, but usually stick to disposables for dinnerware. But since the apartment used to be a vacation rental, it's already stocked with most everything I need."

"Oh, that's right! I hadn't thought about that. Bea's cottages are the same way. In fact, I put a bunch of her stuff in storage to move my own in. If you are missing anything, especially kitchen stuff, let me know. I'm sure she won't mind you borrowing them."

Emma smiled. "I'll let you know. And you know what, I might take you up on that shopping trip after all. I've been thinking about adding some dishes and cups to my traveling gear. Something coastal in that hard plastic stuff so it travels well and gives me that cheery look wherever I go."

"Melamine. I know a couple places that sell sets with all the pretty ocean blues—fish, seashells, boats—whatever you can think of. I've been wanting to get some myself. They're perfect for outside eating, and the ones in my cottage are getting a little faded and worn. The best part is, you don't have to worry about something breaking if a gust of wind takes it."

"You've convinced me. I'm going to be working this weekend to try to get the inventory loaded before the season starts, but maybe a weekend after that—if you have the time."

Alayna sighed. "Some days, I feel like I have nothing but time. Everything with the restaurant is hurry up and wait. I have to rush to get something done, then go for days waiting on everyone else to get things done before I can move on to the next step. The only thing I have to work on every day is menu testing, and even *I* don't want to spend all day every day cooking."

"Well, if you ever need someone to test that menu, I will gladly volunteer, although I'm guessing you have no shortage in that lineup."

Alayna laughed. "There've been a few offers, but if you're serious, I've got a whole seafood thing going tonight. If you don't have plans, I'd love for you to come for dinner. It probably won't be ready until seven thirty or after and Luke and Aunt Bea will be there, but if you're interested in food and some company..."

"I'd have to be crazy to turn down a seafood dinner by a professional chef." Emma felt a blush creep up her neck. "I'm going to go ahead and admit I googled you. Not *that* situation, but your restaurant. You were seriously killing it. Your reviews —even from the nastiest of food critics—were all stellar. I'm so sorry you lost your restaurant."

"Me too. And then in some ways, I'm not. After all, if that nightmare hadn't happened, then I wouldn't have come home. Wouldn't have met Luke. Wouldn't be opening a new restaurant on Tempest Island, which I'm willing to admit now is the only place that ever felt like home after my parents died."

"I can see that. And I'd love to come to dinner. What can I bring?"

"Just yourself. You'll be doing me a favor. I need input before I firm up the menu, and I have to do that soon because I need to get it formatted and printed. I mean, I'm going to have specials and probably different menus for different seasons or maybe one for tourist and one for regular. Or maybe something else entirely."

Emma stared and Alayna laughed.

"Now you see the problem, right?" Alayna said.

"It's important, and you're giving it the correct amount of attention. So can I come early and help with anything?"

"No help needed. Just show up around seven and I'll pass around some cocktail treats and wine, and you can chat with Luke and Aunt Bea."

"Great! I can't wait."

"Me either, and now that I've put another warm body on the schedule, I need to finish my shopping and get home and cooking. I'll see you later!"

Emma smiled as Alayna walked off. She usually avoided this type of intimate setting with other people, too afraid of all the questions that might be asked and all the answers she couldn't give. But maybe she'd been foolish in that. She'd established a background of sorts, and the one thing she'd learned was if people looked uncomfortable—especially sad—then others didn't push. She was a pro at looking uncomfortable and sad. If things got too deep, then she knew how to handle it.

It was high time she started doing more, even if it was only temporary. She'd been living half a life for far too long.

———

MARK PUT the last of the boxes in the bed of Luke's truck and blew out a breath. Luke closed the tailgate and gave him a long look.

"You okay?" Luke asked finally.

"Yeah. And I really appreciate you helping me with this— especially on such short notice. If I'd used my SUV, it would have taken two trips. I... Hell, one is hard enough."

"I'm sure it is. But I'm pretty sure it's supposed to be."

Mark studied the other man, momentarily surprised by his insight. But Luke had shared some of his background with him, so Mark knew the former SEAL was no stranger to loss.

And it wasn't that long ago that Luke and Alayna had stared death in the face. Mark imagined the *what if things had turned out different* scenarios had run through his mind far more than once. Probably would for a while.

"Yeah, I guess it *is* supposed to be hard," Mark said. "But the world's not going to stop for me and Lily. This is just one more step to getting back into life instead of just going through the motions while it happens around me."

"I get what you're saying, but I think you're selling yourself short. You sold your home and moved to the island, kept your business going and even expanded some things, and you've made sure your daughter got through all of it without losing her spirit. So it took you a while to move out some boxes that you didn't even see every day. So what?"

"Ha." Mark let out a single strangled laugh. "I guess I hadn't considered it all that way."

"Well, maybe you should start. You ready to do this?"

Mark nodded. "Yeah, I don't want to take up any more of your evening. I'm sure you've got plans."

"Alayna's cooking more potential menu items to test, but she said she was getting a late start, so I've still got time. Bea's coming over to give her opinion. You're welcome to join us. She said maybe seven thirty."

"I appreciate it, but I've already got Jane working overtime and Lily's not quite to adult dinner status given that her bedtime is eight."

Luke nodded and climbed into his truck. Mark took one final look at the boxes before hopping into the passenger's seat. It was hard. And it hurt. But it was time. Things were changing. They would be better if Beth were still here, but she wasn't. He couldn't keep going through the motions.

And even though Luke had pointed out all the areas he'd managed well, Mark knew his heart had been on hold. He'd taken care of Lily and his business, but he'd locked himself down, even with his friends. He'd spent an afternoon on the ocean with Luke a week ago when Lily was at a party, and he realized it was the first time he'd gone out and done something just for his own enjoyment in over a year.

Starting now, he was going to do better for himself. It was time.

———

ALAYNA PULLED a tray of something that smelled heavenly out of the oven. Luke walked through the patio door at the same time as if he had an alert on her cooking sheet. He made a beeline for the kitchen and stood next to her, taking in the tangy smell.

"Whatever that is smells awesome," he said.

"It's bacon-wrapped shrimp with a mango sauce." She grabbed his hand as he reached for one. "I just took them out. Let the sauce set a couple minutes and that way you won't burn your mouth. Or your hands, since you insist on testing straight off the tray and without using a fork."

"I'm just making sure I get my share."

"By starting before everyone else? I seriously doubt Bea is going to fight you over the last shrimp."

"I don't know. She's pretty tough."

Alayna laughed and popped the tray of crab cakes in the oven. "How did it go with Mark?"

"Good. I mean, as good as that kind of task can go. I'm glad he asked for help. I'm not sure he could have made one trip, much less two. After we got there, he sat for the longest time, not moving. I didn't want to push, but finally the shelter director came out to greet him and he broke out of his trance."

"That's awful."

Luke nodded. "I can't even imagine what he's gone through. When I thought you were going to die, the pain was so intense it took my breath away. And our relationship was brand-new. But to lose a wife—the mother of your child—man, that's pushing people to their limits."

"Bea said he was pretty torn up for the first couple months. She thinks Lily is the reason he held it together at all. The whole thing is so sad. You should have invited him over tonight."

"What kind of man do you think I am? I invited him. But we're eating outside of Lily's bedtime and his sitter couldn't stay any longer. Though I am glad to know that you won't get upset at extra guests."

"If I planned a dinner for just you and me, then maybe ask first. I might answer the door in only my apron and then we'd all be embarrassed."

He looked up at the ceiling as if in prayer. "And you're doing that soon, right?"

She laughed.

"I promise I wouldn't be embarrassed. Well, maybe just a little when I told whoever I'd brought home to Uber back and order takeout, but after that..."

"*Anyway*, tonight is good because Bea is coming, which you already knew. But what you don't know is that I ran into Emma at the island market and invited her. So it would be a bit hypocritical if I got mad at you for inviting without asking."

He shook his head. "I'm not doing the cooking. The chef has total control over the guest list."

"Well, I guess there is that. And if you don't get out of my way, I'm not going to be feeding anyone."

"What can I do to help?"

"Can you wipe down the table and chairs outside? The

weather is so nice, I'd like to have the appetizers out there at least. If it holds, we can have the whole meal there."

"On it."

But instead of walking off, he wrapped his arms around her from behind and kissed her neck.

"I love you, Alayna," he said. "And I'll never take a single moment we have together for granted."

"I love you too," she said as she leaned back into his chest, safe and secure in his arms.

# CHAPTER FOURTEEN

EMMA RAPPED LIGHTLY ON THE DOOR, FEELING A LITTLE nervous. Which was stupid. Alayna was the nicest, most hospitable person she'd ever met. She'd already spent an afternoon with her. What was one dinner and a couple more people? Besides, she'd already met Bea. And she'd settled on her backstory and was ready to handle anything they threw at her.

The man who opened the door made her blink. Good Lord, if this was Luke, it was no wonder Alayna had let the relationship proceed so quickly. He smiled at her and, even though she didn't think it possible, grew even more attractive.

"You must be Emma," he said and stuck out his hand. "I'm Luke. Come on in. We're still waiting on Bea, but she's on her way. Alayna's setting up for appetizers on the patio. Can I get you something to drink—wine? Beer?"

"A glass of wine would be nice," she said, and followed him into the cottage.

Alayna was holding a spatula and removing something that smelled like heaven from a tray. She gave Emma a smile as she entered.

"I'm so glad you made it," Alayna said. "Go ahead and make yourself comfortable outside. Bea should be here any minute."

Emma looked over at Alayna and mouthed 'so hot' as Luke grabbed the wine from the refrigerator. Alayna grinned and mouthed back 'I know.'

Luke handed Emma a glass of wine and grabbed his beer off the counter. "Telling us to make ourselves comfortable was Alayna's polite way of getting us out of the kitchen. Which just means we get to pick the comfortable chairs since we're outside first."

Emma laughed and followed him out where he flopped into one of four perfectly matched chairs. A few minutes later, she heard Bea's voice inside and then the bookstore owner joined her and Luke and on patio.

"I'm glad to see you," Bea said to Emma as she sat down with a double pouring of wine. "How are things going at the surf shop?"

"Great," Emma said. "The accounting was a mess, but the business is really straightforward and there's not a ton of vendors, so it's not difficult. Just time-consuming, and the setup part is tedious."

Bea snorted. "Not difficult, she says. Aside from cutting checks weekly and doing payroll, I do my books and inventory once a month. Nelly hovers nearby with a bottle of whiskey and a crucifix. And we're not even Catholic."

Emma laughed. "They should give out both along with a finance degree."

"Was that your major?" Bea asked.

Emma had already anticipated this question and had a reply ready. "It was but I quit school after my parents... Anyway, most of what I know was learned on the job. I've worked for some really smart people and was happy to take positions at a lower rate than market in exchange for some educational time with them. It was super lean early years, but I do decently enough now. I've almost always found decent pay and my expenses are low. And I've had some luck with the stock market. I studied it for a long time before I tried my hand at it."

Bea nodded. "That's the way I learned real estate and the book business—people I worked for and with and a lot of reading. But regardless of how you receive the input, you have to have the talent for it or it won't stick. You have a talent for numbers and software, God bless you."

"And what's your talent, Aunt Bea?" Luke asked.

Bea wagged a finger at him. "You better watch yourself while you're living in my house. I could evict you both."

"You love me," Luke said.

Bea grinned. "I do, damn it. But to answer your question, my talent is knowing a good investment when I see it. The bookstore, these two cottages, and a ton of other real estate I've bought and sold over the years. And Alayna. She's the best investment I've ever made."

Alayna stepped out onto the patio and put a tray of appetizers on the coffee table before sitting with them. "I hope you don't change your mind after tonight's meal. I've tried to make things different from expectation so everything is elevated a bit, but not so different that locals will think it's too uppity and weird."

They all stared at Alayna, and she waved a hand at the tray. "What are you waiting for?" she asked. "Dig in. And please don't hold back. If I serve something bad at my opening, I'm blaming the three of you."

Emma picked up a toothpick with a shrimp and popped it in her mouth. The explosion of sweet and heat was so incredible and so perfectly balanced she almost groaned.

"Oh my God," Emma said. "Do you need investors? I can probably afford a one percent stake and I'll take my royalties in food."

Alayna visibly relaxed, then beamed as the others nodded.

"Seriously? You love the shrimp?" she asked.

"This is one of the best things I've ever tasted," Emma said honestly. "Mind you, my expertise is takeout and not fine dining, but I just have to say wow. And I'm going to have another."

"Alayna, this is solid gold," Bea said. "And trust me, the local haters are all amateurs when it comes to food. You could give them manna from heaven, and they'd find a reason to complain. Even if Jesus was the server. But they're not your customers, so it doesn't matter."

"There's nothing like small-community hypocritical pretension," Alayna said. "But we're not going to discuss that on this fine night. We're going to chat about fun things, but mostly and hopefully, how good the food is. And with that said, I'm off to retrieve the crab cakes."

"Did she say crab cakes?" Emma popped a third shrimp in her mouth. "I'm going to be full by the time dinner comes."

Bea nodded. "The problem is that still won't stop you from eating. Why do you think I changed into elastic-waist pants before I headed over here? Did you get a chance to call about the apartment yet?"

"No," Emma said. "Actually, Mark offered me the one-bedroom above the store. Kinda helps us both out. He makes some extra money and I don't have to commute. Plus, I'm on hand for anything that comes up, and it's easiest to do inventory after hours and all when I'm right there."

Emma felt like she was going on a bit, but she didn't want people getting the wrong idea. Then she mentally chided herself. No one was going to get the wrong idea. That was just her increasing attraction to her boss and subsequent guilty conscience talking.

Bea looked a bit surprised but also pleased. "Really? Well, I'm glad to hear that he's moving forward with some things. Hiring you and renting that apartment are two big ones."

Alayna walked out with a tray containing a plated crab cake for everyone and placed it on the coffee table next to the shrimp before joining them.

"That's not all he's moving forward with," Luke said. "This evening, I helped him carry off a bunch of boxes of his wife's stuff for donation."

Bea locked her gaze on Emma, just long enough to make her uncomfortable, then finally, the older woman nodded.

"It was time," Bea said, still looking at Emma. "Maybe hiring you prompted him to get out of Neutral on more things than just his business. He's been stuck there a while. Not that I'm saying there's a timeline on grief, because I'm not. Beth was an incredible person and I feel for Mark and Lily. You're not supposed to go through that kind of loss at their stages of life. But life is for the living. And at some point, you have to get back around to living yours."

"I think all of us know something about that," Alayna said.

Bea reached over and squeezed her niece's hand. "And we all know something about getting on with things."

Alayna smiled at Bea. "With that said, it's time to get on with the taste-testing, so everyone grab a plate. If you're nice about the crab cakes, there's more inside."

"Who wouldn't be nice about crab cakes?" Luke asked, and everyone laughed.

Emma took her plate and settled in for another round of stellar food. Even though she'd been somewhat apprehensive about the night, it was impossible not to enjoy the great food and even better company.

As impossible as it would be not to miss it when she was gone.

———

BEA PUT the last of the dishes in the dishwasher and turned it on. She was stuffed beyond belief and loving every second of it. Alayna tried to send her home when Emma left, but Bea refused to let her niece do all the cooking *and* the cleaning. So she and Luke had cleared everything off the tables outside, washed the stuff that needed hand care, and loaded up the dishwasher with everything that didn't.

Alayna was supposed to use that time to relax but instead, she sat at the kitchen table with her laptop and started making notes about the dinner. She looked up when Bea slid into a chair across from her.

"That was an incredible meal, honey," Bea said. "Your restaurant is going to be the talk of the town."

"If it opens, you mean," Alayna said.

"Don't you worry about that," Bea said. "We'll make it happen. I was glad to see Emma here tonight. I get the impression the girl could use a friend. Doesn't seem like she has any."

"With all the moving around she does, I guess it would be hard to," Alayna said. "It was hard for me to make friends in New York with everyone coming and going."

"How much has she told you about her past?" Bea asked.

"Not a whole lot. Just what you already know—that she has no family left and she's a contemporary nomad, I guess you would call it. And she loves numbers."

Bea frowned. "Do you know anything about her parents? Her childhood?"

"Not really," Alayna said, feeling her heart drop a little. "Why? Do you think something's wrong with her?"

Luke took a seat next to Bea.

"Not wrong," he said. "But she's very guarded and very skilled at deflecting so that you don't notice."

Alayna stared at them in dismay. "I cannot handle forming another relationship with big problems on the horizon. Please tell me she's not a bad guy."

"Not a bad guy," Luke said. "But I'd say she's known trouble."

Bea nodded.

"Well, I know what that's like," Alayna said. "Do you think that's the real reason she moves around so much?"

"It's certainly possible," Bea said. "And also why I get the feeling she could really use a friend."

"Maybe she'll confide in me eventually," Alayna said. "Then I'll know how we can help."

"She might," Bea said. "Or maybe she'll confide in someone else."

Alayna was momentarily confused, then she caught on. "Mark? You think there's something there?"

Bea shrugged. "I'm sure she hasn't failed to notice how attractive her boss is. She's got eyes like the rest of us."

Alayna stared at Bea in dismay and Luke chuckled.

"I'm sure she has," Alayna said, "but why would Mark's being good-looking factor into her suddenly opening up to anyone? I have to prod her to accept an invitation to hang out with me. I can't fathom her pursuing her boss. She's just not that forward."

"Ah, so you *do* think he's good-looking," Luke joked.

Alayna rolled her eyes. Bea laughed, then gave her a reflective look.

"Emma originally stopped on the island for a short vacation," Bea said. "Seeing the *Help Wanted* sign and landing a job wasn't part of her plan. And I get the impression that even though she doesn't do things in a traditional way, that in sticking around here, she's surprised herself."

"And you think Mark is part of the draw?" Alayna asked. "I mean, sure it's possible, but it takes two..."

Bea gave her a pointed look. "Mark leasing her that apartment and donating Beth's things is a big deal. Probably even bigger than what the three of us realize."

Luke nodded, now completely serious. "He was clearly upset and I offered several times to haul the stuff back inside or turn around. Every time, it was like he was going to crack, but he never did. And I could see how hard it was, leaving those boxes, but when we drove away from the shelter, he had this expression of total peace. I have to say it really left an impression on me."

"Do you think the two of them realize?" Alayna asked.

"No," Bea said. "And none of us can say anything about it. This is a very delicate balance they've formed. They both have scars and they need to figure out how to live with them on display. Whatever has happened to Emma is part of her past forever. But it doesn't have to be part of her future."

"That's what I thought, until my past followed me into my present and threatened my future," Alayna said.

Bea nodded. "And that was an awful thing but in hindsight, a good one to have settled, especially as things turned out well for you and Luke. If Emma's got trouble, she's got to figure out a way to end it, because you know better than most that running only delays the inevitable. When it's over, she has to accept that even though it's a part of her, it doesn't have to define her. Then she can be free. The same goes for Mark."

Alayna smiled. Bea had always been wise beyond her years.

Maybe she was right about this as well. At least, Alayna hoped she was.

"Maybe they'll be free together."

———

BY THE TIME the council meeting rolled around on Thursday night, Alayna's anxiety had shot up to New York levels. Luke had tried to distract her with paddleboarding, shopping, and even a sexy dance while tempting her with baked goods, but for the first time, none had interested her. Instead, she'd spent most of the day pacing back and forth on the beach, muttering to herself and plotting the demise of the Whitmores if they succeeded in destroying her dream. At least she'd worked off her next ten meals with all that stomping around in the sand.

She checked her watch for the ten thousandth time, wondering what the hell was holding up her aunt, who should have already been there. Finally, she spotted Bea and Nelly come in the back door and waved at them. They hurried down the aisle and dropped into the seats Alayna had saved for them. Bea glanced up at the city council members, who were getting ready to begin the meeting.

"When you didn't answer your phone, I thought you'd been in an accident," Alayna fussed at her aunt.

"The way she was driving, I'm surprised we weren't," Nelly said.

Bea waved a hand in dismissal. "Got you here, didn't I? That new delivery driver showed up late, and I thought we'd never get him out of there. I don't know why he thinks we want to stand around listening to his girlfriend problems."

"Bea fixed him right up, though," Nelly said. "She told him that the problem was he was too busy talking to other women to bother and get home at a decent hour for dinner with his own. That got him moving."

"Not fast enough," Bea said. "I was hoping to have some time to circulate among the council members before they got started."

"You circulated more people this week than the ceiling fans at the bookstore," Nelly said. "You'll have to settle for glaring at the rest of them from your seat."

They all went quiet as Carlson Whitmore entered the room using a side door. He glanced over at them and frowned, and Alayna tensed. She'd hoped that all of Victoria's complaining to Bea was just her blowing smoke, but Alayna should have known that was a wasted thought. This one-sided war Victoria was waging had been going on for years, and it didn't look as if she were interested in calling a truce. And Carlson was clearly here to do his wife's bidding.

"I'd like to call this meeting to order," Carlson said, and everyone settled down.

For one long hour, council members droned on about things so insignificant that Alayna wondered why someone didn't jump up screaming and tell them to stop wasting precious minutes. Clearly, the council must not have much to do if this was how they spent their time. Even Luke, who was used to standing at attention while other people talked, appeared to be nodding off at one point. Bea had spent the hour glaring from one council member to the next. Every time one of them glanced her way and saw her fixed gaze, they'd immediately look down at the table.

Finally, the regular business was concluded and it looked as if they were going to wrap up for the night. Alayna cast a confused look at Bea. Was Victoria actually going to let this one go? That would be a welcome surprise.

"I have one last thing on the agenda," Carlson said, and all of Alayna's hopes were dashed. "I'd like the council to reconsider the zoning for the commercial space above the bookstore."

"Reconsider it for what?" one of the members asked. "My understanding is a restaurant is going in there, and that meets our standards."

"Does it?" Carlson asked. "That space was previously occupied by an attorney with minimal employees and very few clientele going in and out of the area. The parking behind the building already stays almost full during season. Can we really afford to add more traffic to an already-congested parking situation?"

Bea stood. "You mean the parking lot that *I* own? And that I allow all the other businesses' customers and employees to use for free? *That* parking lot?"

The council members shuffled in their seats as Bea's statement struck a nerve. Carlson wasn't the only one who could make life harder for the local business owners, and most of the council members owned businesses on the island.

Carlson frowned. "You do not have the floor. You'll have a chance to speak before the vote at the next meeting." He turned back to the council as Bea sat down. "There is also some concern from the homeowners in the neighborhood behind the building about the increase in noise during late hours. Loud, drunk patrons can bring down the quality of life to the people who live here year-round. Their needs have to be considered."

Bea jumped up again. "You mean like the party you had last year, where ten times the number of people that will fit in that restaurant poured out onto your lawn, into the street, and destroyed other people's landscaping?"

"As there were no arrests, that is hearsay," Carlson said.

"There were no arrests because you hold the mortgage on

the sheriff's house," Bea said. "Everyone in this room knows what's going on here. Are you going to allow it? Because remember, it doesn't stop with me. What about the next person Victoria finds a reason to dislike? What is the council going to do to them? Close their business down? Is the bank going to call their mortgage? Cancel their lines of credit? This is blackmail, pure and simple."

Everyone in the room started mumbling, and Alayna heard several people call out in support of Bea. Carlson banged his gavel and everyone got quiet again.

"The vote will happen at next month's meeting," he said. "I am proposing we limit the zoning of the space to professional services with normal business hours only. You all have one month to do your own research. Anyone who wishes to speak for or against can present a two-minute monologue prior to the vote. You're all dismissed."

The council members all jumped up and practically ran out the door as Bea stared after them, fuming. Carlson walked right by them, wearing a faint smile. Asshole.

"I just don't understand what he has to gain by any of this," Luke said.

"Revenge," Bea said.

"For what?" Luke asked.

"For Bea being smart and not needing his money," Nelly said. "For Alayna being prettier than Melody and having talent and actual friends. Jealousy is a very dangerous emotion when it overwhelms all else and people have the means to make trouble."

Bea frowned.

Gary walked up. "Nelly's right. There's nothing Bea and Alayna can do to change things. Victoria tagged them long ago as her top rivals, and she's been trying to find a way to take them down ever since." He gave Bea a hard stare.

"Remember my suggestion? Think about it. Think really hard."

As he walked off, Alayna turned to her aunt. "What suggestion?"

Bea shook her head. "That fool wants me to run for mayor."

Alayna, Nelly, and Luke all looked at one another.

"Doesn't sound foolish to me," Nelly said.

"Me either," Alayna agreed. "In fact, it sounds kind of brilliant. The mayor has enough pull to stop Carlson from getting things over on people."

"Then why doesn't he?" Luke asked.

"Because he's Carlson's cousin," Alayna said.

Luke groaned. "You've got to be kidding me."

"I wish she was," Bea said. "They've always had a rivalry themselves but so far, the good mayor has made it a policy to stay out of Carlson's way and Carlson has stayed out of his."

"I think Carlson has something on him," Nelly said.

"That wouldn't surprise me," Bea said.

"Which leaves Carlson with carte blanche to run over the islanders," Luke said.

"That about sums it up," Nelly said.

"Then I'm for you running," Luke said. "You've got plenty of people on your side. Why not do it?"

"What if I don't win?" Bea said. "Then they'll just gloat over knowing they have all the power."

"I can't imagine people preferring to live under the threat of extortion over being able to handle their business freely," Luke said. "Give them another option and surely they'll go for it—especially since unlike this upcoming council vote, they'll be standing in a voting booth with no one watching. He can't come back on them individually if he doesn't know who to go after."

"No, but he can collectively," Bea said. "He holds money over most of the islanders and if he doesn't over the older ones, then he does over their kids."

"He can't just call loans for no reason," Luke said.

"He could find reasons," Bea said.

"So you're saying he's not above shady stuff," Luke said. "Well, good. That means he's probably already been up to plenty. We just need to find out what and use it against him."

Nelly grinned. "Count me in on the dirt digging. I've wanted to take that family down since Jesus was a toddler."

Alayna studied her aunt's pensive expression and knew her mind was rolling around all the potential costs of taking such an enormous step. She'd already put herself in the line of fire by funding the restaurant and offering up her space to do it. Bea had never bowed down to the Whitmores, but she'd never openly declared war, either.

Finally, Bea nodded. "Let's do it."

# CHAPTER FIFTEEN

IT WAS CLOSE TO 9:00 P.M. WHEN EMMA PLACED THE LAST of the boxes from her trunk on the kitchen counter in her new apartment. She didn't have to be out of the motel until the next morning, but she didn't want to be rushing to get her things out before work, so she'd packed up and given Gary back the key that evening. It had taken her all of a minute to carry her one overnight bag into the apartment, and since she was too excited to eat, she'd decided to haul the rest of her things in from her car. She'd given the place a good cleaning on her lunch hour, so the space was ready for occupancy. The thought of being unpacked and settled before the weekend made her happy.

She'd made six trips hauling things upstairs so far, and she smiled every time she walked through the door, still unable to believe her luck. In eight years of moving around, she'd been to some beautiful places but had never taken more than a couple days due to the cost involved. Tempest Island was the best of all of them, and she was actually going to live here all summer. She kept wanting to pinch herself, afraid she was going to wake up and find out it had all been a dream.

"Do you need some help?"

Mark's voice sounded behind her and she jumped.

"Sorry," he said as he stepped inside through the patio doorway. "I didn't mean to startle you. I would have headed over sooner, but bath time was World War III, and I'm pretty sure I've read every book Lily owns twice tonight."

Emma waved a hand in dismissal, trying to act casual even though her pounding heart wasn't remotely relaxed. She'd only seen him a handful of times that day at work, but she'd heard the steady stream of customers coming in and out of the store.

"It's not your fault," she said. "I'm lost in thought and didn't hear you walk in. I hope I wasn't making too much noise."

"Not at all. Lily's bedroom is on the other corner of the building. I just heard the deck creaking while I was loading the dishwasher. I can go grab some more boxes."

"Actually, I'm done. Since the place is fully equipped, I'm not bringing up my kitchen stuff, so mostly it's just my clothes and my linens. I figured I'd use my stuff to swap out with yours."

He scanned the boxes and shook his head. "How do you manage to get everything important in your car? Things are a little better now, but there was a time when Lily was a baby that it looked like we were traveling out of the country just to go get ice cream."

"Babies are a whole different thing. But I guess you just figure out the things you have to have and buy them in quality, like shoes. I have great running shoes. Then everything else is disposable. And I don't collect things, especially breakable things."

"It shouldn't be that hard to get, given that I was in the military and barely had a duffel bag of belongings to cart around back then. But I guess I've gotten used to having more creature comforts, which admittedly is a lot easier when you're in one place."

"You need more comforts when you have a business and a child. But this is all I'm bringing in for now. My car is still out front, though. Is it okay if I move it across the road in the morning before work?"

"Sure. You could move it at lunch even. The pre-wave will start this weekend. That will be the people with no kids who want to get their early season time in the sun before the families descend on the island. The week after, schools start closing for the year and the tidal wave begins."

"How long does it last?"

"Mid-August is when a lot of schools start up again and even for those that don't, parents don't want to be vacationing right before. Too much to do to get ready."

"So the big rush is not quite three months."

He nodded. "After schools start back, we get a second, smaller wave, which is another round of young couples with no kids, singles, and retirees. They're looking for quieter beaches and off-season rates. Business is still solid. It just moves from frantic to steady. And the locals venture out more once the big crowds subside."

"Well, I can't speak for the retail side of things, but your accounting is going to be good to go."

He smiled. "You have no idea how much relief that gives me. Last year was a blur, and we're not even going to talk about the things my CPA said to me when I brought him stuff for my tax return. I'm pretty sure he only kept me as a client because he feels sorry for me."

"Altruism by numbers?"

"Something like that. Well, if you don't need any help, I guess I'll head back for my eventful night of laundry sorting."

"If it makes you feel any better, my event will be clothes hanging."

He laughed. "If you need anything, you know where to find me. See you tomorrow."

She followed him as he headed out of the apartment and waited until she heard his patio door slide shut before closing and locking hers then drawing the shades. She double-checked the interior door and drew the dead bolt before starting for the bedroom, ready to tackle her clothes. The bottle of whiskey on the kitchen counter beckoned to her, and she stopped long enough to pour a shot.

Her pulse was still racing. She'd thought it had spiked because he'd startled her and that was probably initially true. She couldn't remember the last time she had forgotten to stop and lock a door right behind herself. But the longer Mark had stood there making casual conversation, the harder it had been for her to stop thinking about the fact that it was just the two of them, alone in her apartment, and her bedroom was only steps away. Too many unbidden thoughts had flashed through her mind as she'd struggled to maintain polite conversation. Thoughts that she hadn't felt in well...ever.

She frowned. No. Surely, that wasn't true.

She took the whiskey into the bedroom and flopped down on the one empty spot on the bed. She'd had relationships in high school and college. Granted, they were brief and both parties were immature, but it still counted, right? And it wasn't as though she'd been a nun the last eight years, even though she'd dressed as one to make her dramatic exit from her old life. She'd dated casually, had mutually satisfying sex with some, and then moved on with no hearts broken.

But Mark was different. When she was around him, she started thinking about all those things she couldn't have—a home in one place, friends, a life that didn't include looking over her shoulder, a relationship with a man that wasn't surface level. And Mark was an excellent choice for that. He had solid and permanent practically stamped on his forehead.

She sighed, knowing she was only increasing the agony by staying here for the summer. Time wasn't likely to make her feelings go away. If anything, the more she got to know about Mark, the more she liked him. He wasn't at all what she'd imagined in her previous thoughts of her fantasy man, but he was still perfect.

And not an option. Not even a temporary one.

Because anything with Mark wouldn't be casual—not for her. And she doubted Mark would be free-spirited with his feelings either. He'd had a great marriage and he had Lily to consider as well. He was the kind of man who wouldn't start a relationship with someone unless he thought there was a future.

And a future wasn't in her vocabulary.

———

MARK GRABBED a beer from the refrigerator, sat on his couch, and turned on the television. He spent the next few minutes scrolling through the offerings to finally turn on a movie he'd already seen at least ten times.

"Two hundred channels and nothing to watch," he grumbled, although he knew that wasn't the real source of his disquiet.

Lily was fast asleep and had been sleeping through the night for months now unless a storm awakened her. She enjoyed kindergarten, and Jane was doing a better job with his daughter than he could have ever imagined.

Lesson bookings and rentals for the season were already rolling in, and it promised to be another good one even if he never got that whole video thing off the ground. But this year, he wouldn't have to worry about the accounting end of things. He could spend all his time on the customers and the product offerings, fine-tuning pricing and lessons for the best possible profit.

*And the reason you can do that is because of your gorgeous accountant.*

He stiffened even as the thought rolled through his mind, then looked down at his wedding band. He couldn't deny he'd felt an attraction to Emma the first time they'd met, but she was an attractive woman. It wasn't as if he hadn't noticed beautiful women since his wife died. He was grieving. He wasn't blind.

But this was different.

He'd felt that familiar tug—that spike of joy and excitement when you saw someone who really mattered, and that slow decline back to basic and normal when they're gone. Not that it was anything like what he'd felt with Beth, of course. His love for his wife was long and far and deep and everything else you could describe. He barely knew Emma, so he couldn't feel the same. But there was a spark of all of that—a flicker that could turn into a flame if tended.

*It's too soon.*

He nodded in an attempt to convince himself, but it didn't seem to diminish how much he was looking forward to seeing Emma the next day, and it didn't allow him to relax in the knowledge that this highly desirable woman was sleeping just a couple walls away. Why on earth had he thought it would be a good idea to rent the apartment to her? He didn't have to see her to know she was there. The proximity alone was enough to keep his mind whirling with things he had no right thinking.

*You have Lily to consider.*

*Emma never stays anywhere long term.*

*It's too soon.*

That last sentiment needed to be repeated, because it was the one he was the most iffy on. Was there a rule about when a widower could start finding other people attractive? Or, God forbid, go on a date? And if there were rules, were they published anywhere? And did they vary by region or the age and sex of the one left behind?

He blew out a breath. He'd bet a year's revenue that if there were rules about such things, Bea and Nelly would know them, but no way was he going there with either of them. He was pretty sure Nelly had already not-so-subtly been pushing that agenda. He wasn't about to give her ammunition.

Maybe it was the similarities Emma had to Beth that had captured his attention when other women hadn't. They both had beautiful auburn hair and loved their numbers game. And... Well, he guessed that's where they ended. Beth was a beautiful person and Emma seemed to be as well, but Beth had preferred decorating and baking and Emma preferred outdoor sports. Beth was a huge homebody who had hated every minute of their travel on the surfing circuit. Emma was barely in one place long enough to change her driver's license.

"Daddy?"

Lily's voice sounded behind him and he jumped up, sloshing beer on his hand.

"What's wrong, sweetie?" he asked as he walked over to kneel beside her. "Are you all right?"

"I'm thirsty," she said. "And you didn't bring me my glass of water."

"I'm so sorry. I'll get that right now."

"I can carry it. I want the pink cup."

He found her favorite pink cup and filled it halfway with water, then handed it to her. She took a long drink, then smiled.

"Thank you, Daddy," she said as she headed off.

"Sweet dreams," he said and sighed.

Carrying her own water. What next? Pierced ears? Makeup? Boyfriends?

His shoulders tightened and he headed back to the couch to retrieve his beer. Thinking about raising a daughter was enough to send him to the hard stuff. He said a silent prayer that Lily turned out to be a tomboy and flipped the channels again until he found another movie he'd already seen time and time again.

But as he looked at the screen, it was Emma who played through his mind.

# CHAPTER SIXTEEN

HE SAT IN THE CORNER OF THE FRAT HOUSE KITCHEN, HOLDING A soda. He'd been watching Katarina since she came in, but she was dressed as a nun, and that had garnered her more than a few curious looks. Still, most had given her one hard stare and a laugh, then gone on with their business, but this guy kept studying her and it was making her nervous. She'd thrown a couple of casual glances his way, trying to ascertain if she knew him, but he didn't look familiar.

"Hey baby, you wanna dance—horizontally? I can make you see God."

The arm suddenly thrown around her shoulders made her jump, but while the drunken frat boy who was looking at her with watery eyes might have been a threat of some sort before tonight, at the moment, he didn't rate even a second of worry.

"I've got a boyfriend," she said.

"So?"

"He's an attorney," she said.

Drunk or not, guys seemed to understand legal ramifications, and this one was no different. He shrugged his arm off her shoulders just long enough to fling them around the girl next to her and make her the same impossible-to-refuse offer. She located the back door and stepped *outside on the patio. There were some couples making out, but the noise and crowd level was considerably less than what was inside.*

*She needed to think, and the loud music and even louder students were making it impossible. Not that she blamed them. If she were a normal person, like everyone else in that house, she could be having a good time as well. But her father had killed a man. That set her clearly apart from the norm.*

Don't panic!

*She took in a deep breath and slowly blew it out. There had to be a way for her to get out of town. But she needed money. The ATM had a limit and once she used it, she had to be ready to jet from that site. Her credit cards were useless. She did have a second bank account—one her parents didn't know about. She'd started siphoning part of her retail earnings into it and all of the cash she made on the side by tutoring and writing papers for other students, things her parents were completely unaware of. She'd been stockpiling cash in case her scholarship disappeared or her parents put so much pressure on her to comply with their antiquated beliefs that she was forced to move out and fend for herself.*

*As soon as word got out that she was missing—and her coworkers and other students would start asking questions eventually—the cops would easily find the other account. Which meant she needed to be at the bank first thing tomorrow morning to close it out with cash and use that money to get the hell out of LA. In a way they wouldn't be watching, which meant no plane, train, bus, or rental car. So what did that leave? She could hardly abscond from the state on a bicycle, and she had a feeling that anywhere in California wouldn't be far enough. And even if she managed to get out of the state, what would she do for rent? Or food? Her savings would only last so long, and she couldn't exactly march into a business and give them her real name.*

You need a fake ID.

*A bead of sweat ran down her forehead and she yanked the habit off, allowing some of the evening breeze to filter across her skin. She'd been watching entirely too many movies. Fake ID? What the hell did she know about fake IDs? She'd never even had a bad one to get into a bar. She certainly didn't know how people went about getting a good one. Especially one you could actually conduct adult business with.*

Don't get ahead of yourself.

*Maybe she just needed to go to the police. They would protect her, right? But snatches of monologues Josef had subjected her to came to mind. She'd mostly tuned him out on their dates, but she remembered him bragging about driving his car at double the speed limit on the highway and the cops having to let him go because his dad had so much pull.*

*Was it pull? Or payroll?*

*If her father's real position with Ivan including killing people, then that cast his wealthy boss in an entirely different light. Which meant the cops couldn't be trusted. At least, not the cops in California.*

*So she needed to get out of California and then talk to cops. Somewhere that Ivan didn't have business interests and wouldn't be likely to have people reporting to him. Which meant no major cities—at least not anywhere in the Pacific Northwest. She needed somewhere smaller —somewhere that Ivan wouldn't bother reaching. Definitely not Vegas. She knew he had several business interests there. Maybe Arizona.*

*Which seemed impossible given that she was currently trapped just off campus.*

*"Are you all right?"*

*The voice sounded behind her, causing her to jump. She whirled around and saw the guy from the corner standing there.*

*"I'm fine," she said.*

*He narrowed his eyes at her. "Are you sure? You look... I don't want to offend you, but you look scared."*

*"I...uh, I'm trying to avoid someone."*

*He nodded. "Tonight or for the rest of the semester?"*

*"For the rest of my life?"*

*He frowned. "Are you in trouble?"*

"If he finds me, I am."

"Then we'll make sure that doesn't happen. I can get you away from here."

She took a step back. "What? No. You don't need to—this is none of your concern. And I don't even know you."

He pulled his wallet out and handed her a business card, then showed her his ID.

Levi Hughes.

"That's my mom's business card. She's a social worker and runs a shelter for women, mostly domestic abuse victims. I volunteer there teaching computer courses, so I see and hear a lot. And you have that look a lot of them have when they get there."

"I can't go to a shelter. I have to get out of California. The guy I'm running from has family money. He knows everyone and everyone owes him, even the cops."

It wasn't exactly untrue, she thought. And better for Levi to think she was running from an abusive boyfriend than to know the truth, which would be a stretch for anyone to believe.

He nodded. "I have an uncle. He drives a tour bus between here and Sedona. He always keeps a couple seats open in case my mom needs them. He's leaving tomorrow morning."

Katarina sucked in a breath. "You could get me on that bus? You would do that for me?"

"Of course. And I can give you some money and a contact to help with identification."

She shook her head. "I have some money. I just need to get to the bank as soon as it opens. Before I'm reported missing and things are closed. Will I have time before the bus leaves?"

"What bank?"

She gave him the name and he nodded.

"There's one on the same street as my uncle's business. It opens an hour before the bus leaves. I use it myself. I have my own room here if *you feel okay staying overnight. If not, I could take you to a motel and pick you up in the morning."*

*She had no reason to trust him. For all she knew, he could be using his mother's card to get girls up to his room. For that matter, he could have made the cards himself.*

*He must have seen her doubt because he pulled up his phone and showed her a Facebook page. "That's my mom and there's a picture of both of us. Then here. This is her shelter. See her bio is right there online with her picture."*

*Katarina took the phone and scrolled through the website and Facebook page. At least he and his mother were who he said they were. Which meant she actually had a better idea of who this veritable stranger in front of her was than she did her own father.*

*"I...uh, your room is fine," she said. "But I don't want to get you into trouble or put you out."*

*He smiled. "Every guy here will have a girl—or two—in his room tonight, so no trouble at all. And I have bunk beds. I let a lot of drunk girls sleep it off. It's safer for them."*

*"That's a commendable thing you're doing."*

*He shrugged. "Maybe if someone had done it for my sister, she'd still be alive."*

*Her chest clenched. "I'm so sorry."*

*"I appreciate it. And now maybe you understand..."*

*She nodded.*

EMMA BOLTED UP as the thunder shook the walls. The room was pitch-black and completely unfamiliar. Frantic, she reached for her phone to get some light, and only when she shone it around her did she remember she was in her new apartment.

*Safe* in her new apartment.

She reached for the lamp but it didn't come on. As she'd used it the night before, she assumed that meant the storm had taken out the power. But that was okay. Her flashlight was one of the first things she always unpacked, and it was in the nightstand drawer. She pulled it out and then cast the wide beam at the ceiling, lighting up the entire room. Thunder rumbled overhead again, and she saw flashes of lightning in between the blind slats. Then the rain began to pour, sounding off on the metal roof.

Since sleep wasn't going to happen again until the storm was over, she flung back the covers and headed for the kitchen. She craved a cup of coffee, but it was just as well there was no power to produce one. The caffeine would keep her from falling back to sleep, and as it was only 2:00 a.m. she really hoped the storm eased up in time for her to get some more in. She'd stayed up past midnight, hanging and arranging her clothes and rearranging the kitchen items to suit her better, so she hadn't been asleep long before the storm hit.

She grabbed a caffeine-free soda from the fridge—soda she kept specifically for these kinds of nights—and headed to the living room. She lifted a navy throw blanket from the end of the couch and moved to the other side, farthest away from the patio doors. Lightning flashed through the blinds every couple minutes and the rain continued to pour.

She grabbed her laptop off the coffee table and typed his name in the search bar.

Levi Hughes.

Links immediately populated to the young attorney who was already making a name for himself with the DA's office in Los Angeles. She clicked on his social media page and smiled when she saw the picture of him and his fiancée on a sailboat the weekend before. Satisfied, she closed the laptop and leaned back on the couch.

It had been a long time since she'd had that dream. Since

she'd seen Levi—her savior—again. She literally owed him her life and desperately wished there were some way to thank him. But she couldn't risk contacting him, not even anonymously. She'd kept up with Ivan as well, and although he'd finally come under scrutiny, the DA's office hadn't managed an indictment yet. Which made her wonder just how many government offices Ivan had people working for him in. She was certain that Levi wasn't one of them but contacting Levi would put him at risk. As far as she knew, no one but her, Levi, and his uncle knew how she got out of the state, but those facts had never made it to the police.

After she'd fled California, she'd learned to reroute her internet connection using proxies. Then she'd logged into her school email and her social media sites. There had been a lot of messages from friends, posting about wanting her safe return, but Levi had never attempted to contact her. She was certain he'd recognized her when her face was flashed across the news, but he'd kept his word.

No one had ever known that Katarina Petras—wearing a wig that Levi had provided and clothes picked up that morning at Walmart—had taken a tour bus from Los Angeles bound for Sedona, but had gotten off when they stopped to refuel in Williams, a small tourist town near Flagstaff. In Williams, she'd met a woman whose name and address Levi had given her. That woman had never asked her a single question. She'd simply changed her short, dark brown hair to auburn, given her some clip-in extensions that matched, and provided her with all the documents for her new identity.

Katarina Petras had become Emma Turner.

Over the years, she'd had a lot of different hair colors and styles, but in the last three, she'd returned to that first shade of auburn that she'd had when she ran. And she'd let it grow out to the length that the hair extensions had provided. She liked the color and thought it looked good with her tanned skin.

Sometimes she missed the short dark bob that she'd kept flat-ironed straight, but it was too easy to spot in a crowd, especially framing her bright green eyes. A ponytail of auburn was something people saw so much it didn't even register. But she still kept a collection of wigs. Mostly, she used them when traveling from one stop to another. That way, if by any chance someone was tracking her, there were no random gas station sightings with the potential of camera footage to use to track her car.

In the beginning, she'd changed cars several times, but after a few years with no issues, she'd finally settled on her older-model Camry and had left things alone. But even though she had no reason to think anyone was still looking for her, she was glad that her car would be parked behind the bookstore, where it wasn't visible from the street. That trickle of fear never seemed to go away, no matter how long or how far she carried it.

She opened the laptop again, hesitated, then finally tapped in the next search.

The news reports of her father's murder popped up, all dated a month after she fled LA. And the rumors had circulated afterward, set in motion when the lonely and painfully honest Amy went to the police and told them she'd seen Gustav and another man at the college the night that Coach Mayhern had disappeared. The same night Gustav's daughter, Amy's friend Katarina, had disappeared.

There had been a rash of speculation after Gustav was killed. Some believed he'd seen something related to the coach and Katarina's disappearance and had been taken out for that knowledge. But the DA had been unable to make the necessary connections, and when Amy had died of an overdose a week after her visit to the police, their one witness who could place Gustav at the college and who had sent Katarina off to find him was gone.

Emma knew good and well that Amy would have never taken drugs. She had been vegan, not for philosophical reasons but because she was hyper concerned with her health, as her mother had battled diabetes and kidney issues from a young age. A carjacking was the official verdict for Emma's father's death—no suspects ever arrested or even identified. But Emma knew better. Her father had been killed by the same man who'd killed both Amy and Katarina's mother—Ivan Danek.

She searched her mother's name next but again, she found nothing but the original stories, describing the loss of control and her mother's fiery crash down a mountainside just two weeks after her father's murder. The official conclusion was that she'd been grieving and taking meds for anxiety and to sleep. That she'd likely been foggy—maybe even falling asleep when she'd gone through the guardrail.

Or maybe she'd driven off that cliff on purpose.

There hadn't been any brake marks, so the ME hadn't been able to rule it out but also couldn't claim it a certainty. Emma didn't think her mother would take such action. It was entirely too assertive a move and Helenka Petras had always been the passive, doting wife. But if she hadn't heard her parents' exchange that night, she would have never believed her mother was aware of her father's real position with Ivan. Her mother had obviously been tougher than she'd thought.

And coldhearted.

Emma swallowed the lump in her throat. She'd never been close to her mother, but she'd also never thought the woman could wish her harm. But what she'd overheard told her everything she needed to know about the people who'd borne and raised her.

And all of that was why she'd never gone to the police herself. By the time she felt she was far enough away to risk it, the others started dying, so Emma decided to take Katarina's secrets to the grave. There was no point in her coming forward, anyway. After all, her father had murdered the coach and he was dead. Even if she told the police what she'd over-heard her parents saying, it wouldn't be enough to bring Danek up on charges.

She closed the laptop and shoved it onto the end table, frustrated with herself for revisiting things that were best left in the past. She might not have a permanent future in any one place, but she had a temporary life here and she intended to live it to its fullest. Dwelling on things she couldn't change wouldn't help. It never had. And she still couldn't even think about Amy without tearing up. She hadn't deserved what happened to her. She was the ultimate victim here with no connection to any of them outside of the horrible timing in trying to talk to a friend that night.

The woman in Williams who'd given her the new identity had also provided Emma with several pills—an antianxiety and a sleep medication. She'd suggested if they helped, she should find a doctor to prescribe them again when she found some-where safe enough to stick around.

When Emma had gone almost a week without sleeping more than an hour a night, she'd tried them, but the slightly numb feeling in her body and her mind unnerved her. She needed everything in top working order in case of an emer-gency, and a clear head was her number one priority. The drugs prevented that sharpness that she'd depended on. So she'd gone back to running, added meditation, and learned to operate on minimal sleep. Eventually, she'd found balance again. Except for the occasional nightmares, she'd been doing fine.

Until now. Two nightmares in the same week were more than she'd had in the past few months. She could only assume that the harsh thunderstorms that rolled over the island, coupled with her breaking her long-observed rules, had upped her anxiety. Maybe it was time to add back meditation, as she'd slowly allowed it to go by the wayside.

She heard a clicking sound, then the hum of the refrigerator. The microwave blinked at her, requesting a time reset. She let out a breath of relief. The power was back on. Then she realized that the rain had dropped from fierce to light and she hadn't heard thunder in a while.

She rose from the couch and headed for bed. With any luck, she'd be able to fall back asleep for a couple more hours at least. And maybe when she was off next weekend, she'd see about getting a new car. It had been several years and couldn't hurt to change things up, especially if it relieved some of her anxiety. She'd been thinking about a small SUV for a while now, and she had the cash saved to make the deal. Alayna had already offered to go housewares shopping with her. Maybe she wouldn't mind car shopping with her as well. It would be fun to have a friend along for a change.

She crawled back into bed and pulled the comforter up, snuggling down into the soft mattress as she felt a slight chill run through her. She closed her eyes and forced herself to think about numbers, about accounting, and prayed it would be enough to stop her racing mind and let her sleep again.

# CHAPTER SEVENTEEN

Mark waved at a couple as they walked in the surf shop and told them he'd be with them shortly, then turned back to the computer to finish ringing out the lady buying T-shirts. Another person waited behind that customer, and six more people were milling around the shop, items in their arms. Business had started as soon as he'd opened the door, so the first wave of summer had started a day early.

So far, no one had children with them, so he assumed this was the grandparents, singles, and couples, trying to get their days in before the beach turned to mostly families. Apparently, more than a few had decided to get started on Friday instead of Saturday, but he couldn't blame them. It was an absolutely gorgeous day. Eighty degrees and not a cloud in the sky. The surf was minimal, so not great for the serious surfers but perfect for the waders and the paddleboarders. He'd already rented three paddleboards and it wasn't even lunch yet.

He finished up with the customers at the counter and checked his phone to see if a supplier he was expecting that morning had given him an ETA.

"Do you need some help?" Emma's voice sounded behind him.

The truth was, he could use some as his seasonal helper didn't start until the next day and couldn't make it in today. He'd already checked.

"Front of the house isn't what you signed up for," he said.

She shrugged. "It's just one day. You'll have help starting tomorrow, right?"

"Yes. But I don't want to interrupt your accounting work."

"I'm cruising on that. I only have a couple hours more of input, and then after inventory on Sunday we'll be ready to launch."

He blinked. "You're done? With all the system conversion?"

She smiled and nodded. "The current stuff, anyway. I'll start on the historical stuff next so you'll have good comparisons. It really is an easy software. And I was up super early this morning, so I headed downstairs and got a head start on what I had slated for today."

"Well, I'd be a fool to turn down help but just until this rush is over. Is there any change to how I'm checking people out?"

"Nope. Everything here will be the same as before. Your retail software integrates with the new accounting software. Once I get the inventory done on Sunday and load the month-to-date sales data from the retail system, I'll connect the two and you'll be good to go Monday morning."

"I can't believe it. You're a miracle worker."

"Excuse me," a young guy stepped up to the counter. "I'd like to rent a paddleboard for the day."

"You take that," Emma said. "I can answer questions and ring people up. It's not like I don't know the stock."

She headed to the middle of the store and asked if anyone needed help. Mark felt some of the tension leave his shoulders as he pulled out the paperwork for the paddleboard rental and got the customer started on it. When the guy was done and off with his board, Mark came back into the store to see where he needed to jump in.

But the store was clear.

"Did you kick them all out?" he asked.

Emma laughed. "I didn't have to. I merely assisted in helping them select the tees and other souvenirs they absolutely had to have and then they were happily off."

"That rush surprised me a little. It's usually not like that until tomorrow."

"Maybe they all came in at the same time and you'll be bored all afternoon."

"Highly unlikely, but you never know. You said you were in early? Is everything okay in the apartment?"

"Yeah, that was all on me. The storm woke me up, then I had trouble getting back to sleep, so I finally gave up after a lot of rolling around and messy dreams."

He nodded. "The storm woke Lily up and she crawled in bed with me. I, however, sleep like the dead, so I never noticed it was storming or that she'd gotten in my bed. The storms used to keep me awake, but after a while, you get used to them."

The door to the store opened, and Mark looked over to see Melody Whitmore enter. He struggled to maintain a pleasant expression, but it was hard given the Whitmores' reputation. He had managed to stay out of their sights so far, and that's the way he preferred to keep it, which was why a wave of apprehension rushed over him. She didn't need tourist stuff and if she ever wanted to surf or paddleboard, could easily afford her own equipment. So he had no idea why she'd need to be in his shop, but it probably wasn't good.

"There you are," she said, pasting on a big smile as she

headed for the counter. "I thought you might be out on a board given how beautiful it is today, then I find you closed up in here."

She gave Emma a once-over and sniffed, apparently finding his accountant lacking, then turned back to Mark.

"When you finish with her, I'd like to talk to you about lessons," Melody said. "*Private* lessons."

Emma stared at Melody, and Mark could tell she wasn't impressed. He didn't blame her.

"I'm not a customer," Emma said. "I'm his accountant."

Melody paused for a moment but apparently didn't feel Emma was cause for concern.

"That's nice," she said. "So then you're free to talk now, right?" She clutched his arm and pulled him toward the door. "Let's talk on the beach. It's so pretty today."

"I need to stay in the store," Mark said. "My other retail person doesn't start until tomorrow."

Melody waved a hand at Emma. "She can handle it. You know the saying—the customer is always right." She leaned into him and looked up at him with a sexy smile. "And trust me, there's *nothing* wrong about me."

If it was anyone else, Mark would have taken a step back and politely asked them how he could assist them, making it clear that his personal life was not one of the items on sale, but pissing off the Whitmores could bring things down on him that he didn't need. His business loan was held by the bank Carlson ran, so technically his livelihood and his home were both tied up in the purse that Carlson held the strings to. So far, Mark had managed to avoid issues but if Melody had decided to pursue him romantically, then he had just been tossed into the fire.

"All my boards are rented at the moment," he said and stepped out of her grasp to pull a book out from under the counter. He flipped through the pages, wishing every slot was filled, but unfortunately, he had an opening next week.

"I have an opening for a lesson next Wednesday at two. It's a hundred an hour and that includes the board rental. Would that work?"

She put on a pouty look. "I really wanted that lesson today."

"Sorry, but I can't today. We're slammed here already and the early season starts tomorrow."

She threw a dirty look at Emma. "Maybe you need to hire better help then."

Mark struggled to control his words. "Would you like the Wednesday slot?"

"I have a spa day on Wednesday," she said and waved a hand at her body. "I have to take care of all this."

"I can check the week after," he said, praying that this would be the end of it and she'd find something else to distract her.

"Maybe we could have dinner instead. You could explain it to me and then I could take a lesson later on."

"I have a daughter to take care of after work."

"So get a sitter. That's what parents do."

He couldn't control the rush of anger at her completely dismissive tone. Like Lily was just another hindrance that could be foisted off to suit her.

"My wife only passed a year ago," he said, trying to keep his voice controlled. "I'm not dating. Not now. Probably not ever."

Her eyes widened at his tone, and she gave him another fake smile. "I'll change your mind. Another time."

She whirled around and tossed her expertly colored platinum hair over her shoulder and walked out of the store, hips swaying. Mark looked over at Emma, who was staring after

Melody with an expression akin to smelling something bad, which was appropriate.

"I'm sorry about that," Mark said.

"Don't be. She wasn't pushing herself on me. In fact, I got the impression that she doesn't acknowledge people like me. Who is she?"

"Melody Whitmore. Local spoiled rich girl."

Emma's eyes widened. "Oh! Alayna told me about the Whitmores. They're trying to keep her from opening her restaurant."

Mark stared. "Why would they do that?"

"Apparently, Veronica has always had a one-sided rivalry with Bea, and Melody has hated Alayna since she moved here in high school. I'm sure because Alayna is prettier, nicer, smarter, and more talented."

"That sounds about right."

"Kudos for being so nice. I don't think I could have been."

He blew out a breath. "I hate to say it because it sounds cowardly, but if you get on the wrong side of the Whitmores, they can cause you trouble. In addition to being on the city council, her father runs the bank, which holds the loans for most of the businesses and the homes on the island, including mine. Melody and her mother, Veronica, have plenty of disposable cash and even more free time to figure out new and more evil ways to use Carlson's power."

Emma's expression darkened. "You think Melody would sic her dad on you just because you won't go out with her?"

"I don't know. I mean... I've heard some things. And if they're going after Alayna over some childhood jealousy, then what's to stop them from taking a shot at me?"

"That's horrible. Surely her father wouldn't try to force a recent widower to date his daughter. What does she gain by that?"

"Getting what she wants. I'm pretty sure that's all Melody cares about."

"But ultimately, what does that accomplish? Even if you went out with her, her father can't force you to be attracted to her. Quite frankly, as soon as she opens her mouth, anything attractive is wiped away, which says a lot because she's a good-looking woman until you know her."

He stared at her for a moment, then laughed. "You're so right. God, I can't believe she blew in here like that. My stress level went straight through the roof."

"I can see where being forced to be nice to Melody would stress you out. Maybe she'll leave you alone now."

"Maybe."

"You told her you weren't dating and why. She has to respect that."

He nodded, but he wasn't convinced of that at all.

———

EMMA HEADED BACK to her office, still reeling from the exchange between Melody Whitmore and Mark. Alayna and Bea had aired some grievances with the Whitmores concerning Alayna's restaurant the other night at dinner, and Melody's name had been thrown out there as a contributing factor to the issues, but Emma couldn't believe just how forward Melody had been. She'd practically pushed herself on Mark and was completely rude about his obligations to Lily.

Mark was clearly uncomfortable during the exchange, and Emma had been surprised when he hadn't been more forceful about turning her down. But she hadn't known who the woman was or just how much power the family held over him. Now she understood. What a horrible group of people. They appeared to be the one stinky black spot on the island.

She just hoped that Melody wouldn't cause problems for Mark, but she was worried. Regardless of her looks, Emma couldn't imagine many locals were stupid enough to get involved with her due to her family's reputation. That probably seriously cut into her dating pool—along with her horrible personality.

Emma sat at her desk and looked out the window, then did a double take when she saw Melody out on the beach, draped over the guy who'd rented a paddleboard earlier. He was grinning at her as though he'd won the lottery. Idiot. Emma shook her head, but the reality was Melody had a pretty face and one of those bodies that men seemed to like—all those curves and all in the right places.

Tourist season was probably her prime hunting months. All those young, available men who wouldn't be around long enough to find out how awful she was. Or who figured it out but didn't care because they were only here temporarily, and it wasn't as if she was going to follow them home to ruin their lives.

Maybe Melody would focus on the vacationers and leave Mark alone.

*I'm not dating. Not now. Probably not ever.*

Mark's words echoed in her head and her heart clenched for a second time, just as it had when he'd uttered them. Because while she knew he'd said them in an attempt to shut Melody down, he issued them with such conviction that Emma had to believe it was the God's honest truth. Mark wasn't ready. And how could she blame him? It had only been a year, and he'd been deeply in love with his wife and living a fantastic life that they'd built together. They had a child. He'd obviously managed to get a good enough handle on his emotions to keep his business going and make sure Lily lacked for nothing. But he might never get far enough beyond the grief to want another relationship.

*And even if he did, he's not an option for you.*

She slumped back in her chair and sighed. Talk about someone who'd never be ready to have a relationship. Everyone in her life was temporary. Why allow feelings to form when the future only held loss when leaving them behind? Mark was already recovering from a huge loss. She knew exactly what that felt like and didn't blame him for wanting to avoid it going forward.

But none of that completely logical sentiment changed how crappy she'd felt when she'd watched Melody flirting with Mark, or how happy she'd been when he'd gotten rid of her. And that worried her. Getting attached to the island was bad enough. Her budding friendship with Alayna was going to be hard to sever when the time came. Falling for her boss was something she couldn't allow.

———

LEVI HUGHES WASN'T a violent man. In fact, he'd made it his life's work to fight against violence and those who perpetrated it. But at the moment, he felt like punching something. Six years of working at the DA's office and he still couldn't put together enough evidence to hang Ivan Danek. The man was as slick as he was horrible and unfortunately for Levi, very clever. He had structured all his businesses to cover very well for his misdeeds.

Danek's people were unfailingly loyal and if there was ever a question of that loyalty, they weren't around long enough to display it. It didn't help that a lot of his 'employees' weren't from the US and could simply be traded back to Danek's homeland for a replacement. But Levi suspected many never took another step in this country or any other. He just couldn't find the bodies.

He dropped into his office chair and leaned back, his thoughts veering off to Katarina Petras. Of course, he'd had no idea who she was that night at the party. All he knew was that she was scared to death and needed help. It wasn't until she was reported missing that he knew her name, and even then, it still hadn't all clicked. Then he'd started interning at the DA's office shortly after, heard the buzz on Danek, and found out Katarina's father had been one of his top men.

Mayhern and Katarina disappearing had been two big seemingly unconnected mysteries until poor Amy Copeland had come forward and tied Gustav Petras to the missing Coach Mayhern—a man who'd been under investigation for drug dealing on the campus. Drugs they suspected Danek of supplying.

Then the bodies had started to pile up or people simply disappeared.

Levi didn't know for certain what Katarina had heard or seen, but he could make a really good guess. More than once, it had crossed his mind to look for her, but even if he could find her, it wasn't fair to do so. Given his suspicions that Danek had people on payroll everywhere in the city, he knew he couldn't keep Katarina safe. And really, what could she offer? Even if she'd seen her father with the coach—even if she'd seen her father kill him—her father was the perp and he was dead. Unless Levi could tie Gustav's actions back to Danek, he still had nothing. Being employed by someone wasn't evidence of murder, especially when he didn't even have a body.

And even if he wanted to find Katarina, it wasn't that simple, and that was by design. His uncle had gotten her out of the city, and she'd left the tour to see the woman his mother had used back then to give the women new identities. But that woman had a strict protocol. She never asked anyone's name and kept no records of what the new identity was. For her safety and for the women's.

He blew out a breath. Hell, for all he knew, Katarina was dead as well.

His phone rang and he saw his fiancée's name on the display.

"Please tell me you're good with takeout tonight," he said when he answered.

"That bad, huh?"

"Let's just say Danek put another notch in his bedpost."

"Jesus. What's it going to take to get that guy?"

"A miracle."

"I'll start praying, and after that, I'll order Chinese delivery. Might as well save you the stop. Then you can come straight home and have a shot of whiskey."

Despite the horrible day, Levi smiled. "You know I love you, right?"

"Of course you do. Who wouldn't?"

"I'm leaving now."

He hung up and grabbed his keys. Might as well go home and enjoy his evening with his beautiful woman. Danek had been a thorn in his side for years. Staying at work another hour wasn't going to solve the problem. But as he headed out, his thoughts went back to Katarina once again.

What if he could find her? What if she knew more than he suspected?

# CHAPTER EIGHTEEN

THE DOORBELL RANG JUST AS BEA PULLED A TRAY OF MINI pizzas from her oven. It was poker night and she was really looking forward to a night of gossip and commiserating with the girls.

"It's open!" she yelled.

A second later, Nelly came in with Birdie, Scarlett, and Izzy right behind her. They all carried trays of goodies that they piled on the counter and then everyone went to work, pulling off foil, opening up containers, and fetching dishes. Everyone knew where everything was at everyone else's house, and no one expected to be served. They'd learned early on that the sooner they got the food set up, the quicker they could get to drinking and cards.

Because they'd all complained about having a rough week, Bea had suggested they go with simple appetizers, and everyone had been happy with that. So now, the counter contained a charcuterie tray, chips, salsa, queso, finger sandwiches, a fruit tray, the mini pizzas, and an assortment of cookies. Everyone piled up a plate, poured their drink of choice and headed for the dining table.

"To the Jokers," Bea said, and lifted her glass to make a required toast to get the night rolling. "May we get a good night's sleep."

"May our blood pressure go down," Izzy said.

"May our waists go down with the blood pressure," Scarlett said.

"May our elastic not wear out," Birdie said.

"I wouldn't mind if mine wore out just a little right now," Scarlett said. "I got a lot of food here."

They all laughed and dug into their snacks.

"I know we've all said this was a rough week," Bea said. "I vote we get the bad stuff out of the way while we eat, so we can stick to gossip and bad-mouthing people while we play cards."

"Seconded," Scarlett said.

"I'm going to start," Bea said. "I'm sure you've all heard about the city council meeting last night, so I won't rehash it. The contractor is pushing to have Alayna's restaurant open before the vote next month, which should garner more votes our direction."

"And we'll all be there supporting you," Birdie said. "Along with all the other businesspeople on the island."

"The ones who aren't beholden to the Whitmores, you mean," Nelly said.

"And therein lies the problem," Bea said. "Which is the same problems we've had since the Whitmores got a little power. So Gary approached me with an idea the other day, and I thought he was crazy, but since a little crazy has never been much of a deterrent for me, I've decided to put his idea into action—I'm going to run for mayor."

The table went completely silent as they all stared at Bea, then they all started cheering at once.

"It's about time someone took the Whitmores down,"

Scarlett said. "And you know we're here for anything you need. I've got money, time, a whole lot of boredom, and even more pent-up anger at the Whitmores."

Given that one of Scarlett's ex-husbands had cheated with Melody—a girl less than half his age—Bea had no doubt that Scarlett had a good bit of issues to work out where the Whitmores were concerned.

"Good," Bea said. "Because the first thing we want to start with is digging up dirt, and I don't figure there's anyone more qualified for that than you."

Nelly nodded. "And no one who enjoys it more."

"Most people would be offended by those statements," Scarlett said and smiled. "But I take them as a compliment. I'll get started on dirt collecting first thing tomorrow. By the next poker night, you'll be calling me Hoover."

They all laughed.

"I appreciate it," Bea said. "But until I have to officially announce my intent, I want to keep this a secret. I don't want the Whitmores having any more time to plan a counterattack than necessary."

They all nodded.

"Can I go next?" Birdie asked.

Bea gave her friend an encouraging smile. "Of course."

"I don't know where to start really," Birdie said. "You remember I've been complaining about Tom's many jaunts to the boat store?"

They all nodded.

"Well, in addition to all those trips—where he never bought anything—he was also acting strange," Birdie said. "It seemed like his mind was somewhere else and even though he was never the most romantic man, that aspect of our lives just disappeared altogether."

The other women frowned, probably all making the same leap Birdie had.

"So I confided in Bea that I thought he was having an affair," Birdie said. "And Bea—being the good friend she is, with that direct way she has—confronted him and got the truth out. And he finally told me."

They all looked expectantly at her, except Bea, who already knew.

"He has prostate cancer," Birdie said.

"Oh no!"

"Oh, Birdie!"

"Poor Tom!"

After they'd had a few seconds to process that, Izzy asked, "So what is the prognosis? Does he have a treatment plan yet? Have you talked to his doctor?"

Birdie nodded. "I went with him to talk to the doctor today. Tom already knew everything, of course, but I wanted to hear it myself and ask questions."

"Of course," Nelly said.

"He'll have surgery and some treatment after that," Birdie said. "But the doctor is confident he can remove the cancer and Tom will be around to wander the boat store for many years to come."

"That's a relief," Scarlett said.

"Best possible outcome," Izzy said. "And when he's released for physical therapy, I'll handle it personally. He doesn't even have to come to my clinic. We can do everything right in your living room."

Birdie's eyes teared up. "Oh, Izzy, that would be great. He's so self-conscious about all of this. I know that's normal, but he doesn't want other people to see him sick." A flush ran up Birdie's face. "And he's worried about...things."

Their eyes all widened, immediately understanding the reference.

"Did the doctor say anything about that?" Scarlett asked.

"Only that he hopes that everything goes back to normal but if it doesn't there are options," Birdie said.

Scarlett nodded. "I dated a guy once who had one of those pumps—you know, where you squeeze one of the boys and everything went into immediate salute?"

Nelly's eyes widened. "Good Lord! Are you serious?"

"As a heart attack," Scarlett said. "Modern science preventing failure to launch."

"It's a shame we can't pump our boobs back up," Nelly said.

"There's also a procedure for that," Scarlett said. "I know a thing or two."

"You've *had* a thing or two," Nelly said and they all laughed. "So this pump thing works no matter what?"

"Oh yes," Scarlett said. "That's what made it so great. With the pills, you have to take and wait, so spontaneity isn't possible. The pump makes it all more normal. Well, except for the one time he had a failure. Not a failure to launch, mind you, so we were all good there. But the sail didn't come down afterward."

They all stared.

"You mean he had to walk around like a porn star?" Bea asked. "For how long?"

"Well, the malfunction happened on a Friday night, so until Monday when his doctor could see him and get it drained back into the reservoir," Scarlett said and grinned. "But don't worry, we ordered food delivery and made good use of it."

They all laughed.

Bea shook her head. The things you learned on poker night. Not that she'd had the good fortune of 'sailing' in a while. But to be fair, she wasn't looking for permanent and that made things harder. Most men her age were widowed and looking for a replacement to slot into all those domestic duties their wives had done for the past decades. That whole domestic life thing was probably the biggest reason Bea had never married. It just wasn't her cup of tea. Or can of beer, which would be more appropriate.

"When is the surgery?" Nelly asked.

"In two weeks," Birdie said. "It's bad timing with the season just starting, but this isn't the kind of thing you wait on."

"Don't you worry about the ice cream shop," Nelly said. "Bea and I can manage to split some time over there."

Bea nodded. "And I'm sure Alayna will want to as well."

"And I can help on weekends," Izzy said.

"I'll be happy to fill in," Scarlett said.

They all stared. The only 'job' Scarlett had ever held was marrying rich men.

"What?" Scarlett asked. "I'm friendly and can talk to anyone about anything. And I love ice cream, so they'll take a hit on profits for sure. But this way, I can scope out all the good-looking single men on vacation. It will be a one-stop shop for dessert—both kinds."

They all laughed again, but they also knew Scarlett wasn't joking. She was definitely good with people and could hold a conversation with a stump if needed. And Bea knew she wasn't kidding about shopping for men, either. Man shopping was Scarlett's favorite kind.

Birdie gave them all a grateful look. "I really appreciate everything. We were just going to close the shop and take the loss, but if you guys really think you can fill in, then that would be incredible. If everything goes well, I can probably get away a few hours a week to handle the banking and keep the payables and payroll up."

"You know, Mark just hired that new accountant," Nelly said. "I've heard she's got his whole business back in order in just a week, including setting up new accounting software. I bet he could spare her a few hours to help out."

Bea nodded. "She's really sharp. Probably wouldn't take her any time to get up to speed on the few things you need."

"Oh, I don't want to take Mark's help away," Birdie said. "He's just getting his footing again."

"You were a big help to Mark back when he needed it," Bea said. "Trust me, he'll be happy if he can help, even if it's through his employee."

"Well, if you think so, then I'll drop by and chat with him," Birdie said. Her expression shifted from tense to more relaxed. "I don't know what I'd do without you all."

"You'd have to watch sports on television with Tom instead of eating fat snacks and having drinks with a bunch of gorgeous women," Scarlett said. "Now that the serious stuff is out of the way, give me the gossip on this new accountant."

"Not much to tell," Bea said. "Her parents died when she was in college and she's got no other family, so she's a modern-age nomad. Travels to a city and works for a while, then moves on. Doesn't seem interested in setting down roots anywhere."

"So she's just here for the summer?" Izzy asked.

"That's what she says," Bea said.

"A lot of people come here thinking that, then look for a way to stay," Nelly said.

"That's true enough," Bea agreed. "Alayna has made friends with her and had her over for a taste-testing the other night. She really seems to like it here. She's enjoying her work, and who wouldn't enjoy the island, especially this time of year."

Nelly gave Bea a sly look. "And I think her boss is enjoying her as well."

"Spill!" Scarlett said. "You think there's a romance

brewing?"

"I think there's an attraction," Nelly said. "They're both good-looking people and he rented her that apartment over the store."

"Really?" Birdie said. "That's huge. Tom had asked him before about getting back to summer rental for the place. You know Tom—always thinking about the profit. He couldn't understand why Mark was just letting dollars slip through his fingers. I tried to tell him that he had Lily to consider now that they lived there as well, which Tom sort of allowed for, but he still thought Mark shouldn't be letting the profit go."

"It makes sense that he'd be so protective of Lily," Izzy said. "But renting to an employee is a much better option than strangers changing over every week. Even though I'm sure he could have gotten premium rates from vacationers, this way, he still gets some income but doesn't have to deal with tourist demands and the potential for disrupting his own home space."

Bea nodded. "And Emma doesn't have to rent on the mainland and commute every day. It works out well for both of them."

"So back to the good parts," Scarlett said. "Do you think all that proximity is going to heat things up between them?"

"I hope so," Nelly said. "In fact, I might have been the one who suggested he rent her that apartment."

Bea snorted. "Suggested? I know how your *suggestions* come across. He's probably still trying to reinflate after you steamrolled him."

Nelly waved a hand in dismissal. "I get things done. Methods are unimportant."

"He hasn't been widowed that long," Izzy said quietly. "Even if he's attracted to the young lady, he might not be ready for that kind of attachment."

Nelly gave her a sympathetic nod. "You would understand that better than any of us. But how does someone know when they're ready if they're not out living life and gaining exposure to those opportunities?"

"At first, you just go through the motions," Izzy said. "Then when all the legal and financial wrangling is settled, you do the have-tos. Mine was my business. Mark's is his business and Lily. I don't know that you make a conscious decision to start living again. I think it just creeps in until finally one day, you find yourself thinking about the future without that person you intended to spend the rest of your life with. Then you meet someone and there's that spark—the one you haven't felt in so long that you almost don't recognize it. Then you're flooded with guilt over those feelings and spend so much time arguing with yourself, until one day, you simply stop. And then you take that first hesitant step."

They'd all stopped eating while Izzy spoke, focused on the woman who never had the most to say, but always had something important to say.

"You met someone," Scarlett said, almost breathless.

Izzy nodded, giving them a shy smile.

Scarlett jumped up from her chair and yelled, causing everyone to laugh.

"Well, good Lord, woman, *tell* us!" Scarlett said.

They all nodded and Izzy blushed.

"I met him at my clinic," she said. "He had ACL surgery."

"You're dating a patient?" Nelly asked. "Oh my God. It's just like one of those Hallmark movies."

"Please make it a Netflix one," Scarlett said. "They're *far* juicier."

"There's nothing out of the PG realm for now," Izzy said. "We only met a couple weeks ago, and all we've done is go for coffee after therapy. He was my last patient of the day."

"So tell us the stuff," Bea said. "Scarlett can have another drink and watch Netflix when she gets home."

"Well, he's a year older than me," Izzy said. "He's an aerospace engineer—retired military pilot—and does mostly consulting for the Defense Department."

Scarlett leaned forward, her boobs propped on the table. "What did he fly?"

"F-16s."

Scarlett started fanning herself with one hand. "If you tell me he looks like Tom Cruise, I'm going to have to borrow Bea's shower. I won't be using the hot water."

Izzy laughed. "No. He's got more of a Harrison Ford thing going on."

"Bea, do you have clean towels?" Scarlett asked.

They all laughed again, and Bea reached over to squeeze Izzy's arm. "I'm so happy for you."

"It was just coffee," Izzy said, looking a little flustered.

"It was way more than that," Bea said, and Izzy teared up a little.

Bea's heart swelled for her friend. Izzy's husband had been an incredible man, and their marriage was one of the most solid Bea had ever seen. His loss had been an enormous one to his parents, friends, colleagues, patients, and the medical community. But the biggest loss had been Izzy's. That she had taken coffee with another man—that she had even acknowledged those feelings were possible again—was huge. And Bea couldn't be happier for her.

And at the same time, she wondered why what seemed to come so easily for all her friends had never felt right for her. She had a full life—Alayna, the bookstore, her investments, the best friends a person could ask for—but was she missing out?

It was a loaded question with no immediate answer.

## Storm Surge

*"Individually, we are one drop. Together, we are an ocean."* –
*Ryunosuke Satoro*

# CHAPTER NINETEEN

EMMA GRABBED HER GLASS OF LEMONADE AND HEADED OUT onto the deck with her book, still pinching herself that this was her life. A great job, awesome people, and the most beautiful scenery one could wish for, and literally outside her door. She sank into a lounge chair and gazed out at the sparkling water. Right after work, she'd hurried upstairs, kicked off her sandals, tugged on her swimsuit, and headed straight out into the surf.

She loved running, but the afternoon heat and humidity made swimming a preferable way to burn calories. As long as she was on the island, she decided she'd run in the mornings a couple times a week and swim the other days, weather permitting, of course. She'd always taken care to stay in shape, but swimming used muscles in a different way. And it was fun. Not that she found running odious like a lot of people did. It was actually very calming for her, but there was something about being in the ocean that was therapeutic. It was invigorating and relaxing all at the same time.

After a hot shower, she felt like a limp noodle sitting in the warm sun and cool breeze. How could this be her life? She still couldn't believe it. No, it wasn't forever, but she'd settle for now. And she had an entire day off tomorrow to enjoy the view. She was going to tackle the store inventory and get it all in line on Sunday, which would normally be one of her days off. But it was easier to do the inventory with the store closed, and Mark had told her that if she worked any days on the weekend to swap them out with a weekday, which was perfect.

So the only thing she had to worry about at the moment was what she was going to eat tonight. One of the many advantages of the apartment was the short stroll to food, but it was Friday night and the crowds had already started downtown before Mark closed up shop. She could still call for takeout and probably wouldn't have much of a wait, but she was feeling lazy and didn't even want to slip on sandals or walk down the stairs.

She'd bought the basics the other day at the island market, so she had stuff for sandwiches, salads, and some fruit. Or maybe she'd have breakfast for dinner. She'd always been a big fan of that, and she could make French toast. But a sandwich or salad was easier, required no cooking, and she could be back outside relaxing with her book within minutes.

Mind made up, she placed her book on the table and stood up, stretching her arms above her head and enjoying the setting sun on her face. On the other side of the deck, the doors to Mark's unit slid open and Lily rushed outside, spied her, and waved.

"Dad, it's Miss Emma!" she called back into the apartment.

Mark stepped out with a tray of hamburger patties and hot dog wieners and smiled. "Enjoying the beautiful evening, too?"

"How could I not?" she asked.

Especially now.

The view had been great before but with Mark standing there in his navy board shorts and light blue tank, it had shifted from great to magnificent. His deep tan set off perfectly toned legs and arms, and his blue eyes matched the hue of his shirt. His blond hair fell in waves, creating the perfect beach look. The man could be on a magazine page doing surfboard advertisements. He was the poster boy for the sexy surfer look.

"Dad, can Miss Emma eat with us?" Lily asked. "We have enough for ten people."

He laughed. "We have enough for ten of you, but yes, if Emma would like to join us, we do have plenty."

"Oh no, I couldn't interrupt your evening," Emma said, forcing herself to stop staring.

"You're not interrupting," he said. "That's Lily's job and she's a pro."

Emma's mind rushed with thoughts. She wouldn't mind the company. Lately, she'd been feeling oddly lonely at night, which wasn't her usual state. But was it a good idea to spend so much time in Mark's company? Especially when her mind and body went places that they had no business going?

But Lily was there to remind her of things that couldn't be. And besides, Mark's grill was just on the other side of the shared deck, so if she wanted to stay outside, she was going to be in their company anyway. Might as well eat, especially when a burger sounded much better than what she'd planned.

"If it's no problem, then I'd love to," she said. "I was just debating between a sandwich or a salad."

"Yuck." Lily made a face and Emma laughed.

"I didn't feel quite so strongly against them," Emma said. "But I will admit a burger sounds much better."

Lily nodded. "Dad makes the best burgers and I get half a burger and half a hot dog because I couldn't decide. I swam *forever* today. I'm *so* hungry! I might faint away if I don't eat soon. That's what Aunt Nelly always says."

"I bet she does." Emma couldn't help grinning, remembering the thieving cat at the bookstore and Nelly's hot dog. "What can I do to help?" she asked Mark.

"Not a thing," he said as he slid the patties and dogs onto the grill. "I prepped it all and laid it out on the counter before I came out to grill. I opted out of fries and went for potato chips to save time and hassle, so when I'm done here, we just have to fix our plates and sit down to eat. Lily and I usually eat out here if it's nice."

"That's perfect. I was planning on doing the same. My guess is I'll be out here every evening eating unless it's raining."

He nodded. "I sometimes miss all the space we had in our house on the mainland, but you can't beat the view here."

"Miss Emma, look at the new swimsuit I want." Lily pressed an iPad into her hands and she smiled at the turquoise-and-pink one-piece.

"That's really pretty and the colors are perfect for you," she said.

Lily nodded. "That's what I told Daddy, but he says I have enough swimsuits already. I don't think that can be true, right? Not when you live on the beach."

Emma looked over at Mark, who gave his daughter an amused glance. "I suppose people who live right on the beach should have more swimsuits than everyone else. Maybe you can talk him into just one more for the summer."

Lily sighed. "Only one? Because there's this one that looks like the inside of a seashell..."

"Well, why didn't you say so," Emma said, giving Mark a wicked look. "That makes all the difference."

"I know," Lily said. "Daddy always says to ask Santa for stuff but that's only once a year. I don't know why he only comes once a year. I'd come every day for the cookies."

Emma laughed. "Me too."

"I told you to pick out another suit today from the store," Mark said.

Lily made a face. "There's no turquoise. I tried to tell you I should do the picking for kids, especially girls."

"I'll consult with you on my next order," Mark said.

Lily, apparently satisfied with his response, took the iPad back and climbed into a patio chair, content with her online shopping. Emma made a note that another swimsuit probably wasn't a bad idea for herself. Her sole traveling one was looking a bit tired and if she planned on being in the water several times a week all summer, then she could definitely use another. Maybe even a splurge on two since she was saving on expenses with no commute, and she got a generous employee discount to boot. And Lily was right, after all—people who lived on the beach should have more swimsuits.

*And you never know who is going to see you, living right here.*

But that didn't have to be a consideration unless she wanted it to be. She knew Jane took Lily swimming every afternoon when the weather allowed and that Mark joined them after he closed down the shop. Before she'd moved into the apartment, she'd been swimming in the area in front of the motel, which meant she hadn't run into them unless she walked by the shop. But today, she'd donned her suit and walked some ways away from the apartment before entering the water. She told herself it was so she could get in a good round of much-needed exercise without any distractions, but she knew the truth.

She was avoiding personal time in Mark's company.

She already spent the workday with him, although she saw him far less today with the store busy. But living one wall away and with a shared deck, she was bound to see him a lot more in the evening too, and she'd needed some time away from him this afternoon. Time to clear her mind from her bad dreams and all the desires that would never come to fruition.

Lily lifted the iPad to show her a pretty blue top with white lace around the bottom, and she glanced down at her worn shorts and tank and frowned. It wouldn't hurt to do a little sprucing up on the rest of her wardrobe. Casual clothes were cheap and traveled well and since they fit her work dress code, it wouldn't be a personal-only sort of splurge.

*And you'd look cuter.*

But that didn't matter. She held in a sigh. If she just kept telling herself that, she might start to believe it.

"All ready," Mark said and held the platter up.

Emma felt a flash of guilt as she forced all thoughts of tempting her boss with new T-shirts and swimsuits out of her mind. She smiled as she rose and followed them inside. It was just a meal between employer and employee. Or tenant and landlord. It didn't mean anything.

But Emma couldn't help hoping that it did.

———

MARK TUCKED LILY in her bed and pulled the covers over his sleeping daughter. She'd had a long day and eaten well, then crashed in the patio chair shortly after eating. When he headed back into the kitchen, he found Emma washing dishes.

"You don't have to do that," he said. "I was just going to let it sit in the sink and deal with it tomorrow, *after* I empty the clean dishes from the dishwasher."

"I don't mind," she said. "And you have to work tomorrow. This way, you don't come home to dishes. Unless Jane takes care of that stuff, too."

"No. I've asked her to not do anything but take care of Lily.

I don't want her to feel taken advantage of. And I want her focus to be my daughter and not my imperfect housekeeping."

"That's nice, and rare. I remember doing a lot of domestic duties when I babysat as a teen, and I wasn't even a regular for people. I swear they saved up dishes and dust just so they could mention 'if you happen to have time' before they headed out the door. It wasn't implied that I had to do it, but my tips sure were better when I did."

He grabbed a dishcloth and started drying the dishes after she washed. "Yeah, I'm not going to be that guy. Jane has her hands full with Lily, and I don't want her sitting in front of the television all day or holding electronics. I know it's the digital age and they have their place for everyone, but as long as Lily can be outside and active, I want her to be."

Emma nodded. "It's a healthier lifestyle. That's why I took up running in junior high. I hated days when it was raining and I had to use the treadmill. Running outdoors is so much more interesting. I still prefer it."

"What's your standard?"

"Five miles or so, four to five times a week. I did long-distance running in high school. Used to do a lot more daily back then, but this is just to keep in shape, not compete. I'm dropping a couple days while I'm here and swimming instead. Different muscles and I like the changeup. And swimming is preferable in the evening when it's so hot and humid. I'll stick to running in the morning."

He nodded. "I still try to get in two to three miles a couple times a week. Maybe one morning, I can join you for part of your workout."

"Sure," she said and handed him the last of the dishes. "Well, I guess I'll head back to my side of the building. Thanks so much for inviting me to dinner."

A surge of disappointment coursed through Mark, and he

realized that he didn't want the evening to end. "I was going to have a beer and sit out for a while," he said. "I have some wine too, if you'd like to join me. That glider at the end of the deck is the perfect place to watch for shooting stars. I sit out there most nights unless it's raining."

"Oh." She looked a little surprised by the invitation. "What about Lily?"

"She's dead to the world, but even if she wakes up, she knows where to find me. And the interior door has a high dead bolt. The only way she gets out of this place is through the deck."

She gave him a shy smile. "Okay then. I'd like that."

"Beer or wine?"

"Wine, please. And I'm going to nab another of those chocolate chip cookies that Lily made."

He laughed. "I'm guessing Jane had more to do with that than Lily, but she's taken an interest in baking lately and Jane is great to indulge her."

"Well, I'm happy to benefit from Lily's newest pursuit and Jane's commitment to being the best nanny ever."

"You say that until you know what Lily's next command-ment is—she wants a pony."

"Oh, yeah, that one would have to be a no if Lily was my daughter."

"You don't like horses?"

"I love horses and for years, I wanted to be a jockey, but I'm horribly allergic. Just being near them makes my eyes water and swell shut, then I break out in this horrible rash all over my neck and face. We discovered this stellar response when my parents finally gave me riding lessons for my eighth birthday."

"Oh wow. That sucks. Well, you won't have to worry about

Lily's latest plan to harass me. Not like we have a place to put a horse in the store or our apartment."

Emma laughed. "No. I think a goldfish might be a better option. Maybe you could get a seahorse."

"That's actually a great thought."

He poured her a glass of wine and grabbed a couple cookies for himself before they headed back outside. They both sat on the glider, eating cookies and enjoying the sound of the surf. Mark was painfully aware of how her leg sometimes brushed against his as they moved the glider back and forth. He could feel the heat radiating from her body and had the overwhelming urge to touch the bare skin on her perfectly toned arm.

The moonlight sparkled on the ocean and the sound of the surf echoed across the empty sand. For a while, they were both quiet, and Mark closed his eyes, feeling the salt air on his face and saying a prayer of thanks for just how great his life was. Yes, he'd had a huge loss, but he still had Lily and his business and lived in a place he loved.

*And now there's Emma.*

He shot his employee and tenant a side glance. The kind of thoughts he'd been having about Emma didn't belong in his mind. Mainly because of the other two words that had filtered past him—employee and tenant. Mixing those things with a relationship were never a good idea but right now, it was a horrible one. Emma wasn't permanent. And he wasn't ready. It had only been a year.

*The heart is on its own timetable.*

Nelly's words echoed in his mind. She'd said them a couple months after Beth had passed, when he was lamenting having a hard time focusing and finding joy in anything except his daughter. She'd meant them in relation to grieving then, but she'd also said, 'And when the time comes, you will love again.'

He'd barely even registered the words at the time because the absolute last thing on his mind was getting involved with another woman. In fact, if you'd asked him that day, he'd have said he would never even be attracted to another woman that way again. Not after Beth. Not after losing her.

And yet...

Here he was, his entire being coming alive over a woman he didn't really know. It wasn't just a physical thing, although Emma was certainly beautiful. But he'd seen plenty of beautiful women in the last year and none of them had left a mark, even the ones who were clearly flirting. There was something about Emma...her genuine smile and the way she interacted with his daughter, her desire to fix things and make them work better, her obvious joy with the island and—although he'd never understand it—her fascination and talent with numbers. They all made her so much more than the gorgeous mostly-stranger who sat at his side.

"I can't tell you how happy I am that I put out that *Help Wanted* sign the day you were walking by," Mark said, finally breaking the silence. "Last week, I was stressed every minute thinking about the season starting and all of the things I couldn't and didn't want to do, but that all had to be done. My stress level is down so much, I almost feel lazy."

Emma smiled, clearly pleased with his comments. "I'm glad I was taking a bit of time off at the right moment. I love fixing an accounting mess."

He laughed. "Well, I definitely accommodated you on that one."

She shrugged. "Yours actually wasn't that bad. It was mostly just organization and the software setup, which are things I really enjoy. But knowing your situation and that I was making things better for you in more ways than just with your CPA makes this job more fulfilling than most. I'm not usually anywhere long enough to get to know people and help them out of a bind. You gave me an opportunity to do both. I've missed it. I've missed a lot of things, I guess, with the way I live."

She stared out at the water, the smile slipping from her expression as she talked.

"It's hard traveling around a lot," he said quietly. "I had my crewmates in the Navy, and Beth joined me my second year and after on the pro circuit, so it wasn't anything like what you do. But just the idea of waking up most mornings and not being in *my* place was somewhat unsettling to me. I never got used to it. It felt like I was always moving toward something but never arrived. Does that make sense?"

She looked at him, her eyes widening a bit and nodded. "That's exactly it."

"I know you've said your family is gone, but that's just biology. You can make your own family wherever you want to. The people I've met here—especially the older ladies like Bea, Nelly, and Birdie—became my family and really stepped in when I needed support but would never have asked. Have you ever thought about staying somewhere?"

"Honestly, no. I mean, not until now."

The tension that he'd been holding in his shoulders slipped away as she said the words he'd been desperately hoping would come. He shifted on the glider, turning toward her, and before he could change his mind, he leaned in and brushed his lips against hers. When he finished the kiss, he pulled back just enough to see her expression, praying that he hadn't made the situation uncomfortable for both of them.

But she was staring at him, her face flushed and eyes reflecting the same desire he felt.

He moved in again, this time lifting his hand up to cup her face and deepening the kiss. She matched his intensity and shifted her body against his as their mouths locked into a sensual dance. Emotions he didn't know he still possessed coursed through him. Passion and desire, all blended into a frenetic overload.

"Daddy?" Lily's voice sent them flying apart and a couple seconds later, his daughter walked out onto the deck, rubbing her eyes.

Mark jumped up. "What's wrong, honey?"

"I'm thirsty. You forgot my water *again*."

"I'm so sorry. You go get back in bed and I'll bring it to you."

She gave him a sleepy nod and headed back inside. Emma, who'd been sitting, almost frozen, throughout the entire exchange, jumped up and rushed past him.

"Thanks again for the dinner," she called out as she went. "You go take care of Lily."

Before he could formulate a reply, she closed her sliding door and the light in her living room clicked off. Mark stared up at the night sky and ran one hand through his hair.

What the hell had he done?

# CHAPTER TWENTY

EMMA DREW THE SHADE ON THE PATIO DOORS, TURNED OFF the living room lights, and hurried down the hallway to the bedroom. After she pulled the bedroom door closed and locked it, she headed into the bathroom and flipped on the lights. Her reflection in the mirror startled her.

Her face was flushed and her lips were a tiny bit swollen from the kissing. She could still feel his hand on her cheek and yearned for it to be there again. Good Lord, what would have happened if Lily hadn't interrupted? She was pretty sure she knew and wasn't ready to process that quite yet. Things couldn't have gone all the way over the line but tucked away on the deck in the dim light, they could have gone far enough.

She splashed some cold water on her face and then flopped onto her bed, still trying to process the last few minutes. Of course, she'd been cognizant of her attraction to Mark—had admitted it to herself and was mentally fighting it. But she'd been completely unaware that the attraction was reciprocated. He'd just told Melody earlier that day that he'd probably never be ready to date and then that night, he'd kissed Emma as if he were the hero in a romance novel.

Thank God they'd been sitting, because her legs might have buckled.

So was Mark lying to Melody? Or had he just gotten caught up in the moment and tried something on that he would regret tomorrow? For all she knew, he was regretting it right now, especially since she ran off like a scared teenager. She blew out a breath. How in the world was she supposed to act normal around him now? Even if he retreated back to boss and landlord status, he knew she was into him. And if the kiss was just a big lapse in judgment and he wasn't really into her, then it was all that more embarrassing.

Frustrated, she headed back into the living room and sat on the couch in the dark with her laptop. Sleep was out of the question until her racing mind settled, so she might as well do some surfing. The possibility of needing to move on might come about sooner than she'd thought. If she needed to order some things, she'd better do it before she left this address.

*He asked you if you'd ever thought about staying.*

*He kissed you.*

She leaned back against the couch and considered their entire interaction again, trying to eliminate Beth from the equation. If a man had asked her those questions before—had made that kind of romantic overture before—what would her assessment be? Ultimately, she would have assumed he was interested. And when men prior to Mark had made those sort of advances, she'd put up barriers and planned her escape.

*But that's because you never felt the same way.*

And that was true as well. She'd had relationships, of sorts. It wasn't as if there hadn't been any men in her life the past eight years, but she'd never had a kiss affect her the way Mark's had.

*Which is all the more reason to pack up and leave.*

She sighed and brought up job listings in New Orleans. She

didn't want to leave, but if things between her and Mark got really strained, she wouldn't have a choice. The most she could do was pretend the kiss didn't happen and see if he was willing to play along. But she knew it would take everything she had to be around him every day and not want a second round. Still, if she wanted to remain on the island for the summer, she had to get back to thinking of Mark only as her employer. If she couldn't manage that, then she'd have no choice but to move on.

She scanned the listings long enough to ensure that employment wouldn't be a problem in New Orleans, then shifted to her email—the one she gave to a choice few people she'd worked with and become somewhat friendly with along the way. She already stood out a bit for having no social media. Having no email either would have looked completely odd. So she had the one she used for business stuff, like job applications, another she used for her personal stuff like investments and banking notifications, and a final one that she gave to everyone else.

The coworkers who bothered to check in after she'd moved on usually only did so a time or two, but she kept the same email active just in case anyone ever had something important to relay. She usually checked it once a week or so, and lately, there hadn't been any email at all except the occasional spam that got through the filter.

This time, there was a lone unread email received earlier that evening and she recognized the email address of Becky Livingston, a girl she'd worked with in Tampa. They'd been casual friends and had gone for drinks a couple times a week after work. She'd liked Becky, a woman she suspected had her own rocky past and because of that, had never minded talking only of the present and never pressed Emma for details about her life. Emma figured Becky had been running from something herself and had taken the angle that if she didn't ask other people questions, they wouldn't ask her questions.

She clicked on the email, figuring that Becky was doing the general check-in to see how things were and maybe bring her up-to-date on any of the workplace gossip. But as she read what Becky had written, she felt the blood drain from her face.

HI EMMA,

*I hope you landed someplace cool and are doing well. I know we never really spoke much about personal things when you were here, and I figure we both had reasons for that. But a guy showed up at the store Wednesday looking for a girl. He had a picture. She was younger and had short black hair, but those eyes were yours. Everyone else just shook their head. I don't think they recognized the photo at all. I did, but I shook my head along with everyone else.*

*I didn't like the feeling I got from the guy. He claimed to be a lawyer looking for an heir, but he was lying. My past has made me adept at knowing a liar when I see one. And I know dangerous. He was both. Like I said, I know we never talked about that sort of thing, but I'm guessing this guy is the reason for your silence. I have one in my past as well and this 'lawyer' set off all those same vibes. I saw him again today in the coffee shop across the street. Maybe he's checking other businesses in the area, or maybe he thinks you're still here and we're covering for you.*

*Anyway, I snapped a pic of him because two can play, right? It's blurry because I had to take it from the stockroom upstairs and in between the blinds. Let me know if there's anything I can do. And please let me know that you're safe, but nothing else. I can't be forced to tell what I don't know. That's the first thing people taught me when I ran.*

*I pray that you're somewhere safe and will remain so.*

. . .

*YOUR FRIEND,*
*Becky*

THE BURGER she'd eaten earlier rolled in Emma's stomach as she read Becky's words. It was her worst nightmare coming true. There was no way a lawyer was looking for her. Her parents' 'estate', such as it was, had been willed to her, and if she wasn't an option, then it all went to distant family in the old country. She knew because she'd discovered the documents in her father's office drawer one day while looking for paper clips. But at the rate her father spent, there couldn't have been much to leave, except maybe debt. Certainly, there weren't assets worth conducting an eight-year search when there were alternate heirs available.

Only one person had a reason to want her found so many years later.

She clicked on the picture Becky had sent and sucked in a breath. It was a bit blurry and some distance away, but there was no mistaking the man sitting at the table with the tall coffee in front of him.

Josef Danek.

Emma's forehead broke out in a cold sweat and she rushed to the bathroom, sick to her stomach. Why? After all these years, why was he looking for her? She was no threat to his father and never had been. It was her own father that she'd seen murder someone. And even though she knew it was Ivan's bidding that her father did, she had no proof.

*You have to get out of here!*

She sank onto the cold tile floor and leaned against the vanity cabinet. But go where? She'd been headed to New Orleans, but if Josef had been following her trail for a while, then he'd suspect that's where she was going. Since Mark hadn't called for references, literally no one knew she was here. Which meant she was actually safer on Tempest Island than she would be in the city.

*No. You'd be safer in Idaho.*

That was the key. Her idea of disappearing in big cities wasn't flawed. She just needed to deviate from the obvious path she'd been on and bounce around like a ping pong ball. Which meant instead of New Orleans, she could head to the middle of the country and start her routine all again, but this time not moving on to the nearest big city.

Even Ivan didn't have access to things like employment records at a federal level—at least, not that she knew of—so a new identity wasn't necessary. But it might not be the worst idea. She knew how to find organizations that helped women now. And knew they all had their sources that could provide a new identity for her. But that would mean navigating all her investments and her banking, her driver's license, insurance, and the credit card to a new identity. It was definitely a hassle and would generate questions that she didn't want to answer, but it was possible.

A single tear ran down her cheek and she swiped at it, mad at the world.

Why was this happening to her? She didn't deserve it. She worked hard. She didn't hurt people. She didn't take advantage. She helped when she could.

*The sins of the father...*

Although it was appropriate, it seemed entirely hypocritical as her father hadn't believed in God. He hadn't believed in anything but Ivan Danek, and look where that had gotten him.

It wasn't fair. She didn't choose her parents and certainly didn't choose what kind of people they were. But she was answering for their choices. She'd been answering her entire life. And now their choices had almost caught up with her.

She tucked her knees up to her chest and wrapped her arms around them. Then she lowered her head and wept the way she had the night she'd run.

It took her another hour after reading the email to get a hold on her emotions. She'd always lived as if Ivan was still looking for her, but she'd never really thought that was the case. But now, it was her worst nightmare coming true. And it wasn't even one of his hired goons tracking her. It was his son. For Ivan to send Josef, that meant he was taking it very seriously even after all this time.

When her pulse finally stopped racing, she chided herself for not immediately responding to Becky. Her friend needed to know that she had to lie low until Josef had moved on. If Josef suspected for just a second that Becky knew something, he would do anything to get it out of her. And then she'd be disposable. Just like Emma's mother and father. Just like Amy.

She pulled an old notebook out of her nightstand and grabbed her cell phone. She located the number she had for Becky and dialed, but it was no longer in service. Crap! Becky had a prepaid phone like Emma did and probably changed numbers periodically for the same reasons. Given Becky's own sensitive situation and since she'd sent an email rather than calling, Emma figured Becky hadn't made a note of her phone number when she'd changed phones.

She hit Reply and typed in a response.

*I need to talk to you as soon as possible. I don't know how often you check this email, but I'm giving you my number again as I just tried yours and it's no longer in service. Please call me as soon as you get this. It doesn't matter what time. And please stay far away from that man.*

She sent the email and waited for all of five seconds before clicking the Refresh button. Of course, there was no answer, and she couldn't really expect one. Becky probably had a special email account just as she did and she might not check it regularly. Emma could only hope that given the situation, Becky would start checking it more often, but for now, this was all she could do. The only other way to get hold of Becky was at work tomorrow, and that was assuming she was working.

Which meant she had a really long night ahead of her because no way she was going to be able to sleep. It was just as well that she didn't work tomorrow, because she'd need the day to pack up everything and figure out how she was going to tell Mark that she was leaving.

The kiss!

She groaned and flopped back on her bed. He was going to think she was leaving because he'd kissed her. And there was absolutely no way to correct that notion without telling him the truth, which she couldn't do. The man had given her a job and a place to live, and she was going to repay him by running out on him at the worst time possible. She hadn't even completed his accounting setup, and the season kicked off the following week.

*Stop!*

She drew in a deep breath and slowly let it out. This frantic decision-making had to cease or she was going to make mistakes. Josef was in Tampa, not on Tempest Island. He had no reason to even consider venturing this way. She had time to formulate a plan—to research the job market and housing situation in other cities, which was a far better idea than tossing everything into her car and fleeing in the middle of the night like a criminal. She just needed to calm down and concentrate on an exit plan. One that included finishing the load on the accounting software on Sunday and having a place to go and the route lined out before she left. And a new car was a must now. She'd do that tomorrow.

Her pulse had settled down a bit, but her mind still raced.

She should have known better than to think she could be happy. Actually have a life that was almost normal. Her parents had eliminated that possibility. Any hopes she'd had that Danek was no longer looking for her were dashed. She'd been smart to be careful all these years or things might have been dire a long time ago.

Now she had to be smart again. She'd rushed away from her home eight years ago with nothing but the clothes on her back and an envelope of cash. But she'd also had help. Now she was on her own. She couldn't hope that help would magically appear the way it did at that fraternity party. But she was older and smarter and had more resources now. And she had an entire country to hide in.

Surely that would be enough.

# CHAPTER TWENTY-ONE

MARK OPENED THE PATIO DOOR AND WALKED ONTO THE deck as the sun was rising. It was way too early, and even the second cup of coffee he was holding probably wasn't going to get him moving the way he needed to be. If yesterday was any indication, the store was going to be busy today, and he could count on one hand the hours of sleep he'd gotten. And even those hours hadn't been good ones. He'd tossed and turned and dreamed when he'd managed to sleep, rendering it mostly useless.

He glanced over at Emma's patio door and saw that the blinds were still drawn shut. Not a flicker of light could be seen between the slats, which made sense. After all, she didn't work today, and it was too early for anyone to be up besides the dolphins and apparently him. He sat his coffee on a side table and sank into the chair next to it.

*What the hell was I thinking?*

It was the question that had plagued him all night long, even in his dreams. He hadn't come up with a good answer while he was sleeping or awake. There was the obvious one, of course. He was attracted to Emma and he'd done what any man who was attracted to a woman would do—he'd made his move and hoped it was reciprocated.

And it had been.

Then Lily had interrupted them and apparently, Emma had time to think about what she was doing rather than just respond. And her thinking had her shooting off the deck and into her apartment as though she'd been fired from a rocket launcher. Had he completely misread her expression? Her body language?

He didn't think so. She'd matched his kiss with equal passion and had even leaned into him. That wasn't the response of someone who didn't want to be there. But why flee as if she'd done something wrong? Or maybe she thought *he* had done something wrong.

He frowned. Maybe he *had* been out of bounds on this one. He was her boss and her landlord. Did she feel that she owed him? Surely that wasn't the response of a person who felt obligated but had no desire.

He ran one hand through his hair and sighed. Good Lord, things were complicated. So much more complicated than when he'd met Beth.

*You told Melody that you'd never be ready to date again.*

The conversation popped into his mind and he sucked in a breath. Emma had been standing right there when he'd said those words. He hadn't meant them. Not really. He'd just said what he thought it would take to get rid of Melody. But if Emma thought he had meant them, and then he'd kissed her that same night, what did she think his motives were?

He groaned and closed his eyes, wondering how his life could have become so messy and complicated in a matter of seconds. Regardless of intentions—his or hers—he had to apologize. He shouldn't have put her in this position and wouldn't blame her if she packed up and left. He hoped she wouldn't, as she was doing a fantastic job and seemed to really enjoy living on the island.

Until her boss hit on her.

He was an idiot. He had no idea when he'd lost his mind, but he needed to find a way to get it back. Immediately.

———

EMMA PEERED up around the corner of the building, trying to see between the slats of the upstairs porch to see if anyone was up there. It wasn't the easiest thing to accomplish with all the furniture casting shadows across the deck. If someone was sitting in one of the chairs and not moving, it would be practically impossible to know.

*Someone.*

The word filtered through her mind as if she were avoiding random people when the truth was the only person she was avoiding was Mark. She'd slipped out before the sun came up, figuring that a good long run might help keep her mind off the unanswered email, but she'd ended up walking more than running, the exhaustion from a sleepless night starting to catch up with her. She could have forced it, but forcing exercise when the body wasn't ready for it was the quickest route to injury. The last thing she needed was to twist an ankle and not be able to walk or drive for a week or better.

So she'd walked to the east end of the island, not wanting to go west and risk seeing Alayna. She didn't know if the chef was an early riser, but she had a good idea that her military man was. The last thing she could handle right now was coffee and a chat, and if Alayna had spotted her, Emma imagined she would have invited her in for both. When she'd reached the end of the road, she'd taken off her shoes and walked back toward downtown at the edge of the water where the incoming tide rolled right over her feet.

Before she reached the surf shop, she'd headed back to the street, slipped down the sidewalk in between the buildings, and that had led to her current position—crouching behind a building like a Peeping Tom. She sighed and stepped around the corner. This was pointless. She couldn't avoid Mark forever and even if he was up having coffee in his favorite chair, it wasn't as though she had to speak to him. She knew everything there was to know about how to be polite when she didn't want to be. A pleasant 'good morning' was all that was required before heading into her apartment. And she was wearing sunglasses, which also helped. It was possible she could even get away with a forced smile and a quick nod, she thought as she paused again at the bottom of the stairs.

*Just go!*

Taking in a deep breath, she bolted up the stairs, letting out a whoosh when she reached the empty porch. She hesitated only for a moment, but it was long enough to recognize the flash of disappointment before she hurried into her apartment and straight for the refrigerator. She polished off half a bottled water before taking a break to chide herself.

*You're acting like an idiot. Lurking around corners. Sprinting up stairs and then feeling sorry for yourself when the person you're trying to avoid is nowhere in sight.*

It was official. She was finally having that nervous breakdown she'd thought was coming for years, but the timing made absolutely no sense. She'd been living under an assumed identity for eight years, her family had been murdered, and one of the potential killers was tracking her. She'd witnessed a murder, for Christ's sake. And yet the thing that had her the most terrified was a kiss from an available man she was horribly attracted to.

She checked her watch and pulled her phone out of her pocket. It was only 7:30 a.m. but the store in Tampa had a class at 8:00 a.m. on Saturdays. If Becky was set to work today, she would be in early to do the setup for the instructor. Hopefully she'd answer the phone.

Emma dialed the number and let it ring until it went to voice mail. Frustrated, she hit the number again. This time, a breathless Becky answered on the fourth ring.

"Becky, it's me," Emma said.

"You got my email," Becky said. "Are you all right?"

"Yes. And thank you so much for sending it."

"That guy isn't an attorney, is he?"

"Not even close. And you're right about him being dangerous. The absolute worst kind."

Becky sucked in a breath. "You mean..."

"His father... Let's just say he's collected a lot of bodies and I don't think the apple fell far from the tree."

"Oh my God, Emma! I think he was in my apartment yesterday."

Emma clenched her phone so tightly her hand ached. "No! Are you sure?"

"I'm sure someone was in there. This place is old and doesn't have alarms, but I do things...set things a certain way, put clear tape on doors. I know it sounds crazy—"

"Not to me."

"I know it wasn't anyone from maintenance because they always leave a card and there wasn't any reason for them to be in there anyway."

"Was anything missing?"

"Nothing. In fact, he was really careful to put things back right. A normal person probably wouldn't have noticed."

Emma's chest clenched. The last thing she wanted was to

bring something like this down on someone who already had a similar struggle.

"I'm so sorry this happened," Emma said. "It's all my fault."

"Don't say that! It took me a lot of years to stop blaming myself for what bad people do. You're not responsible for this. The guy doing it is. I'm just glad he had such an old picture and that you look so different now. But someone else is going to recognize you, eventually. And they might talk."

"I know. I'm sure more than one person already has or he wouldn't be so close."

"He never gave your name so that makes me think he doesn't know it, which is something. I assume Emma isn't your given name."

"No."

"How long have you been running?"

"Eight years."

"Oh my God! I mean, I always figured you were lying low because of a guy but, eight years? That's crazy. I've been thinking it was time to move on and this just decided it for me. If he's been after you for eight years, then anyone he thinks might know something would be nothing more than collateral damage. And he must not have believed my denial, or he wouldn't have been in my apartment. I'll finish up my shift today and clear out."

"I hate that you're in this position."

"Like I said, I was getting ready to make a change anyway, and I don't do that whole notice thing. We don't exactly work the kind of jobs where it matters. Besides, the boss's sister just blew into town and needs a job. Me leaving makes it easier on everyone."

"Do you need money? I can send you some."

"I'm good. I haven't been at this eight years, but I've done it long enough to know to save most and spend little."

"I wish we didn't have to live this way."

"Me too. Maybe one day... Anyway, I'll put your number in my phone and text you. It will say something about a food delivery, but that will be me. Then you'll have my new number. I don't usually store things like that...because, you know. But this is different. Take care, Emma."

"You too."

Becky disconnected, and Emma's phone signaled a text coming through. She checked the message.

*Jon has picked up your order and will deliver it by 8:00 a.m.*

Brilliant. She left the text in place, not wanting to load Becky's number into her address book. If anyone ever looked at her phone, they wouldn't think anything of it. She turned off the phone and dropped it on the bed, the tears already forming again.

Why did she and Becky have to live this way? Becky probably wasn't her friend's real name any more than Emma was hers. Constantly moving. Changing phone numbers. The whole fake text thing. It wasn't right. People—especially people who'd never done anything wrong—shouldn't have this life.

But what *should be* and what *was* did not intersect. And Emma needed to make some decisions now. The first one would be to acquire a new car. The next would be where to go in it. She definitely had to deviate from the way she'd moved the past couple years. Sticking to the coastline was no longer an option. The smart thing to do would be to drive to the middle of the country, then pick another direction from there. Or instead of moving in a line down interstates, she could move in a giant circle. Or just throw a dart at a map on a wall. No pattern at all would be the best way to hide.

But first, the car issue. She grabbed her laptop to browse the local used car inventory. That way she could narrow down the places she needed to go and thereby reduce the irritating process of dealing with used car salesman, who so far, had lived up to the stereotypes. She queued up the websites and started cruising through the small SUVs. It was a couple hours until anyone opened, so she had plenty of time.

Time she could be using to pack, but something was keeping her from starting.

She opened a new tab and pulled up Levi Hughes's Facebook account again.

What if...?

She shook her head and closed the tab. She had no business sending her mind to impossible places.

———

JOSEF TOSSED his overnight bag into the trunk of his Mercedes and prepared for a long day of driving. His search of the employee's apartment had yielded nothing. Literally nothing. The woman didn't have so much as a personal photograph or a single memento from her past. It was as if she were on vacation herself, living with the barest of items and nothing to indicate who she was, much less if she knew Katarina.

A person who had deliberately hidden her own identity wasn't likely to give out information on another woman. And even if this woman had known Katarina, it was highly unlikely she'd know anything about where she'd gone. Katarina had been very careful. In the eight years he'd been hunting her, no one had ever come right out and said they knew her, but he'd gotten enough feedback—even the tiniest of frowns when they looked at the old photo—that led him to believe he was on the right path.

The next big city was New Orleans, and he had no doubt Katarina was headed that way. He had to be getting close. It would take a while to cover New Orleans. There were a myriad of opportunities for employment and best he could tell, Katarina had stuck to small, privately owned businesses. New Orleans was loaded with specialty shops like that, but there was no downside in having to spend some extra time in that city. It was filled with entertainment options—especially women.

He hadn't had a woman on tap in a while. And definitely not regularly since Miami, which was a buffet of hot girls looking for a man with the right set of car keys. Maybe he'd find a temporary girlfriend first, then he could take his time exploring the city. After all, he was supposed to be on the road looking for new business opportunities, and what better place for expansion than New Orleans? He hadn't discovered a good investment in a while, and it was time he kicked something back up that direction or he might be pulled from this assignment. That wouldn't be good.

Because he didn't want anyone else settling this score.

# CHAPTER TWENTY-TWO

EMMA CLIMBED BACK INTO HER CAR AND SIGHED. ALAYNA slumped into the passenger's seat and shot an aggravated stare across the car lot.

"Why do they work so hard to be odious?" Alayna asked.

Emma had to smile at the choice of the word *odious*. It was so perfect.

"They're used car salesmen," Emma said. "I'm pretty sure it's in the job description. Maybe they take classes."

"They certainly all have the same bullshit lines. Like some fifty-year-old, balding man with a spare tire you could ride to Texas telling us how pretty we are is going to sell a car. Good Lord, has anyone checked a calendar?"

Emma laughed. "There's one more place to look and if this one is as bad as the others, I'm going to scratch the whole idea for now."

"It's so frustrating," Alayna said. "I mean, if even one of those cars you looked at was decent, we could have put up with some of the nonsense, but whoever wrote those ads really pushed the edges of their 'great condition' comments. I was thinking that after I got the restaurant up and going, I would get something different. Maybe a Jeep, because beach and all, but I'm probably going to have PTSD after today and will be driving that sad Honda until it falls apart."

She knew Alayna was joking, but Emma was definitely feeling some stress with the car hunt. It wasn't a requirement that she find a new car before she left the island, but it would be one less thing to worry about. One less thing left to track her by. Worst case, she'd leave in what she had, but she knew she could reduce her stress by finding something different. But the last thing she was going to do was take a chance on something that might not be reliable. Emma's safety depended on being able to jet at a moment's notice. She couldn't afford a car that would require constant repair.

"I might have to up my budget some," Emma said. "With a couple more thousand, I might be able to get something with some warranty left."

Alayna nodded. "With all the roaming around you do, you need something you can depend on. I had to buy something I could afford in order to leave New York and my budget was beyond limited. I prayed the entire drive down here that the car would be okay. I mean, it checked out, but you never really know until you start driving cross-country how something is going to hold up."

"Exactly. Well, at least you made it and if it craps out now, you have a ton of people around who are happy to give you a lift."

Alayna laughed. "Yep. I even hitch rides from strangers at the ice cream shop."

"That worked out for both of us." Emma remembered every detail of the weekend before when she'd met Alayna and spent the day making a new friend. It seemed as if it had been so much longer. Was that because of the almost immediate comfort level she'd had with the other woman and the island?

Or was it because of the huge number of things that had happened over the past week?

Emma didn't realize she'd sighed until she felt Alayna's eyes on her.

"You want to talk about it?" Alayna asked.

"About what?" Emma feigned ignorance.

"Whatever's bothering you. And don't say nothing because I know that look. I *wear* that look. Is everything okay at the surf shop?"

Emma nodded because her job was the one thing that was going right. "I've almost got the software loaded and ready to go. I just need to finish up inventory tomorrow and get the input done, and Mark will be in accounting heaven starting Monday."

"I'm sure he's happy to have that off his plate. Aunt Bea said his wife used to handle all that end of the business and it wasn't really his thing. It was fate, you stopping for a visit here when you did."

Emma wasn't convinced on the concept of fate. When your life was one big unknown, it was hard to imagine that there was a plan and a purpose for it all.

"So if it's not the job that's bothering you, what is it?" Alayna asked. "Is the apartment working out okay? Are you and Mark getting along?"

Emma must have reacted to his name because Alayna stared at her for several seconds, completely silent.

"Oh, I see," she said finally.

Emma scrambled to get Alayna off that train of thought. No way did she need other people trying to manufacture a romance that was never going to happen.

"That's not it," Emma said.

"Sure it's not. I know and wear that look too—every time I see Luke. Even back when he was annoying the hell out of me when we first met. For the record, you can be annoyed and still think someone is hot."

Emma laughed. "Yes. That's absolutely true, but I'm not the only one who's noticed how hot my boss is."

Alayna's eyes widened. "Tell! It's a rare event when I get to find out something before Aunt Bea."

"Well, it just happened yesterday, so you might beat her to the punch on this one, especially since Mark was fairly put off by the whole exchange and probably won't be talking about it. At least, he appeared to be."

Alayna frowned. "Who was it?"

"Melody Whitmore. I didn't want to say anything because I know she's your mortal enemy. Everything you guys said about her the other night at dinner already had me convinced she was trouble, but seeing her in action took things to a whole other level."

Emma described Melody's obvious play for Mark in great detail. Alayna was shaking her head before she finished.

"She's unbelievable," Alayna said. "The man just lost his wife. I know it's been a year, but still. And he has a daughter to consider. Why on earth would he be interested in someone so obviously dismissive of his child?"

"I thought the exact same thing! And trust me, Mark looked mad enough to spit when she threw out that babysitter comment like Lily was an inconvenience that could be pushed aside when Princess Melody commanded it. The worst thing is, I don't even think Melody gets that her viewpoint is completely inappropriate."

Alayna considered that for a moment. "Maybe because she doesn't have that kind of relationship with her parents. I think she was mostly raised by nannies. I mean, whatever raising Queen Veronica allowed them to do."

"Doesn't look like a lot."

Alayna nodded. "She was also kicked out of boarding school and the local private school, which was how she ended up in public with me. Clearly, her parents thought handing her everything she ever wanted was the way to go. It's not really surprising that she expects the rest of the world to do the same. Not that I'm excusing anything."

"It's an explanation, not an excuse. I get it. Well, I hope she doesn't convince her parents to try to hand her Mark, because he doesn't need that aggravation."

Alayna sighed. "Why do they have to live here? Why can't they buy their own island to lord over?"

"I imagine because it would be only them and having no one to persecute would mean a lack of things to do. It doesn't sound like they contribute anything else. How did that town meeting go the other night?"

"Like we expected. Carlson is pushing to change the zoning for Aunt Bea's building so the upstairs is restricted to office use only."

"Can he do that?"

"He can't, but the city council can. They vote next month."

"Oh my God. What are you going to do?"

"Work like hell to get the place open. A zoning change has never passed on an existing business. It's a really bad look and Carlson's cousin, who is the mayor, is coming up for reelection. If Carlson casts shade on city decisions, it will create problems for his cousin. Add to that, we all think at some point Carlson will challenge his cousin for that job and yeah, we have a better shot at preventing the rezoning that way."

"So people won't buck the Whitmores to their faces, but they will at the polls."

Alayna nodded. "Especially if they think there's a threat to existing businesses, which all of them either have or have family who does. Still, if I can't get the restaurant open before the city council vote next month..."

"Oh my God, I've only been here a week and I already hate those people. They're absolutely horrible."

"True. But Carlson's not the only one who can make things difficult for people. Bea can as well. She owns the parking lot behind the bookstore. She could restrict it to private use or start charging for parking, and every business on Main Street would feel that with a loss to customer base, especially in the off-season when they're depending on locals to cover expenses.

"But she doesn't want to do that," Emma said, already knowing Bea wouldn't want to punish the others because of the Whitmores.

"No, and I seriously doubt she ever would. But she threatened it at the council meeting, and based on their expressions, it hit home. If they change zoning and Bea converts to private parking, the council will have to answer to every business owner and resident here."

Emma shook her head. "All of this because their daughter is a loser?"

Alayna frowned. "I don't know... I think the problems even precede Melody's birth. I've asked Bea about it, but she's unusually vague. She just talks about Veronica taking a disliking to her and her friends like Melody did with me. And since Bea never needed Veronica or Carlson for anything and refused to kiss their butts, they cast her in their villain role. But sometimes I think it goes deeper than that and she just doesn't want to say why."

"Well, regardless, I think everyone knows who the real villains are."

"Oh sure, but he who holds the mortgage has the power."

"I wish there was something I could do to help. Should you

be there working today? I didn't mean to pull you away when things are down to the wire."

Alayna shook her head. "There is nothing I can do right now. I'm not qualified to help with the construction stuff. I can clean when they're done and Bea is going to help paint, so I'll cover the bookstore for her when she does that, but otherwise, I'm kinda stuck sitting around. And I'm not good at sitting around, so trust me, you're helping me by getting me out of my head and giving me something else to focus on."

"I get it. Well, if you think of anything else I can help with, let me know. It's the least I can do for exposing you to the dark underbelly of the used car world on the mainland."

Alayna held up crossed fingers as Emma pulled into the last car dealership on her list.

"This is the one," she said.

Ten minutes later, they stood in front of the Hyundai Tucson that Emma had wanted to see as Emma stared and considered. The salesman—too young to be jaded or scammy —stood silently next to them and let her think. It was a welcome relief. And the car seemed fine, but it just didn't feel like the one. Emma had never been 'into' cars, per se, but she did spend a lot of time in them, so she preferred to have something she enjoyed, at least to a reasonable extent and for a reasonable price. The Hyundai ticked all the boxes, but she still hadn't worked up the enthusiasm for a test drive.

"If this one doesn't grab you," the young salesman said, apparently sensing her lack of excitement, "I have a RAV4 that we just got in. It's all-wheel drive and has a sporty look. It's a little more expensive..."

"What color?" she asked, not interested in flashy colors.

"Silver," he said. "Still looks great but will stay a lot cleaner than black."

"Let's take a look," Emma said.

She'd already been considering an all-wheel drive vehicle because they could handle ice and rain so much better. And since she never knew where she might be and what kind of weather she'd be living in, it made sense to get something that could handle everything the US could throw at her.

They followed the salesman down the next aisle, and he pointed to the sporty-looking crossover at the end of the row. Emma took one look and loved it. It had great curb appeal but in silver, wasn't going to attract unwanted attention.

"It's only two years old," the salesman said. "I took it in on trade myself. The couple loved it but are expecting another child and they needed more room. Low miles and there's still a year left on the manufacturer's warranty."

"How much?" Emma asked.

He named a figure that was several thousand more than she'd originally budgeted, but the Hyundai was older and didn't have remaining warranty, nor was it all-wheel drive.

"Let's take it for a spin," Emma said.

Alayna looked a little surprised—maybe because the price point was outside of what Emma had stated when they'd started or maybe because it was the first time she'd been moved to even drive something.

"I do like this," Alayna said as the salesman hurried off for the keys. "But are you sure about the price?"

"I can afford it. Yes, it's more than I wanted to spend, but it's also got things I wasn't factoring into the price of the other cars. And I'm going to be really honest here—I like the way it looks and am vain enough to admit it."

Alayna laughed. "Hey, you spend a lot of time in your vehicles. You should at least enjoy how they look. And ride, of course. I mean, you change the major things in your life all the time. It doesn't hurt to have one enjoyable constant."

Twenty minutes later, they all climbed out of the car and

Emma looked at Alayna and smiled. The car was everything she'd wanted and more. It even had heated seats, although she knew they were probably of limited use in Florida.

"Let's talk about my trade-in," Emma said. "It's high miles, but I have all the service records."

"That's great," the salesman said. "It always helps. We have a couple of incentives for financing right now. If we can make the numbers work, do you have any idea what kind of term you'll want?"

"I'll be paying cash," Emma said. "Well, a check anyway. I don't have a suitcase of money in the trunk."

He grinned. "Checks work. Let me have the keys and I'll take it back for an inspection."

She handed him the keys and as he drove off, Alayna gave her arm a squeeze.

"Do you love it as much as I do?" Alayna asked. "Please tell me you do because if you don't buy it, I'll be sad because I can't."

"I love it," Emma said. "That's the first time I've ever said that about a car, but this one is perfect for me. Just the right size, and a hatchback will be so much more convenient."

Alayna nodded. "And Toyotas are so reliable. Bea had a 4Runner for a long time. It had over a hundred fifty thousand miles on it when she finally got something new, and it was still running great."

"Reliable is definitely the top priority, and that additional year left on the warranty alleviates a lot of worry about used car buying."

"Do you think they'll lowball you on the trade?"

"Of course, but it's to be expected. My car's got a lot of miles, and it was an older model when I bought it. Unless it's just something beyond absurd, I think I might have found my new car."

An hour later, Emma drove off the lot in her new SUV, and she felt great. It was a small ray of sunshine in an otherwise crap day, but she'd learned a long time ago to take her wins when they were offered. She'd be leaving her lovely apartment with the most perfect view soon enough, but at least she'd be more comfortable and safer. It was a small consolation but it was better than nothing.

"I'm so glad you were able to make this work," Alayna said.

"Me too. It's much more comfortable than my other car. Long drives won't be as bad."

"Hopefully, you won't be making one for a long while."

When Emma was quiet, Alayna looked over at her.

"You're not thinking of leaving, are you?"

"Not with you in the car."

Emma's joke fell flat, which didn't surprise her.

"You said you were staying the entire summer," Alayna said.

"I know. And that's what I wanted."

"But not anymore?"

"I don't think I can stay," Emma said, unable to keep the misery out of her voice.

Alayna stared at her for a bit, then nodded.

"When I heard on the news that Warren had escaped police custody, my first thought was running," Alayna said. "I didn't want to bring trouble onto Aunt Bea."

"Why didn't you?"

"Because I realized that leaving wouldn't protect her. The wrong people would always assume she knew where I was. The only way I and anyone I cared about would ever be free was if I made a stand and ended things for good. It was either that or spend the rest of my life looking over my shoulder. And if I was going to make a stand, then what better place to do it than the one that mattered most with the people who mattered most surrounding me?"

Emma stared straight ahead, Alayna's words weighing heavy on her.

"You know, living in the moment is great," Alayna said quietly. "Unless you're the type of person who craves stability and security. Then living in the moment is great for vacation and the random day off, but if I lived that way every day, I'd always feel that not only was something lacking but that I was running a marathon with no finish line. That I was constantly reaching for something just outside my grasp. So ultimately, I'd live with disappointment every minute of the rest of my life."

Emma's heart clenched. Alayna has articulated so well what had haunted Emma for so long. The lack of foundation. The lack of a real future. The lack of, well, Emma.

As long as she ran, nothing changed.

But Alayna had family and friends and a man she cared about behind her. She already had a future in place—she just had to fight for it. Emma didn't have anything to fight for but herself.

And she still wasn't sure that was enough.

# CHAPTER TWENTY-THREE

MARK HEADED FOR THE FRONT DOOR OF THE SHOP, READY to lock up, but before he made it, Melody Whitmore strode in and this time she wasn't alone. Veronica Whitmore, who'd never set foot in his shop before now, gave the place an uninterested glance and sniffed before turning her attention to Mark. Based on her frown, he had a feeling he came up as short as his shop did.

"Hi, Mark," Melody said as she sidled up to him and clutched his arm. "I was telling Mother about the super-cute boards you had and how you've promised to give me private lessons."

As soon as Melody laid a hand on him, his entire body tensed. If he had to make a list of women he never wanted to touch him, it would start with Melody. But under her mother's scrutiny, he couldn't exactly pull his arm out of her grasp and run, even though that's exactly what he felt like doing.

"I said I'd be happy to put you on the books for a lesson," he said. "But I need to check availability."

Melody set her mouth in a pout. "But you could make

some time for me outside of your regular schedule, right? I mean, given our relationship and all."

"I'm afraid I don't have any time other than the open slots. I have a store to run and a daughter to raise."

"Doesn't that college girl keep your daughter?" Melody said, her tone as dismissive of Lily now as it had been the day before.

"When I have to work," he said between clenched teeth. "But Jane is not her parent. I am, and more importantly, I enjoy doing it. I'm not interested in doing things that reduce the amount of time I spend with Lily, especially during the summer when it's already limited."

Melody was forcing a smile, but she'd picked up on his tone. So had Veronica, and the older woman was now staring at him as if he were something that had accidentally gotten stuck on the bottom of what he was certain was a designer shoe.

"Melody, let the man's arm go," Veronica said. "I don't know why you insist on wasting time with people who aren't your peers. One of these days, you'll learn to be more discerning with the men who make passes at you. Clearly, he cannot support you in the way you deserve."

Mark choked back an indignant cry. Veronica knew good and well Melody was the pursuer here, but she wasn't about to admit that her daughter was getting turned down by someone Veronica considered beneath them. Good God the entire family was ridiculous.

"Mother!" Melody said, pretending to chastise, but Mark saw the sly smile that appeared for a second and then was gone. "But I suppose she's right. I'm really not interested in having to share my man with anyone, and I certainly don't want to spend my free time with a kid. I'm sorry, Mark, but this just isn't going to work out for me."

Mark stared at her. Unbelievable.

"Let's go, Melody," Veronica said. "We have a reservation and you need to change shoes. If you're going to wear open toe to dinner, then at least put on the Pradas."

"Ta-ta," Melody said and waved over her head as she followed her mother out of the store.

Mark ran over and locked the door behind them, then lowered the blinds and leaned back against the door and blew out a breath.

"What the hell was that?"

———

EMMA SAT ON THE DECK, holding an unopened bottle of water and staring at the ocean, hoping it offered up the answers she needed. Where was a working crystal ball when you needed one? She knew what she wanted to do but didn't know if it was the right thing to do.

Alayna's words had haunted her all afternoon.

Was this her place to make a stand? Alayna had roots on the island, so it made perfect sense for her to take up arms here. But Emma had barely darkened the doorstop. And Alayna had family to stand with her, not to mention the hot SEAL who'd been at the right place at the right time. Who did Emma have to back her up?

She knew Alayna would support her decision to stop running—that had been implied in the advice she'd issued that afternoon—but Emma didn't want to drag other people into her mess. Unfortunately, she'd been unable to come up with another option, and given that she'd been searching for one for eight years now, she was finally willing to admit that she couldn't fix this alone.

Run and keep running, or stay and ask for help. It came down to two choices.

The question was, did her existence here put anyone at risk? Amy's death still weighed heavily on her, and even though there was nothing she could have done to prevent it, Emma still felt guilty that Amy had lost her life over being in the wrong place at the wrong time. And Emma knew that Amy had gone to the police because she was worried about her friend's disappearance. She'd paid the ultimate price for being a good person. If Emma stayed on Tempest Island would Alayna be in danger? Mark? Or worse, Lily?

Common sense told her that Josef wouldn't risk involving other people because it was more to cover up. If he located her, he was more likely to wait until she was isolated and then strike. With his father's money backing him, he had all the time in the world to lounge around until the perfect opportunity. He's already been after her for eight years. Hours, days, or even weeks wouldn't matter at this point.

But Emma couldn't exactly go stand around in public all day every day, either. She was safe in the store and in the shops downtown, but she was alone in her apartment at night. If Josef came after her there and Mark heard, he'd come to her rescue. It was just the kind of person he was. And Emma had no doubt that while Josef wouldn't seek to eliminate Mark intentionally, he wouldn't hesitate if Mark got in the way.

If she stayed, she should move out of the apartment.

But where could she go? Unless she took to camping in the middle of the woods, there would always be someone around who might try to help and end up in the same position Amy had.

*Unless you take him out first.*

She blew out a breath. The nine-millimeter she carried was one of the first things she'd acquired when she took off. It was easy enough to pay cash at a gun show, and she took a couple lessons at a range from an older gentleman who'd been retired from the Army. She knew how to shoot, and she wouldn't hesitate to do so in her defense or in defense of someone else. But she hadn't practiced in a while and could use a refresher. Alayna said Luke had given her lessons and really improved her response time and accuracy. Maybe he'd be willing to give Emma lessons as well.

But waiting for Josef to attack her and hoping to shoot him wasn't exactly a plan. This wasn't going to end as long as she maintained the defensive position. It had protected her for a long time, but unless she wanted this life forever, things had to change.

She had to become the heroine in her own story.

Before she could change her mind, she went back inside and grabbed her laptop. She sank onto the couch and accessed the LA district attorney's website. She located Levi's profile page and clicked the Contact button. Then she typed.

*Hi Levi,*

*We met years back at a fraternity party. I was the nun. You were helpful with some advice on a legal issue back then and I see that you've done well in your career. I was hoping to arrange to speak to you so that I might get your advice on an old problem that keeps resurfacing.*

*Thanks!*

*Emma*

SHE TOOK a deep breath and slowly blew it out, then hit Send, her hand shaking as she pressed the track pad. Waves of emotion coursed through her—fear, relief, excitement—all contributing to the bout of dizziness and nausea she felt.

But she'd taken the first step to leaving her past behind.

There was no turning back now.

———

MARK CLIMBED into his SUV and waved at the mother of Lily's best friend and said a quick prayer on her behalf as she walked back inside her home. The brave soul had allowed her daughter to have an end-of-school sleepover and had taken on five delighted girls. Mark was both thrilled to have a night completely to himself and terrified for when the time came for him to return the favor.

So far, he'd only attempted a single-friend sleepover, and he'd hovered all night between wanting to call an exorcist or simply move out. How girls managed to scream ten octaves above normal for so many hours on end, he had no idea. And even joyful screams were rough on the eardrums, especially closed in their small apartment, and definitely in the middle of the night when everyone should be sleeping.

Now, the question was what to do with all this free time.

He said a silent prayer of thanks that Melody Whitmore hadn't somehow known he'd be alone that night. She'd probably have tried to strong-arm him into going to dinner with her and her parents. Not that Veronica would have been up for the idea, but Mark figured when push came to shove, her parents didn't tell Melody no. Apparently, the entire family had a problem with the word.

Hopefully, the exchange they'd had this afternoon had nixed her pursuit of him. He'd been seriously worried when Melody had started in right there in front of her mother, but when Veronica had turned it all around—making Mark the unsatisfactory pursuer and Melody the prize—he figured it might have worked out to his advantage. Melody could pretend to be the one who found Mark lacking and continue her good standing with her mother, while Mark could try to forget the exchange had ever happened and not have to hide when he saw Melody on the street.

Since he didn't have dinner duties, he stopped for Chinese takeout on his way home. Lily wasn't a huge fan, so he usually limited his indulgence to his lunch hour. But during season, he preferred to eat light during working hours because he spent so much time with lessons. A heavy meal was not his friend, but a heavy dinner on the deck was just what the doctor ordered after the day he'd had.

He had just given his order when the door opened and Alayna walked in. She gave him a smile as she stepped up to the counter. The teenage boy taking the order looked at her like a lovestruck puppy.

"Your usual?" he asked.

"That would be great," she said and gave him a big smile. He blushed and practically ran to the back with the ticket.

"I think he's in love," Mark said as he slipped into a chair at a vacant table and motioned for her to sit.

She laughed and took a seat across from him. "He's way too young for me but a really good kid. Hopefully he finds the perfect girl when he heads off to college in the fall. But I heard I'm not the only one with an admirer around here."

Mark panicked at first, thinking Emma had complained to Alayna about the kiss. Then he saw the teasing expression on her face and realized she'd gotten the scoop on the Melody Whitmore incident. The first one, anyway.

"You talked to Emma," he said.

"We went car shopping today. So the spoiled princess of

Tempest Island has set her sights on you. I don't know whether to pray for you or tell you to see a Realtor."

"No kidding! She had another go at me this afternoon, but I'm hoping that one was the end of it."

He told Alayna about the exchange.

"Wow," she said when he finished. "Of course Veronica turned the whole thing around on you. She'll never believe that men aren't lining up to date her perfect daughter. Even though the fact that she's never had a long-term boyfriend that I'm aware of should be an indication."

"I'm sure she just assigns them all the 'unsuitable' tag and tells herself the right man hasn't come along yet."

"The right man for that nightmare hasn't been born yet. I'm not sure what kind of guy would put up with her."

"One who was equally nasty and wanted the connections."

"That's a good point. At least most of the women here are nice. I'm sure you have your share of admirers...you know, for when you're ready."

"I don't know about that."

"So how's Emma working out?"

Mark was a regular guy, but even he knew when a woman was fishing. And Alayna had an agenda mentioning available women and then segueing right into Emma. No way he was biting on that loaded subject, especially after last night.

"She's done a great job getting everything sorted and set up," he said. "It's a huge stress relief, especially with the season under way."

She nodded. "I've been hinting that maybe she should think about sticking around here—you know, give up this whole nomad thing for a bit of the good life here on the island. What do you think?"

"I, uh, well... That's up to her, I guess."

"But you'd be happy if she stuck around for longer than the

summer."

"Sure, although I'm not certain how much full-time work I'll have long term."

Alayna shrugged. "I'm sure there are other reasons she might want to stick around. Jobs are great, but they're not everything."

"Says the workaholic chef."

"Yes, but if the Whitmores get their way and my restaurant never opens, I'm still sticking around. Bea and Luke are here. As long as I have my friends and family, I'm good. It took me a while to figure that out, but I'm not about to forget it. This island has a way of changing hearts and minds. Maybe it will change Emma's as well."

"I agree that the island is a special place, but people still have practical concerns, and earning a living is one of them."

"Beth worked for multiple businesses, right? I don't see any reason why Emma couldn't do the same. God knows, I'm not about to do my own accounting, and just between you and me, Aunt Bea needs to hire someone as well or her liver isn't going to make it through another tax season."

Mark laughed. "I feel her pain."

"Mr. Phillips," the teen at the counter called and held up his order.

"Looks like it's dinnertime," Mark said and rose to pick up his food. "It was good talking to you. Say hi to Luke for me."

"I will. And think about what I said. I'm pretty sure Emma would consider staying if she knew everything her future might include."

She gave him a knowing look and he forced a smile before hurrying out.

Because he'd had entirely too many uncomfortable exchanges with women that day, he let himself in the front door of the shop and took the interior stairs up to his apart-

251

ment. That way, if Emma was on the deck, he didn't have to face her. Then he felt like a coward and a fool the entire way up the stairs.

He placed his food on the counter and pulled a beer from the refrigerator. The upside of his kind of work was that he was already dressed for relaxing when he got off work, and since Lily was occupied for the night, he was going to skip his evening swim. He eyed the patio doors and weighed his options. Then he cursed himself for being stupid, pulled out his container of food, and headed for the door. He couldn't spend the entire summer hiding in his apartment, and he certainly had to deal with Emma at the store and potentially in front of other people. It was better to clear the air now than wait until they were at work.

And if she was outside, that's exactly what he was going to do.

———

EMMA HEARD movement on the deck and peeked between the blinds and spotted Mark sitting in the glider at the end of the deck. He held a container of Chinese food, and a beer rested on the table next to him. She didn't see or hear Lily, which was rare, so she wondered if his daughter was at a friend's house. It was too early for her to be asleep and if Lily was awake, everyone around her knew.

*Now is your chance to talk to him.*

She blew out a breath. All afternoon, she'd been thinking about what to say to Mark, and she had yet to come up with a good way to introduce the topic or explain it without dumping her problems on someone who didn't need more trouble in his life. And men like Mark didn't simply nod and leave things alone. They tried to fix them, and the last thing she wanted was Mark putting himself and Lily in danger because of her. The second-to-last thing she wanted was him thinking she was moving out because he kissed her.

God, what a tangled mess. This is why she'd had rules. *Good* rules.

Before she could chicken out, she shoved the door open and stepped outside. No turning back now without looking like an idiot. She'd just have to figure out a way to explain her situation—at least to the extent that Mark would understand why she needed to move to the mainland until her situation was resolved.

*You're assuming it ever will be.*

She forced that negative thought from her mind. Now was not the time to think about how badly things could go. If she got mired into that pit, then she'd end up running again. Mark looked over as she approached and gave her a tentative smile. Why did he have to look so cute, even when it was clear that he was worried?

*And that's your fault.*

"Can I sit?" she asked.

"Of course," he said and scooted over to make room on the glider. "Would you like some Chinese takeout? I always buy too much."

"I thought Lily wasn't fond of Chinese."

"She's not, so when I have the opportunity, I tend to overdo. She's at a slumber party to celebrate the end of school."

"A slumber party of five-year-olds?"

He nodded. "I've already prayed for the mother, and for myself when I have to reciprocate. It might be easier to move away."

"Speaking of moving—"

"Wait. Before you say anything, I have to apologize. My

behavior last night was out of line. You're my employee and my tenant, and I should have never gone there. I don't blame you if you want to move, but I'm hoping you'll at least stay at the job. I promise things will be nothing but professional from this point forward."

Emma didn't know what to say. She hadn't been expecting an apology, but she probably should have. Even though she hadn't known Mark for very long, she had a good idea what kind of person he was. But part of her was also disappointed. Maybe he'd just been caught up in the moment. Maybe it was just a case of him missing his wife and what they had and Emma being there and being similar in certain ways.

Which sucked, but also made things easier.

"You don't have anything to apologize for," she said finally. "But I do think it's best if I move to the mainland...just not for that reason."

He frowned. "I don't understand."

"There are things about me you don't know."

"Well, since I know very little about you, that stands to reason."

Emma took a deep breath and slowly blew it out. "I mean bad things. Things about my past."

"Are you in trouble?"

"No. Yes. I mean, I am but I'm not the cause. Or maybe I am— Oh my God, this is so hard to explain."

"Maybe start at the beginning?"

She nodded. The beginning was where she had to go, but how did she explain her entire horrible life in one conversation? Even if she hit only the important items, how did she decide what they were when everything that she was today was a sum of the whole? Finally, she decided that the most direct approach was best. Then Mark could ask questions.

"I saw my father kill a man."

# CHAPTER TWENTY-FOUR

MARK STARED AT EMMA, JAW DROPPED AND NOT A CLUE AS to how to respond. Surely he'd heard incorrectly. Because in the vast list of things that he'd imagined she might say, witnessing a murder hadn't even been in his consciousness. Witnessing her father committing a murder was so far out of his realm of thinking that he was having trouble comprehending it even when she'd said the words.

But because she sat there staring at him—her expression a mix of fear, worry, and embarrassment—he knew she wasn't making it up. And that meant he had to say something, but for the first time in his life, he couldn't find words. Unfortunately, he had to come up with something or she was going to bolt— that much was clear.

"I..." he began. "I don't...I'm..."

"I get it. It's overwhelming and not what anyone wants or expects to hear. You're the first person I've ever told."

He blinked. "The first person...ever?"

She nodded, clearly miserable. "I shouldn't have. I'm sorry. This is exactly why I've never stayed anywhere long enough to get attached to people. Because no one should have to live with this. I know firsthand how horrible it is and I never wanted to impose it on other people."

"Impose? Good God, Emma! You think by telling me this horrific thing in your life that you're imposing on me? What the hell kind of person would I be if I was aggravated rather than concerned? Do you really think so little of me?"

"I think the world of you...and Lily. That's why I can't stand the thought of putting either of you in danger."

"Danger? You mean your father is after you? I thought when you said you'd witnessed a murder you were running from the memories, not from a human being. Wait, that's not exactly true. It did cross my mind that you might have been avoiding an old boyfriend, maybe even a husband—someone who treated you badly. But this... This is beyond what I could have thought. How long have you been running? Does he know where you are? Why is he still looking? Do we need to go to the police? What can I do?"

He knew he was throwing a ton of questions at her but once his startled mind had started spinning, he hadn't been able to slow it down. But it was the last question that made her crumple. Her hands flew up to cover her face, and she started to sob. He put his arms around her and drew her close. He could feel her heart racing and struggled to find the words to soothe her, because were there really any words for this?

They sat that way for a while, Emma sobbing and him holding her, then finally she leaned back and wiped the tears from her face with her hand.

"Tell me," he said gently.

And she did.

He listened without interrupting, but it was hard. There were times he wanted to know more, but this wasn't the time to ask. Emma needed to get the entire story out—the story she'd never told anyone before. But it was hard to listen when the only option of comfort was to squeeze her hand, especially when there were times he was so angry he wanted to get up and punch something.

How could parents do this to their own child? Every time he thought about how scared Emma must have been when she ran, he thought about Lily, and he was angry all over again. Her face was flushed with the effort of telling the story and her hands shook. At times she wept but never stopped talking.

Finally, she stopped and drew in a deep breath, then blew it slowly out.

"And you're sure it's this Josef that your friend in Tampa saw?" he asked.

Emma nodded. "The photo she sent was from a distance, but it's him. Even after eight years, he still looks the same."

"But why would they still be looking for you? If your father killed the coach and he's dead, what could you possibly do to Danek at this point? No one can prove he ordered the hit, and men like Danek just say their family, friends, employees, or whoever were acting on their own and they know nothing. Without proof that he was the one calling the shots, you shouldn't matter."

"That's logical, and when I took the job here, that's what I had decided. That surely it was over. That I could finally call a place home and mean it. You don't know how much I wanted to believe that. But that is definitely Josef, and there's no reason for him to be looking for me unless his father ordered it. Trust me, I don't get it either."

"But you sent an email to that attorney with the DA?"

"Yes, but I don't know that he can do anything. I mean, clearly the DA hasn't been able to hang anything on Danek. Who knows how far his reach is?"

Mark ran one hand through his hair and blew out a breath. "Okay. Let's back up and think about things we can control.

First off, I never called your references, so no one knows where you are, right?"

"I never tell anyone, and I didn't tell Becky when I talked to her."

"And since you've always stopped in big cities, then there is no reason for Josef to look for you here."

"That's what I'd like to believe, but I can't ask you to take that risk."

"I was a soldier...and a damned good one. Do you know what it's like to be asked to stand down when someone needs protecting?"

"I have a good idea, but Lily also needs protecting. She has to come first."

His gut twisted because he knew she was right. He couldn't do anything that put Lily at risk, but even though the situation was as serious as it gets, it still didn't sound as though Josef would ever figure out where Emma was. Based on what she had told him, Tempest Island was a complete deviation from her norm. Josef wouldn't expect such a drastic change after eight years of not changing her MO. But was that enough to take the risk? If it was just him, he'd say yes in a heartbeat. But he had to think of Lily.

"I can't put Lily in danger," Emma said. "What if Josef finds me? What if he tracks me down here—where I live?"

"Even if that happened—and it doesn't sound plausible given everything you explained—why would he risk doing anything with Lily there?"

"Lily being harmed is not the only risk to her. If you stepped in and were injured, or worse, killed, then Lily would have no parents. No family at all that was capable of raising her."

He cursed and slammed one hand on the glider, making her jump.

"I'm sorry," he said. "I didn't mean to scare you. That's the last thing I want to do."

"You startled me. You didn't scare me. Look, Mark, I didn't tell you all of this so that you could fix it for me. I told you because I didn't want to leave and have you think it was because of last night. It's not. But I knew if I left, that's what you'd think because not even in your wildest imagination could you have come up with the truth."

"That's for sure. But you can't expect to tell me all of this and then me just sit back and do nothing. Emma, I kissed you because I wanted to...because you make me feel things I haven't felt since Beth. Things I never thought I'd feel again. And I'll be damned if some murdering asshole is going to disrupt my life just when I got it going again."

He stared at her, instantly chagrined. She never said a word, just stared at him, her mouth slightly open and her eyes wide.

"I mean," he said, "if you're interested in me that way. Because if you're not, then that's fine too, but I don't want you to quit working with me or move. And I'm still going to help you. Okay, yeah, I'll be disappointed, but that's not on you. That's all me and I just don't want—"

She moved in and planted her lips on his so quickly that it took his breath away.

He wrapped his arms around her and drew her in, as he'd longed to do since the moment she'd started sharing her horrific story. This woman was incredible and she didn't even know it. The things she'd overcome. The decisions she'd had to make at such a young age. And the intelligence and emotional maturity she'd had to develop and use with every single thought. His respect for her and his empathy for what she endured increased a million times over. No one should have to live this way.

Especially not someone like Emma.

When she broke off their kiss, she laid her head on his shoulder and just clung to him. He could feel her heart pounding wildly with his own. Neither of them had been expecting this, but one thing was finally clear to him—both of them wanted it.

They had to fix this. He couldn't handle losing someone he cared about again.

Emma couldn't believe that she'd told Mark everything—and she'd kissed him! Every careful rule she'd made regarding her life had been completely thrown out the window. It was the first time in her life she'd done something without calculation, and it was exhilarating and scary. Was this how normal people lived? Able to act on their feelings rather than worrying about the effect every action taken and sentence uttered had on their future?

She clung to him, her face on his shoulder, pressed into his neck, and for the first time in her life, she felt as though she belonged. This was where she was meant to be—right here in this man's arms. She was as certain of that as she was that the sun would rise tomorrow. It was an overwhelming feeling.

Finally, she leaned back so that she could lock her eyes on his, worried that he'd had time to think about all of this and realized it was a bad idea. But instead, all she saw was worry and caring. And resolve. Mark was a man who could be depended on. He was the kind of man who got things done.

"I..." she started, then hesitated, trying to find the right words. "I've never felt this way before, about anyone. I would say it's because I never allowed myself that luxury, and that's partially true, but the fact is no one has ever made me feel like I needed to break my rules. No one has ever felt worth the risk. But you have to be sure. Because I can't ask you to take a risk with me over things that aren't your responsibility. And I can't ask you to put Lily in harm's way."

He shook his head and put one finger over her lips to stop her.

"The only risk here is losing you," he said. "And that's what will happen if you run again. I know we haven't known each other long, but the way I feel about you isn't temporary. I truly believe we could have a future together—here, on the island that we both love. We just have to make sure you're safe and then we can decide how we want our lives to be."

She choked back a cry. "I think just sitting here with you is pretty perfect."

He placed his hand against her cheek and gently brushed his lips across hers. "So do I," he whispered.

Her body was already alive with his touch, but suddenly, the heat coming off him and his lips on hers sent shock waves through her. Never had she wanted a man like this. She'd never even known it was possible to feel this way. And while their future was definitely in question, what Emma knew was that they had this night.

This one perfect night.

And because it might be all they ever got, she covered his hand with hers, looked him right in the eye, and whispered, "Stay with me tonight."

———

MARK AWAKENED early Sunday slightly confused. The morning sun was barely streaming in between the blinds, casting a dim glow over an unfamiliar room. Then he felt something shift in the bed next to him and it all flooded back. He was in the apartment.

With Emma.

He turned over and gazed at her face—eyes closed, a long strand of her auburn hair falling across her cheek. Her tan had deepened in the last week, and she looked so healthy and vital. And Lord, that was only two words that he would use to describe her. Energetic, tireless, and creative were another three.

He felt like the luckiest man alive, and he was pretty sure he wasn't biased in that thinking. He'd listened to enough people complain about their relationships to know that people didn't often connect on this level. He'd been fortunate enough to feel that way about two women. He'd lost one. He wasn't going to lose another.

Emma shifted and her eyes fluttered open. She looked up at him and gave him a slow, sexy smile.

"That might have been the best sleep I've gotten since I've been here," she said.

He laughed. "There wasn't much of it. Not that I'm complaining."

"But it was quality sleep. And there was no storm, so no bad dreams."

His heart clenched when he thought about what kind of bad dreams Emma probably had. He couldn't imagine seeing something like what she had and living with it every day. He'd been a soldier in a war, but that didn't compare to seeing your own father gun someone down as part of his job. The betrayal of such a thing—of knowing that your entire existence was a farce—was overwhelming. And then living every day of your life looking over your shoulder and pretending to be someone else.

"You are an incredible woman," he said. "Everything you've managed for all these years. Most people would have crumpled under the pressure."

"I think people do what's necessary when survival is on the table."

"Yes. But they don't necessarily do it well. Your life might be unconventional, but you've constantly increased your education and skill set along the way and improved your options with every move. Most would have been waiting tables forever, not actually developing a career while running for their lives."

She sighed. "I guess, in the back of my mind, there was always that hope, you know? That one day, I could stop running and everything I'd done would matter."

"It does matter. And that day is today."

He leaned down and kissed her gently and she placed a hand on his chest. He deepened the kiss and lowered his body onto hers, unable to believe that he'd found this a second time. There were so many things they had to do. So many plans to make, precautions to take. But they could all wait.

Because this moment was right now. And it was perfect.

———

EMMA CLENCHED the steering wheel as she drove across the island toward Alayna's cottage. She was anxious but at the same time, happier than she'd ever been. Telling Mark had been cathartic beyond anything she'd ever imagined. But now, nerves were edging into that elation as she thought about what to tell Alayna.

She knew her friend would understand better than anyone the choices she'd made and the stress she'd dealt with, knowing that someone so close to her wasn't the person she'd thought they were. Alayna knew firsthand not only the terror, but the embarrassment and disappointment and the enormous blow to self-confidence that something like that did to you. Alayna wouldn't judge. She would just ask what she could do.

And yet still, Emma worried. So many years of going it alone had left her comfortable on her own island. Well, maybe not comfortable. Maybe *capable* was a better word. A necessary capability.

*Which you no longer need because you have friends. Friends who will help.*

She blew out a breath. Just that thought was so overwhelming. It was the place she'd always wanted to be but never thought she'd find. And now, this was it—her opportunity to finally push away her past and have her real future.

And it scared the hell out of her.

She pulled into Alayna's driveway and parked her new SUV. Alayna had the door open before she even got to it and gave her a brilliant smile, as only Alayna could, before waving her inside.

"I've already had my coffee fill for the day," Alayna said. "But if you'd like some, I could make you a cup. I know you've got inventory to get to. If that doesn't move you, I have fresh pineapple juice. Just finished squeezing it."

Emma blinked. "You squeeze your own pineapple juice?"

"It's so much better that way. And healthier, which means the cinnamon rolls I'm about to offer you are balanced out. Sort of. At least, that's Luke's argument."

Emma laughed. There was no one on earth like Alayna.

Her friend.

"I'd love some of that pineapple juice, and I agree with Luke on the cinnamon roll argument."

"Great!" Alayna pulled a pitcher from the refrigerator and poured them both a large glass of juice, then removed a tray of cinnamon rolls from the oven.

"I popped them back in to keep them warm after Luke left

for the base because I never like to eat first thing," Alayna said. "So they should still be nice and gooey."

Emma took a deep breath as the smell of cinnamon had her mouth watering. "You made these from scratch?"

"Don't tell me you do that can thing like Luke."

"Actually, I'm too lazy to even bother with the can. I just buy them from a bakery."

Alayna laughed as she popped two rolls onto plates and waved Emma toward the patio. "Mine are better. So let's head outside into this perfect weather and you can tell me what you need from me."

"What do you mean?"

"I know that look. You've made a decision—a big one. I'm ready to help. So let's do this. Let's sort out your life over pineapple juice and cinnamon rolls."

Emma laughed. How had she been so lucky to find Mark and Alayna at the same time? They sat on the couch on the patio, both facing the water, and Alayna placed one hand on her arm and squeezed. Emma hadn't been certain how much she was going to tell Alayna before coming here, but that single action made up her mind.

She told her everything.

When she was done, Alayna hugged her tightly, still sobbing as she had several times during Emma's story. Finally, she released Emma and wiped her eyes.

"I know most people would say something like 'I can't believe it,'" Alayna said. "And maybe a year ago, I would have said the same thing, but not now. I knew that day when I told you my story that you had one as well. You were so guarded, so careful, and behind that confidence was that layer of fear that you lived with every moment. I know what that looks like because that was me."

Emma nodded and even though she'd expected nothing less from this awesome woman, relief coursed through her.

"I knew you'd get it," Emma said. "I liked you from the moment we met, and then after I heard your story, I felt a connection with you that I couldn't describe. And I'm somewhat ashamed to admit it—jealousy."

Alayna shook her head. "You should never feel ashamed for wanting a normal life. That's all it was. I'd broken free from a horrible situation and have a wonderful future ahead of me. You want the same. Good Lord, Emma, who wouldn't? Especially after what you've been through."

"I know, it's just that I never thought I could and now I want it so badly... But I feel like I'm making another mistake by putting people at risk."

Alayna nodded. "I get it. You know that I do. But Mark is right—he never checked references and you've deviated so far from your norm that no one should be looking for you here."

"He shouldn't be, but what if he does?"

"Then we settle it, and you get to move on with your life. Here. With Mark and me and the job you're made for on the island you love. It's time, Emma. Time to take a stand. For you."

Emma sniffed, feeling the tears coming again. "I'm so overwhelmed. With you and Mark and all the kindness everyone has shown me. And I don't want anyone hurt."

"No one will be hurt—least of all you. You'll just continue to keep a low profile. You said you contacted that attorney with the DA's office, right? He'll know what to do. And he might have a way to find out where Josef is, so you can rest easy."

"I hadn't even thought about that. I'm going to send you some photos. I pulled them from Josef's social media. It's him and his father. I want you to share them with Luke and Bea. I know you'll need to tell them about all of this, and that's okay."

Alayna shrugged. "They already had an idea that something was up."

Emma stared. "What do you mean?"

"Just that they thought you had trouble and that's why you never stuck around. But they also thought you were the victim, like me. This will be a shock, given that it involved your father, but not a surprise, if you know what I mean."

"Yeah, I get it. Thank you so much, Alayna. For everything. I don't know how I can ever repay you."

Alayna grinned. "You can start by telling me about last night and Mark. I was in the surf shop yesterday getting new sunglasses when Lily told me all about the slumber party she was headed to. Which means you and Mark were all alone in that big building...sharing secrets."

Emma felt the blush creep up her neck and onto her face, and Alayna laughed and threw her arms around Emma and squeezed.

"Never mind. You don't need to say a single word."

# CHAPTER TWENTY-FIVE

As he often did on Monday mornings, Levi stopped to pick up coffee for himself and his paralegal. He was running late and always felt guilty when he didn't show up on time. His paralegal, despite working on finishing her law degree and having a young child, managed to be early and organized and looked as though she'd been put together by hair and makeup on a movie set. One day, he'd be brave enough to ask her for the secret, but he was afraid it started with rising at some hour he'd consider obscene. He'd always been more of a night person.

His paralegal gave him a broad smile as he handed her the coffee and the apology, then gave him a quick reminder of his schedule for the day. He had an appointment that morning down at the LAPD to go over some details with the investigating officers before putting together his case recommendations for his boss. His afternoon was clear, but as he had a big trial coming up, his boss had been trying to give him some extra time every day to prepare.

He opened his blinds to let the morning sunlight in, then listened to voice mail while queuing up his computer.

Nothing from voice mail needed immediate attention, so he jotted down a couple notes for later and clicked on his email. He was happy to see some of the case documents he'd been waiting on from the forensics team were there for his review and that he could now renew his car warranty for less money.

He downloaded the forensic files, deleted the car warranty spam, and checked the last entry. He didn't recognize the email address, and it didn't appear to belong to a business, but since the description was simply 'Legal question,' he figured it was one of the fairly common inquiries he got from individuals. The really simple stuff he answered himself and if they needed help, there were several attorneys he referred out to, depending on what kind of legal situation they needed help for.

He started reading the email and jumped out of his chair, squeezing his coffee so hard the top popped off and it spilled all over his desk. He yelled and his paralegal rushed in, then ran back out and returned a couple seconds later with paper towels. She moved to tackle the mess on his desk, but he grabbed her shoulders and stared at her, unable to control his excitement.

"This might be it!" he said.

"What might be it?"

"The way to take Danek down!"

"What are you talking about?" she asked.

"I can't say just yet. And I'm so sorry about the mess, but there's someone I need to talk to. Cancel my appointment this morning and tell the DA I had something important to do."

"Will you be back this afternoon?"

"Probably. Maybe."

He grabbed his keys off the desk and ran out the door, leaving his confused paralegal standing in the middle of his office, still clutching a handful of paper towels. He dialed his contact, an FBI agent, as soon as he jumped into his car.

"You're not going to believe who I just got an email from."

———

MARK GLANCED BACK at the hallway that led to the offices, then finished ringing up the customer at the counter. Two more stood behind him, and his summer store help was hustling among even more customers in the crowded store. It was a good thing to be so busy—a necessary thing—but he couldn't help wishing they'd get a break so that he could go check on Emma.

Lily had returned from her sleepover before lunch on Sunday, and his day had then been consumed by the whirlwind that was his daughter. Emma, despite everything else going on, had insisted on finishing up the inventory and accounting so that he'd be ready to launch with the new software on Monday. He'd tried to argue, but she refused to take the day off and he couldn't exactly stand guard over her with Lily in tow. And since it was a beautiful day with a small surf, Emma had insisted that he give Lily the surfing lesson he'd promised.

Sunday night, he'd grilled hamburgers and after Lily was asleep, Emma told him about her conversation with Alayna. She and Alayna had decided on a story to distribute to select islanders with the photos of Josef—an old boyfriend with a violent streak. Alayna assured them that's all it would take for them to button their lips and report back if anyone showed up looking for Emma. Mark had never doubted that the islanders would support Emma, but it was a relief to know that so many people would have their eyes open. Then they'd talked late into the night about everything *but* Emma's dire situation, getting to know more about each other.

With every word, Mark had felt his heart beating stronger. It had been so hard not taking Emma's hand and drawing her inside, but they didn't want Lily to know. Not yet. Not until they had a better handle on things. But Mark already knew that Emma was everything he'd never thought he'd have again. His love for Beth had been deep and strong, and the bond between the two of them—especially after Lily arrived—was like something out of a fiction novel. But it had been real. All of it. And suddenly, even though he'd thought it could never happen again, those same feelings were there. Just there. Hitting him like a freight train. It was thrilling and scary all at the same time. But he knew more than anything that he wanted this. He wanted Emma to be part of his life. Part of Lily's life.

He wanted forever.

He'd been cheated out of forever once. He wasn't going to allow it to happen again.

The weekend had been both wonderful and hard, and now he had to spend an entire day working with Emma, trying to pretend everything was normal. Which it wasn't. The attorney hadn't replied to Emma's email over the weekend, but he would be back in his office today and hopefully, something would happen today. Would the attorney remember Emma? Surely he would after the lengths he'd gone to in order to help her. The real question was, could he do anything to help?

More than anything, Mark hated this defensive position they were in. He was far more comfortable with an offensive strike. This waiting for things to happen wasn't his bag. The military hadn't exactly trained him to sit back and wait. Granted, everything had been very structured and thought out, but he'd had an active role in beating the enemy. The military had never taken a 'wait until they strike' approach, and he wasn't sure he was capable of taking one now.

Another frustrating thirty minutes passed before the store cleared of all but two customers and Mark signaled to his salesperson that he was going into the back. He headed straight for Emma's office, knocking on the door before he entered so that he wouldn't startle her. She turned around in her chair and gave him a shy smile and then shook her head.

"Nothing yet," she said. "But it's only eleven o'clock, and they're three hours behind."

"Crap. I hadn't thought about the time difference."

"I know. The waiting is so hard and I don't know why. I've effectively been waiting for eight years, but now that I've decided to do something, I guess I want it all to happen right now."

"You want to get on with your life. A real life. I want that too."

"Let me check again."

She pulled out her laptop and did her bypass so that the IP address wasn't registered, then checked her email. Her pulse jumped when she saw the email reply that had hit her inbox just minutes before.

"It's here," she whispered.

Mark shut her office door and rushed across the office, then leaned over the desk as she clicked on the email.

*EMMA,*

*OF COURSE I REMEMBER YOU! That night was as epic as your costume. It was great to hear from you, and I'll be glad to try to help with your legal issue. Can you give me a call? I find these things are generally easier to explain with a conversation rather than a lot of typing. And that way, I can ask questions as we go. Here's my cell number. If you let me know when you plan to call, I'll make sure to block off that time.*

*Levi*

EMMA CLUTCHED the desk as she read, one layer of stress dissolving as a different one took its place. He remembered! That was the first hurdle, although she hadn't figured he could forget.

"So this means he wants to help, right?" Mark asked, and she could hear the anxiety in his voice.

She nodded. "He's giving me his cell and asking for a call time so he can be somewhere private. Or maybe with other people who can help."

"I hope he trusts the right people."

"He's an extremely good judge of people. He clued in right away that something was wrong with me that night. I think he's spent most of his life studying people so that he can figure out what they were thinking or about to do. His older sister was... They lost her to a stalker who turned violent when she wouldn't date him. She was only nineteen."

Mark's stomach rolled. "That's horrible. And it explains why he was so invested in helping you."

She nodded. "I don't want to talk while I'm at work because I don't know how long it will take, and I'd like to have you in on the conversation—if that's okay, of course. Can Jane keep Lily late?"

Relief engulfed Mark when Emma said she wanted to include him in the call. Then he frowned. "Jane has night class for summer school, but I can get someone to watch Lily for a couple hours. I need to be there for this."

"Okay. Then seven o'clock? That gives us time to close the shop and for you to get Lily with a sitter. And it will be four in California, so maybe it won't disrupt too much of Levi's day."

He nodded and she started typing a reply, then she closed her laptop and turned to face him. He looked as anxious as she felt, but who could blame them? There was so much riding on this.

He leaned over and kissed her gently on the lips.

"I have a good feeling about this," he said.

The warm brush of his lips on hers made her heart clench. She'd never wanted anything or anyone as badly as she wanted Mark and Tempest Island.

She just prayed Levi had a solution.

———

Josef stepped out onto the balcony of his motel room that evening and looked at the crowded streets of the French Quarter. It was the start of summer and New Orleans was bursting with tourists. He smiled as he watched a group of scantily clad young women enter the bar across the street. This place was prime hunting ground. So many women looking for a good time. Maybe it wasn't as overflowing as Vegas or Miami, but there was something to be said for atmosphere here. It was more old-world than flashy, but the parties raged just as hard.

He'd been driving for hours that day, so the first thing he'd do was take a shower. Then he'd put on his nightclub clothes and head out to find a girlfriend for the night. He had an appointment with a Realtor for the upcoming week to look at several businesses for sale—the sort of businesses that might prove useful for laundering. His father expected results and had been growing more and more impatient with Josef recently. He was not the kind of man who tolerated failure, especially from his own son. A few more businesses to add to Ivan's increasing portfolio would give Josef a little breathing room.

He was just about to head into the shower when his cell phone rang. He frowned when he saw the display. It was Marek, a childhood acquaintance from back in LA. One who worked for Ivan now as his father had for years before he'd passed. Josef had never liked Marek much. He was loud and liked to throw money around for attention. Since that was Josef's domain, he didn't appreciate someone else in his group trying to one-up him. Obviously, there was only one son of Ivan Danek, and that meant Josef was at the top of the food chain. Everyone else knew their place. Except Marek.

Still, Marek didn't call often, so Josef's curiosity was piqued.

"Marek," Josef answered. "What can I do for you?"

"Your father called and asked me to meet you over in New Orleans to assess some businesses."

Josef felt the rage he often felt for his father course through him. "I appreciate the offer, but I'm good."

There was a slight pause. "It wasn't an offer. It was an order."

Josef silently swore. He didn't need oversight. He was a grown man and just as capable of seeing to his father's business as his father. And definitely more capable than Marek, who wasn't in line to inherit any of it.

"Fine, but I just arrived myself. I have one appointment tomorrow morning and two more later in the week. And there are still some others that I'm reviewing financials for. You'd need to be on a red-eye to make the meeting tomorrow morning. It's at 8:00 a.m."

"Christ, that's a little early, isn't it?"

"That's when the Realtor could fit me in, and I asked for

the first available. If that's a problem for you then maybe you could mention it to my father and he will rethink his choice."

Marek sighed. "I'll be there. I'm in Florida, so I can drive over tonight."

Josef stiffened. "Why are you in Florida?"

"Vacation, actually. I met this hot number in Vegas, and I've been overdue for some time off. She had a friend who vacationed on an island down here and said her friend was always raving about it, so we came down here to check it out. But I got to tell you, man, it's no Miami. There's zero club scene—bunch of old people and kids running around. Not my bag at all."

"Uh-huh. And will you be bringing this hot number to NOLA?"

"No way! We were supposed to leave tomorrow anyway. She can just go back without me. It's no big deal—just a bit of fun. So where are you staying?"

Josef gave him the hotel name. "I'll meet you in the lobby tomorrow morning at seven thirty."

"Got a big night planned, I bet. Lots of pretty women in the French Quarter. That place is definitely more my vibe."

"It's a nice city."

Marek laughed. "Nice city, my ass. It's a buffet. That's why you like it. Plenty of great food, drinks, and hot women. It will be a welcome change after seeing a bunch of senior and mom bods all week. Oh hey, I did see one hot number coming out of the surf shop. Looked like that girl you went out with a couple times—Gustav's daughter, I think?"

Josef tightened his grip on the phone. "Really? She looked like Katarina?"

"Yes and no. I mean, her face looked similar and her body was that lean athletic type, but this girl had long auburn hair.

Much nicer than that short black shit Katarina wore. I never got it. It was like she was trying to be unattractive."

Since that thought had already occurred to Josef and he had wondered if Katarina was specifically trying to be unattractive to him, it wasn't a conversation he was interested in having. Especially with Marek.

"Hmmm," Josef said. "What was the name of this senior-and child-filled island? I want to avoid it."

"Tempest Island. Pretty place, but like I said, nothing here for guys like us."

"Doesn't sound like it. Anyway, I've got to run. I'll see you in the morning."

Josef pulled up a map on his phone and located Tempest Island. It was a tiny place—not at all like the other stops Katarina had made. Surely Marek was wrong. But there was that niggling doubt in the back of his mind that reminded him that Marek had a memory for women like he did for nothing else. Every scrape Marek had gotten in from elementary school on was about a female. It was his biggest addiction.

It couldn't be a coincidence that Katarina had been in Florida just weeks ago and now Marek had spotted a woman who looked like her in the same state, and in line with her trajectory of moving around the coast. Her stopping point might be outside of her norm, but maybe she'd decided to change things up. Maybe she thought she was safe.

He was going to disabuse her of that notion.

# CHAPTER TWENTY-SIX

EMMA PACED HER APARTMENT, WHICH TOOK ALL OF FIVE seconds, then turned around and paced again. She'd done it so many times since she'd gotten off work that she was surprised there weren't worn spots on the hardwood floors. She'd tried meditation, stretching, and even a shot of whiskey, but nothing had taken her nerves down from the stratosphere.

Never in her life had so much ridden on a single phone call.

She heard footsteps running up the stairs outside and a couple seconds later, Mark slid the patio door open and stepped inside.

"Lily is all set," he said. "Alayna and Luke are watching her. They're going to take her paddleboarding, so she's thrilled."

Emma blew out a breath. "That's great. Now if time would just speed up."

"It's only ten more minutes."

She stared at him and he put his hands up.

"I know!" he said. "Do you have any idea how difficult it was to make small talk with Alayna and Luke, when the whole time, all of this was racing through my mind? You know they probably think we asked them to babysit so we could have a romantic evening, right?"

"Probably. But there's no point telling them about the phone call until we know if anything will come of it. It's bad enough that our hopes are up. I don't want to get everyone else excited before we know what our options are...if there even are any. I mean, hell, I wish we were having a romantic evening, so no problem with them thinking it."

He took her hands in his and squeezed. "We'll have the rest of our lives for those."

She stepped into him and wrapped her arms around him, feeling a tiny bit of her tension diminish in his embrace. Nothing would make her happier than for his words to come true. But so many things had to be resolved. Just thinking about them made it all seem insurmountable.

"We're going to make this happen," he said softly.

She blew out a breath and broke the embrace. "I'm going to splash my face with some water and have another shot of whiskey."

"Whiskey?"

"Yeah. That's not a problem, is it?"

"Only because you haven't offered me any."

She gave him a small smile. "It's right there on the counter. Give us both a generous serving and then we'll make this call."

She headed into the bathroom and splashed some cold water on her face, then patted it with a washcloth. She gripped the vanity and stared at herself in the mirror. She looked old, tired, and stressed, and since that's exactly the way she felt, there wasn't any point in trying to improve the situation. She just needed to make this phone call, and pray for a solution.

She headed back into the living room where Mark was already seated on the couch, two glasses of whiskey on the coffee table next to her cell phone. She picked up her glass as she sat next to him.

"You're not having a shot?" she asked when he didn't pick up the other glass.

He pointed to the end table next to him at the two glasses sitting there and she let out a single laugh.

"Good idea," she said. "Are you ready?"

He nodded and squeezed her hand before she put down the glass and picked up her phone. She dialed the number Levi had given her and didn't even realize she was holding her breath until he answered and it all came out in a big whoosh.

"This is Levi," a familiar voice answered. "Are you all right?"

Seven words and yet the explosion of emotions they induced was incredible.

"I am at the moment," she managed, feeling suddenly and completely overwhelmed.

"I have to say, I never expected to hear from you. I was afraid..."

"I know. A lot of bodies piled up after I ran. I'm sorry it took me until now to contact you. I feel guilty—"

"Don't even go there. You had every reason to be afraid and honestly, I don't know that I could have done anything for you back then. Not more than I did, anyway."

"But you think you can now?"

"I do, but first I have to tell you that I have a friend here with me—an FBI agent. He leads a task force that is assigned to bringing down Ivan Danek. You can trust him. He's my cousin and we've been working together for a very long time."

Emma felt a tiny bit of tension leave her shoulders. Levi had brought reinforcements, and not just anyone, but family.

"Okay," she said. "Where do you want me to start?"

"From the beginning. I need to know what precipitated you running. I have some ideas, but I need the facts."

Emma took a deep breath and told him about what she'd seen at the football field that night. When she was done, there was silence for a couple seconds.

Finally, Levi spoke. "I figured all of those things were tied together but I wasn't sure if you saw anything or just overheard something. I'm truly sorry you had to witness that. I'm more grateful than ever that you walked into the party that night."

"I'm the grateful one. You literally saved my life. If you hadn't clued into my needing help, there's no way I could have gotten away."

"Well, you've clearly done an excellent job using the little help you were given."

"Yes. And I'd hoped that time would eliminate the need to live looking over my shoulder, but turns out, it's a good thing I have been."

She heard him suck in a breath.

"They're still looking for you?" he asked.

"Yes." She told them about Josef.

"I don't really understand why he's still after me all these years later," she said when she finished. "How can I hurt Ivan? Yes, I saw my father kill Coach Mayhern, and I recognized the other man as one of Ivan's employees. And I overheard my parents when I checked the security cameras, but all that gives you is my word. I can't give you hard evidence that Ivan was involved. And my parents are both dead."

"Ivan doesn't like loose ends, even the tiniest of them."

"I know," Emma said, choking back a cry. "Amy...there was no point..."

"No. There wasn't. What Amy saw wouldn't have been enough to convict your father, much less Ivan. It just proves how vicious Ivan is and why I was thrilled to know you were still alive."

"However long that lasts."

"Until we're both old and gray if I have anything to do with it. That's why I asked my cousin to be here. Now that we know what we're dealing with, we're going to come up with a plan."

"What do I do in the meantime?"

"Stay where you are and stay alert. It sounds like you're in a great place to avoid Josef and with people around you who will be on watch. That's the optimum situation. Meanwhile, my cousin will dispatch some agents to get eyes on Josef while we figure out how to utilize this information to bulk up the case against Danek. I want you to know, you're not the only good card in our hand. Taken independently, we never had enough evidence to move forward, but adding you to the list might be the difference we needed."

Emma felt relief wash through her. They were going to make a plan and they had other evidence. If she could tip things in Levi's favor, then that would be the answer to her prayers.

"Another thing," Levi said. "Can you start documenting everything that happened that night? Write it all out, with every detail you can think of, and I mean everything. Those things that seem unimportant all support your credibility."

"I actually already did that. I started while I was on the bus leaving LA. I don't know why, but I thought maybe someday it would be important and I knew I'd forget things."

"Seriously? That's incredible. And you still have that file?"

"Yes. I've had cloud storage for years. I don't look at the files from back then...you know...but it's still there."

"Can you forward it to me?"

"Of course. And I have to ask—if we're successful in taking down Danek, how much trouble am I in? I mean, I've been living under a fake identity, including Social Security card. I have payroll checks, a retirement account. Am I going to prison?"

"Good Lord, no! Yes, some of the things you've done are illegal, but they were also necessary. No prosecutor is going to bring you up on charges, especially not in my office. If we did, I'd have to go up on charges too since I helped you acquire that new identity and knowingly withheld information about an active police search. Besides, we're not in the business of putting the victims behind bars. We're here to protect people like you."

The last bit of tension that Emma had been holding in her shoulders left and she put her hands over her face, trying to keep herself from crying.

"Thank you," she managed.

"It's me who should be thanking you. We're going to fix this. And you're going to have the life you always deserved. You counted on me once. You can do it again."

The tears that had been threatening to fall the entire call spilled out as soon as she put the phone down. Mark gathered her in his arms and held her as she cried. Tears of fear, relief, sadness, regret, and hope all fell as he held her.

There was a light at the end of the tunnel.

And it was her awakening from her living nightmare.

When she'd cried herself out, she released Mark and studied him. The care and concern were so visible on his face that she didn't even have to ask how he felt. She knew.

"I can't believe this might be over soon," she said finally. "It's what I've always wanted and now that it's here, it's almost overwhelming."

He nodded. "And scary, I bet. I mean, you want a different life, but the one you've had is the one you know and the one that kept you safe. This is a huge step. I'm so in awe of you.

Everything you've done and are about to do. You're an incredible woman, Emma. Or should I call you…"

"No. Emma Turner is who I am and who I want to be."

"I'm glad. Because I really like Emma Turner."

She smiled. "Then let's set her free. Pass me my laptop."

He handed her the laptop from the end table and she popped it open and went through her usual song and dance.

"You do this every time you use your laptop?" he asked.

"Only when I'm accessing the email I give to former coworkers and employers or other things that might give away my identity or location. In this case, the cloud storage is a duplicate of one I had in college, so it probably isn't really necessary, but it's habit at this point. After I ran, I dumped everything from my old one to this one, just in case I ever needed anything, then added my online journaling to the new one when I was finally able to handle putting it all down."

"Because your parents or Danek would have accessed your old storage."

"I'm sure that's one of the first things they would have checked, right after tracking my cell phone, credit cards, and bank account. I haven't used it since I finished those journal entries, but I've kept the subscription to hold these files. I don't keep anything else there because… Well, to be honest, because I don't want to see those files. Just seeing the icons stresses me out."

"That's why I put all those boxes of Beth's stuff in this apartment. I couldn't bring myself to get rid of them but every time I looked at them, it hurt."

She took his hand and squeezed. "We both know loss. I think that's one of the reasons I feel such a connection to you."

"Yes, but we're both more than our losses."

"Absolutely."

She drew in a deep breath and accessed her old files. She'd never created a folder for her journaling, so all the files from the night she'd run and afterward were on the main page, and there were a lot of them. Rather than create one document for all her thoughts, each entry was a separate file that covered a different part of her life. She knew there were several files about that night—one for her conversation with Amy, another for what she saw at the stadium, and more for her run across campus, how she got to the party, and meeting Levi. Probably fifty documents in total.

"I numbered them rather than named them," she said.

Mark shook his head. "Yeah, I can't imagine trying to assign names to those files. But numbering is good."

She nodded. "I'll create a new folder and copy everything that Levi needs into it, then send him the whole thing."

"What's this one?" Mark pointed to a file with a different extension than the others.

She looked at the file name, which was just a series of numbers and frowned. "It looks like an audio, but I didn't record anything."

She clicked on the file and when she heard the voices, the blood drained from her face. When she'd checked the cameras that night and heard her parents talking, she'd somehow recorded them.

Mark's eyes widened as he realized what he was listening to and when it was over, he put his hands on her shoulders and looked her directly in the eyes. "This is horrible *and* wonderful. It's proof of everything you're saying. Don't you see? The voices can be verified. They named everyone—Danek, the other man who was with your father, Mayhern, you—it's all spelled out right there."

She blinked twice, trying to break out of the shock. "Oh my God!"

He nodded, looking excited. "This is everything. You have to send Levi this file and call him again. Do it right now."

Hands shaking, she pulled up Levi's email, attached the file, and hit Send. Then she grabbed her phone, and for the first time in eight years, she felt the scales tipping in her favor.

———

IN HER LOVELY cottage on the beach, Alayna flopped onto her couch and blew out a breath. "Oh my God."

"That was intense," Luke agreed as he sat beside her.

"The restaurant business is intense. That was one of those rings of hell things. How can someone so little have so much energy? How does Mark do that every day?"

"The universal 'they' claim you get used to it."

"Not buying it."

Luke chuckled. "So I take it this is all that's required for our 'how do you feel about kids' talk?"

"It is for now." She looked over at him. "Is that a problem?"

He shook his head. "I'm not ready now. Not sure if I ever will be. Maybe we should get a dog first and try that on for size."

"The hours when the restaurant opens will be brutal, especially to start, and you sometimes have war games that require you to be gone for days."

"War games?"

"I know what you're teaching those guys to do. I've seen movies."

He laughed. "If my men could do what you see in movies, they wouldn't need me."

Alayna pursed her lips. "I sometimes think about a cat. Then I remember the stunts Shakespeare pulls when he's holding a grudge and I think again."

"Like what?"

"Well, this weekend, the pet store was out of his favorite food. Aunt Bea got him the same brand but a different flavor and he refused to eat it. When she came in the next morning, he'd unrolled every roll of toilet paper and paper towels in the bookstore."

He stared. "A cat did that?"

"Well, it wasn't Aunt Bea or Nelly, and they're the only one with keys except me."

He jumped up from the couch. "I have an idea. Stay here."

She watched as he hurried out the patio door and down to the beach. He bent over, then came jogging back inside and held out his hand. Inside was a perfect white seashell.

"I don't get it," she said as she took the shell.

"It's the Tempest Island version of a pet rock. I figured this was something we could handle."

Alayna flopped back on the couch, laughing. "This is why I love you."

He leaned over and kissed her. "I know."

Someone knocked on the front door, and Alayna and Luke looked at each other. Alayna shrugged so Luke headed to the door and opened it up to Bea, who held up a bottle of wine.

Luke grinned. "You heard we were babysitting."

She nodded as she headed into the kitchen to uncork the wine and pour some for the three of them. Alayna waited until she'd flopped into a chair in the living room before quizzing her.

"Is something wrong?" Alayna asked.

"Yes," Bea said. "But I don't know what."

"Well, if you don't know, I doubt anyone else does," Alayna said. "Is this your problem or mine or someone else's entirely?"

"Emma's."

Alayna blinked. "But I thought you'd be thrilled that we

were babysitting—didn't you and Nelly think Mark and Emma would make a great couple?"

Bea nodded. "And if I thought he had you babysitting for romantic reasons, we'd be having a completely different conversation."

"What makes you think he didn't?" Alayna asked.

"I was leaving the bookstore when he came back with Lily a bit ago and saw him in the parking lot."

"Okay...?"

"Let's just say he didn't have that freshly serviced look."

Luke spit out his wine and Alayna stared at her aunt in dismay.

"Good Lord, Aunt Bea!" Alayna said.

"I'm just saying," Bea said, "that I know he was home and I'm sure Emma was too, and that look on his face was worry, not relaxation. I've seen it too many times lately and worn it myself some to know what it looks like."

Alayna blew out a breath. "I guess you're right. I mean, I didn't even think about it because I wasn't thinking about... I figured they had a date—you know, one of those getting-to-know-you things since Emma finally leveled with everyone."

Bea frowned. "Something's up. I can feel it. He was trying way too hard to appear normal."

"You think Emma talked to that attorney?" Luke asked.

"Maybe," Bea said. "Anyway, I'm going to get out of here in case the two of you have service appointments, but I just wanted to put that out there. Let's keep a close watch on Emma. I have a bad feeling."

She rose from the couch. "Enjoy the wine. I'll talk to you tomorrow."

She headed out of the cabin and Luke followed her to lock the door behind her. Alayna looked down at the coffee table at the shell Luke had brought her earlier and thought about what it represented. Choices. Everything they'd overcome. The future they had ahead of them.

And she said a prayer that Emma was going to get her own shell choices soon.

———

LEVI PACED the apartment he shared with his fiancée. It was 2:00 a.m. and he hadn't managed to sleep yet. What he had managed was to make that worn spot in his socks a complete hole and consume an entire jar of peanuts without even realizing it. But he couldn't stop his racing mind. Just when he had hit a low point—thinking he'd never come up with enough for a case against Danek—Katarina had materialized.

Their initial conversation had him excited enough, but when she'd called back and told him about the audio file she'd never known she had, he'd almost run outside and done cartwheels. As it was, his fiancée had been subjected to three hours of conversation on that one subject, although he had eased it for her by bringing home her favorite wine and Italian takeout, complete with cannoli. He'd learned long ago that there was little she wouldn't forgive for cannoli.

"Can't sleep?" His fiancée's voice sounded from the doorway of the bedroom.

"No. My mind is racing."

She nodded. "I can imagine. This is huge—the kind of huge most people in the DA's office never see in an entire career. Add to it that you actually assisted a key witness in her escape from the man and it's become personal."

He shook his head. "I had no idea who she was when I helped her. Not until the news reports started up about her disappearance. When her link to Danek broke, I can't tell you how happy I was that I decided to skip studying and spend an hour at that damned party. If I hadn't..."

She walked over and hugged him. "But you did. Sometimes you have to accept that things happen for a reason. I think you were meant to meet Katarina that night. It's all coming full circle now."

He held up crossed fingers.

# CHAPTER TWENTY-SEVEN

JOSEF SMILED AS HE GUIDED THE RENTED YACHT INTO THE marina on Tempest Island. As much as he hated to admit it, Marek had finally proven useful—his memory for women, anyway. Josef had headed to Tempest Island immediately after their tour with the Realtor at the beginning of the week, not expecting much. After all, Marek had only seen Katarina a handful of times, and that was over eight years ago. The odds of him randomly coming across her and recognizing her, even though she'd changed her appearance, were so slim they shouldn't have even mattered.

But Josef hadn't been able to shake the feeling that it meant something.

So he'd driven to Tempest Island and spent a day wandering around the tiny beach town. Even if Marek *had* seen Katarina, there was always the chance that she was gone now. She could have even been vacationing like Marek. That would make more sense than attempting to live in a place like this. There was nothing here. Sure, there was the beach, but it was crowded with middle-aged couples and their screaming kids.

There was no nightlife to speak of. Within minutes of arriving, he'd understood why Marek hadn't been impressed.

He'd started to turn around and leave right then, but something had kept him from doing so—that niggling doubt that maybe Marek had been right. So he'd walked the island and sat on the beach in a ball cap, sunglasses, and earbuds and pretended to listen to music while he studied people passing by. He'd avoided doing business on the island, afraid that Katarina might have friends who would tip her off, so he'd bought a lawn chair, towels, and water on the mainland and hauled them in every day. After a day and a half, he'd been ready to call it quits.

Then he'd spotted her.

He was just about to head back to New Orleans, and there she was, coming out of the bookstore. He had just gotten into his car and almost dropped the drink he'd been holding when he caught sight of her. Marek was right—she'd changed her hair, and damn it if she didn't look even better than before. She'd been hot when she was younger, and she was even hotter now. She had that runner gauntness, but her curves had filled out some, giving her that athletic but feminine body that he always went for.

Then he remembered how she'd betrayed him. Betrayed his family. And the anger that had been building for eight years was back in place. The desire to grab her and throw her in his car was overwhelming, but he couldn't risk such an action in front of so many people, not to mention the cameras on the street. So he clenched the steering wheel until his hands ached and watched as she walked in between two of the buildings just down from where he was parked.

He waited a couple seconds, then jumped out of his car and hurried after her. The path between the buildings was empty when he peered around the corner, so he eased his way down the sidewalk toward the beach. At the end of the path was a set of stairs that led to a deck. He stopped at the edge of the building and scanned the beach, but he didn't see her anywhere. Then he heard voices on the deck above him. A child, asking about hot dogs, a man responding. And then Katarina. She might be able to disguise her appearance, but she couldn't change her voice.

He'd returned to his car and pulled just past the Main Street stores and parked. Then he headed for the beach with a towel and a bag containing water and binoculars. He found a spot behind a lifeguard tower where he could peer around and see the deck but could easily tuck back and remain hidden from their view. He'd watched all evening until they'd finished dinner and then the man and the girl had gone through patio doors inside and Katarina had gone through another set of doors next to them.

Was she involved with the man? Or was she sharing a meal with a neighbor? The upstairs must be two separate units given the way they'd turned in that night, but they'd seemed very chummy given that Katarina couldn't have been on the island for very long. He hadn't seen any interaction that indicated a relationship—they'd never even touched, much less kissed—but even from a distance, he'd gotten the impression that there was more to their interactions than what he could see. Regardless, the man and the child weren't his problem, so he'd returned to New Orleans for a couple days, looked at the other properties, and put together a plan to get Katarina away from the prying eyes of the townspeople and the vacationers.

A plan that allowed him to deal with her the way he'd always wanted to—long and slow.

The boat was a stroke of genius on his part. It not only

offered the perfect way to escape cameras and people, but it also allowed him the ability to dispose of the body where it was unlikely to ever be found. All he had to do was wait for the right moment—that moment when the fewest number of people would see her leave with him—and he'd make his move.

As soon as he'd wrapped up his business in New Orleans Friday morning—making deals for two of the three properties he looked at for his father—Josef had headed back to Tempest Island. Marek had returned home, but Josef had called his father and asked him to meet him in Florida, insisting that he'd found something that his father had to see in person and that would top every acquisition Josef had ever made. He hadn't told his father about Katarina yet. He wanted it to be a surprise when he picked up Ivan that evening and he saw what Josef had accomplished.

Josef couldn't help smiling. This would prove his worth. Prove that he had the dedication and patience to see the important things through. That he was capable of something that Ivan's top men had never managed. That his loyalty to his father and what he'd built was absolute.

And the first thing Josef would do when he was in charge was cut Marek loose.

———

EMMA SHUT down her computer and stretched her arms over her head. It was Friday, and she was looking forward to her weekend off. Monday had been so stressful that every day after had felt almost like a vacation. The relief from talking to Levi and knowing that he and the FBI were working on a plan. And then the incredible find of that audio file. It was all so unimaginable, but everything about her life had been since that night.

Every day, Emma had awakened with excitement. This

might be the rest of her life—the perfect place, perfect job, perfect friends...perfect man. She couldn't help smiling when she thought about Mark. They'd spent every evening together on the deck, grilling and playing with Lily and chatting. They were careful to show only friendship in front of Lily because it was too early to say anything. With the potential for a trial across the country looming, Emma didn't want Lily getting too attached and then have to leave for weeks or months.

Oh hell, who was she fooling? The three of them were already attached. Every minute she spent with Mark, Emma was even more convinced that she'd found her person. And Lily was an absolute delight and clearly missed having a woman around in the evenings. But things weren't settled yet and until they were, they were going to remain friends only in public and in front of Lily. They had, however, managed to steal some kisses at work and a couple at night after Lily was asleep.

And every single one of them had left Emma wanting more.

She headed for the front of the building and poked her head in the store. Mark was signing a couple up for paddleboarding lessons and several more customers were milling around. There was still almost another hour to go until closing, but it appeared that Mark had cut his assistant loose for the night, probably figuring things would continue to taper off now that it was approaching dinnertime.

"You need help?" she asked.

He looked back and shook his head. "Not here, but if you could go upstairs and relieve Jane, I'd be eternally grateful. She has a date tonight and said that because it's raining, she needs more time for her hair. I have no idea what that means, but I'm sure she'd appreciate getting to leave early."

Emma grinned. "No problem."

The rain that had moved in that evening was supposed to

clear out overnight, but right now, it was coming in giant sheets, so Emma took the interior stairs up to the apartment landing. She knocked on the door to Mark's apartment and hoped they could hear her over the loud music playing inside. A couple seconds later, a harried-looking Jane opened the door to let her in.

"I'm so sorry," Jane said. "Were you standing there long?"

"Not at all. Mark asked if I could relieve you on Lily duty so you could attend to hair duty."

Jane gave her a grateful smile. "First date, you know. And it rains. With this baby-fine hair of mine... Anyway, I really appreciate it. I should warn you—she's a real firecracker today. No outside play time to wear off all that energy. I was just teaching her my aerobics routine, and she decided she needed a different set of leggings for it so she's digging everything out of her closet."

Emma laughed. "I'll figure out something. I'm wishing you an excellent hair night. And an even better date."

Jane grabbed her purse off the kitchen counter and gave Emma a quick squeeze before heading out. "Your mouth to God's ears," she called over her shoulder as she hurried out.

Lily burst into the living room and broke into a smile when she saw Emma.

"Where's Daddy?" she asked.

"The store's still open, so I'm going to stay with you until he gets off. If that's okay."

"Of course. Miss Jane was teaching me how to do 'robics. She says it's painful, but I don't know why. I thought it was fun."

"I think it only gets painful when you get older."

Lily nodded. "Miss Jane is old. Almost as old as you and daddy."

Emma laughed. "We're practically ancient. So what do you

say we stop the aerobics and I teach you to stand on your head."

Lily's face lit up. "Really? Maybe I'll get good enough and can do it on my paddleboard."

"I'll just bet you can."

Forty-five minutes later, Emma's phone signaled an incoming text and she called for a break. Lily had tumbled over at least a hundred times but had managed to get her legs up for a good five seconds on the last attempt. Emma had no doubt she'd be head-standing with the best of them before the night was over.

She grabbed her phone from the kitchen counter and saw a text from Mark.

*You guys up for pizza?*

"Lily—your dad wants to know if you'd like pizza for dinner."

Lily rolled her eyes. "Well, of course. Why does he even waste time asking? I'm starving!"

She smiled and texted back.

*Sounds great.*

*OK. Locking up now. Will be there with dinner in a few.*

"Look, Miss Emma," Lily said, and pointed outside. "It stopped raining. Can we sit outside for our break? I need to buy a headstand pillow. Our rug isn't soft enough."

"I'm sure any of your pillows will do."

"No. It has to be a special pillow just for headstands. And it has to be blue, like the water."

"Okay, well, you look at pillows, and then you can discuss that with your dad when he gets here."

Lily's shoulders slumped. "Daddy never understands. Colors are important."

"I'll put in a good word."

Lily brightened. "You will?"

"It was my idea to teach you headstands, so it seems that's the least I could do."

"I really like you, Miss Emma. You're nice and pretty and know things. My mom was nice and pretty and knew things too. You would have liked her."

Emma's heart clenched. "I'm sure I would have."

Lily grabbed her iPad and ran for the door. "Hurry up! You can really hear the waves after a storm."

Emma tucked her phone in her pocket and headed outside. Lily was already in one of the patio chairs, furiously typing on her iPad. Emma took a seat in a chair next to Lily and pulled out her phone to check the weather.

"It's been a long time." A familiar voice sounded from the stairs to her right and Emma felt the blood rush from her head.

She looked over as Josef stepped onto the deck, and bile rose in her throat.

"Who are you?" Lily asked.

Josef smiled. "A friend. I'm here to give her a ride."

Lily, who could obviously sense something wasn't right, frowned. "But Daddy is bringing pizza."

"She'll have it some other time," Josef said and looked at Emma. "Isn't that right? And you won't need your phone. I have mine."

Emma knew exactly what he was conveying—the only way she could protect Lily was to leave with him. Otherwise, Lily could become yet another casualty of knowing her, like Amy.

Emma turned to Lily and handed the girl her phone. "I need you to keep this for me, okay?"

"But why? Why are you leaving? You're supposed to stay with me until Daddy gets home."

"He'll be here soon," Emma said and prayed she could get away before Mark showed up. She had no doubt that Josef wouldn't hesitate to eliminate both of them in order to get to her. "I need you to go inside and lock the doors. Keep looking at pillows and your dad will be here in no time."

"But where are you going?"

Emma had no doubt that Mark would put two and two together, but just in case there was any inkling of doubt, she said something that would seal the deal.

"My friend is going to take me to a stable to see about horse riding lessons," she said.

"Really?" Lily perked up a little. "Can I go too?"

"Not this time, but if it works out, I'll bring you next time. So tell your dad I had to go to horse riding lessons, okay?"

"Okay, Miss Emma. But you're going to miss the pizza."

"We've got to go," Josef said and clenched her shoulder.

When he leaned against her, she could feel the hard metal of the gun against her arm. She hurried up from the seat.

"Go inside and lock the door," she said. "It won't be long until your dad gets here."

Josef grabbed her arm, his fingers digging into her skin so hard it made her muscles ache, and he pulled her toward the stairs. She cast one last glance back as Lily closed the patio door and waved. Emma lifted her hand and choked back a cry, knowing she'd never see the beautiful little girl again.

————

LEVI LOOKED up as his cousin walked into his office and immediately stiffened when he saw the look on his face. "What's wrong?" he asked.

"My guy located Josef yesterday. He's in New Orleans."

Levi nodded. Since Emma had left Tampa and had been making her way around the Gulf Coast, New Orleans was the next logical place to stop.

"So he bypassed her, which is good, right?" Levi said.

His cousin shook his head. "My guy was supposed to keep eyes on him at the hotel, but Josef disappeared this morning. A charge came up on his personal card an hour ago. He rented a yacht. On Tempest Island."

# CHAPTER TWENTY-EIGHT

MARK RAN UP THE STAIRS ONTO THE DECK, CLUTCHING TWO pizza boxes. Since the rain had stopped, he'd half expected to find Lily and Emma outside, but the porch was empty. Lily jumped up from the couch as he made his way to the patio door and she hurried to unlock it. He headed for the counter to dump the pizzas, then gave Lily a curious look.

"Where's Emma?"

"She had to go with her friend."

Mark frowned. The only friend he was aware of was Alayna. "What friend?"

Lily shrugged. "Some man. I didn't like him. He never smiled. I have her phone too. The man said she didn't need it."

A wave of terror rushed through him and he knelt down and held Lily's shoulders. "Did she say where she was going?

"Uh-huh. She said she was going to horse riding lessons and if she likes it, then I can go too. Can I go, Daddy?"

"Oh my God." Mark jumped up and pulled out his cell phone and dialed Luke's number.

"He's got her," Mark said as soon as Luke answered.

"What? How?"

Mark repeated what Lily had said.

"And there's no way this could be a surprise for Lily?" Luke asked.

"Emma is allergic to horses. Severely allergic. That was her way of letting me know everything is wrong."

Luke cursed. "That FBI guy was supposed to be getting eyes on Josef, right? Call Levi and see what they know. If the FBI can tell us where to find him, we can get her back. We'll be there in five. Alayna can stay with Lily."

Mark asked for Emma's phone, his hands shaking as he took it from Lily and accessed Levi's number. Lily, sensing something was seriously wrong, started to tear up and Mark sat on the couch and pulled her onto his lap, stroking her hair.

"Emma?" Levi answered.

"No, it's Mark. He's got her. He's got Emma."

"Shit! My cousin just told me they tracked down Josef on Tempest Island. I was just about to call Emma and tell her I've called local police and the FBI is sending agents."

"Well, it's all a little too late. Where is Josef?"

"He rented a yacht. Hold on, I wrote it down—Island Bay Marina, but—"

Mark tossed the phone on the couch and ran to his bedroom closet to unlock his safe. Lily followed him, now crying.

"Was that man bad?" she asked. "Is he going to hurt Emma?"

Mark crouched down, trying to think of what to tell his clearly frightened daughter. He'd always stuck to an age-appropriate version of the truth and decided now shouldn't be any different.

"Yes, he is a bad man," he said. "But Daddy and Luke are going to find her and make the man leave."

"But if he's a bad man, why did Emma go ride horses with him?"

"Because she wanted to get the bad man away from you."

"Oh. Like Mommy would have."

His heart clenched. "Just like that."

"Mark!" Luke's voice sounded from the front of the apartment.

Lily bolted for the front and Mark removed his pistol from the safe and shoved it in his waistband before hurrying into the living room to greet a tense-looking Luke and clearly upset Alayna. Lily had already launched into the chef's arms and she'd gathered her up and was rubbing her back as Mark quietly filled Luke in.

"The marina can track the boat," Mark said. "I just need a way to get to it if it's left the dock."

"I've got you covered," Luke said. "Let's head out to the marina and I'll make a call on the way. Alayna, I think you should take Lily to Bea's house and wait there."

"That's a good idea," Mark said. He didn't think Josef would return, but with Lily safely tucked away with Alayna and Bea, he could fully concentrate on rescuing Emma.

Alayna gave them a quick nod and headed out ahead of them, clutching Lily's hand in hers.

"Come on, honey," she said. "We'll go visit my Aunt Bea. She's always got the best snacks and she has a huge television. I bet we can find cartoons."

Lily looked back at Mark, her eyes filled with tears, and his heart broke. But he couldn't comfort her. He had to save Emma or the heartbreak would be a million times worse.

"What is Levi doing?" Luke asked as they rushed out to his truck.

"They're sending FBI agents and contacted the locals but

the FBI is hours away and the locals aren't really trained for hostage rescue."

Luke nodded. "We're going to get her back."

"We have to! I know it's crazy because I haven't known her long, but I can't fathom my life without her."

"I get it."

Mark blew out a breath. "Yeah. I guess you do."

Luke pulled out his phone and made a call to someone who went by a call name. He quickly explained the situation, requested a boat and gear, and disconnected.

"My buddy will meet us at the marina with everything we need," Luke said.

"I guess it's good to have the kind of friends you do."

"Oh yeah." Luke glanced over at him. "What did you do for the Navy?"

"Search and rescue."

"Good. We might need it."

Mark gave him a single nod and tried to focus on getting Emma back. If he let his mind wander down the many potential bad outcomes, he'd lose his edge. And the edge was what kept you alive and winning.

Luke pulled into the marina parking lot and slid to a stop. They were out of the truck and running a second later. Even though the facility was officially closed for business, a light was still on in the office. They raced to the door and Mark was thrilled when he saw the manager at his desk. Luke banged on the door and the man hurried up.

"We're closed," he said as he opened the door.

Mark pushed in and pointed to the computer screen with the GPS system pulled up. He didn't know the man well, but there was no time to rectify that. "A man named Josef Danek rented a boat from you. He kidnapped my girlfriend. I need to know where that boat is."

The manager's eyes widened and he looked over at Luke, who nodded. Apparently, the two men's reputations were enough to get him moving. He hurried to his chair and pulled up the list of boats and accessed the one Josef had rented.

"I saw him pull out of the marina not long ago," the manager said. "There—he's accessing the pass."

"He's headed into the Gulf," Mark said, his stomach clenching.

"Go to channel 77 on your radio," Luke said. "I need a constant feed of where that boat is going. I'll radio in when we're off."

"But 77 is commercial," the manager said.

"And not likely to be busy this time of day," Luke said. "I'm sure the coast guard will forgive us."

Luke's phone signaled an incoming text. "We're up," he said and they hurried out.

Mark saw a man waving from the end of the dock, standing next to a Zodiac with a center console. He knew immediately that it was military issue. The man gave Luke a quick salute.

"You sure you don't need me, sir?" he asked.

"The less you are involved the better," Luke said. "Plausible deniability. If anyone asks, I requested equipment to plan an exercise."

The man gave Luke a single nod, then hurried away.

"Oh, man, I don't want to get you in trouble either," Mark said.

"Don't worry about me. I've got a favor or two I can call in if things go sideways."

"You mean things like having a civilian onboard a military-issued boat to go rescue another civilian?"

"I see it as having a former search-and-rescue expert consulting on how to conduct a mission at sea in an incoming storm."

Luke motioned to Mark to cast them off and a couple seconds later, they were pulling away from the marina. Then Luke changed the channel on the radio and asked for an update on the location of the yacht.

"Cleared the pass and headed out to sea, due south," the manager said.

Mark took a seat, trying to control his impatience as Luke slowly powered through the no-wake zone. It was only seconds, but felt like forever, when Luke finally kicked the throttle in and the boat leaped out of the water. They had no plan, other than to find the yacht. Mark had plenty of rescue experience, but it was usually military personnel or equipment, and they weren't being held hostage. But if they could get close enough to the yacht, Mark already knew he'd figure out a way to board, and then he'd take down Josef, freeing Emma once and for all.

He just hoped it wasn't already too late.

———

EMMA STRUGGLED to free herself from the ropes on her wrists, but they didn't budge. Josef had taken her from the apartment to the marina where they'd boarded a yacht. She'd thought about bolting when they'd gotten outside, but she knew Josef wouldn't hesitate to go back for Lily as leverage, and the little girl in the apartment alone was a sitting duck. Once they'd gotten on the boat, he'd tied her wrists and backhanded her so hard she'd fallen onto the floor. Then he'd dragged her into a closet with not even a sliver of light coming through and locked her in.

She'd heard the boat start up and felt them leaving the marina. They'd stopped several minutes later with the boat still running, then continued on at a fast clip until it slowed to take on the rise and fall of the Gulf's waves. She already knew her fate. Josef had made it clear when he'd bound her that he was going to take from her what was his due, then shoot her and toss her overboard. Emma knew that he'd said those things because he loved when people were afraid of him. She also had no doubt he was telling the truth.

Josef was going to kill her.

This was where her eight-year nightmare ended and unfortunately, it wasn't the ending she'd hoped for. The only thing she could do was keep trying to work on the ropes and hope she could fight Josef off when the time came. She'd taken self-defense courses over the years, and Luke had given her a refresher one evening when he was training Alayna. But she knew she was no match for Josef, who'd been studying martial arts his entire life. Plus, he had a gun. That tended to push every advantage to one direction.

She'd felt around in the tiny space for something she could use to wear down the ropes, but the closet was completely empty. There wasn't even a sharp edge on a wall or shelf to use. She twisted her hands again and cursed when the rope dug into her flesh. But it moved! She twisted her hands again, wincing at the pain, but it didn't feel as tight as before.

Suddenly, the door to the closet flew open and Josef stared down at her. Emma looked up at his smug, evil expression and wished she had a weapon. Never had she hated someone more. He reached down and yanked her up, wrenching her shoulder.

"Stop whining," he said. "You've got worse than that coming."

He shoved her forward toward the main living area of the yacht, and she pulled desperately, still trying to break free from the ropes. Maybe if she could get them off, she could jump off the boat and swim for land. Assuming they weren't too far offshore and assuming she could find an indication of where land was. It would be dark soon, if it wasn't already. But without her arms loose, it wouldn't matter. The Gulf was too much to tackle with just her legs.

"You've lucked out," Josef said as she walked through the galley that led to the back deck. "I had a good time planned— you know, to make up for all those dates where you put me off —but the boss says I have to just wrap up business and clear out."

Emma glanced out a porthole and her heart sank as she saw the dim light outside. No way she'd even be able to spot land, much less swim for it in the dark, which was right upon them.

"I'm so sorry you have to adhere to your usual boring work of killing people so they can't expose your father for the murdering criminal he is," she said.

Josef laughed. "My father is a genius. But he's gotten softer as he's gotten older. He actually thinks we could bring you into the fold."

They walked out onto the deck and he shoved her down on a bench.

"So I have a onetime offer for you," Josef said. "You can give up this foolish running and take a role with my father's organization, or you can die here. It's a great deal. Honestly, I don't even know why you'd be trusted to toe the line, but I guess killing you later is just as effective as killing you now."

Emma blinked. Of all the things she'd expected to hear, this was not one of them. Join Danek's organization? Good Lord, why? He'd killed her father without qualm. Why on earth would Ivan want Gustav's daughter working for him? Was his ego really that big?

"You're crazy," she said.

Josef nodded. "I think it's crazy too, but it wasn't my idea."

He stepped close to her and leaned over, running his finger down her face and onto her chest. "But I can't say I'd mind the perks. You look nice with that hair and the tan. You're a bit ragged for my lifestyle, but I could get you cleaned up. Maybe I'll undress you and start now."

"That's enough, Josef," Ivan's voice boomed from the cabin and a second later, he stepped out onto the deck.

Now Emma understood what the stop was for. Josef had picked Ivan up away from the marina, probably at a private dock where no one could see him.

"Katarina has done an admirable job evading us," Ivan said. "The organization can always use people who are clever and adaptable."

Josef shook his head, clearly disgusted at the thought.

"You've got to be joking," Josef said. "She's a liability."

"But she could be an asset," Ivan said. "And that's the offer."

"I spent eight years finding her—doing something that your other men could never do—accomplishing it long after you'd given up," Josef argued.

"And your efforts will be rewarded," Ivan said, "even though they went against my direct orders to let the situation go."

Emma stared, certain she'd been dropped into the twilight zone. None of this—except Josef's attitude—made any sense.

Ivan turned to her. "So what will it be—asset or liability?"

"You mean I could be an asset like my father?" she asked. "The man who served you for years and whom you killed without a second thought?"

Ivan shook his head. "Your father's death was long overdue, but I couldn't have two accidental deaths so close to me in such a short time frame."

"Two deaths?" Emma asked. "But you killed my mother as well. No one believes that car wreck was an accident."

"Of course it wasn't an accident," Ivan said, and then smiled. "But it also wasn't your mother."

"What?" Emma stiffened. "What are you talking about? They matched dental records."

"And if that dentist was indebted to you, it's a simple matter to have those records switched."

A wave of horror rushed through Emma. "You killed a woman in place of my mother? Why?"

"Not just any woman," Ivan said. "I killed my wife and told everyone she'd returned to her family in the old country. You see, long ago, in my village in Czechoslovakia, I met a girl—a beautiful girl, full of joy and promise—and I wanted nothing more than to be with her. But I was already betrothed and the marriage was necessary to get me into the US and to form my connections in this country. My wife was the key to everything and for many, many years, I had to pretend that I was devoted to her. But as her family and connections began to acquire prison sentences, die off, or leave for countries with no extradition laws, they and she became less important. I knew it was finally my time to have the life I wanted. With the woman I wanted."

"You and my mother?" Emma couldn't contain her shock. "But my father..."

"Was necessary to get your mother to the US," Ivan said. "Women don't work for my organization and even if that were not the case, my wife would never have tolerated one as beautiful as Helenka working beside me. So we found a suitable man, and I took him on."

"Oh my God," Emma whispered, her stomach rolling in disgust. Her own mother and Ivan Danek. Emma had known her life before she'd fled had been a lie, but she'd never known to what extent.

She looked at Josef. "And you're okay with this—with your father killing your mother?"

Josef shrugged. "My mother had me because an heir was

needed, but she had no interest in raising me. I'll be sadder when my nanny dies."

Emma knew what she should do. She should lie and say she'd be part of their evil empire and then plan her escape some other way. But she saw the gleam in Josef's eye and knew that any part she played would be short-lived. Josef wouldn't share with her unless he could own her, and if she agreed to Ivan's terms, she was certain that would be part of the deal.

"You said women don't work for your organization," Emma said.

"For your mother, I would make an exception," Ivan said. "I deny Helenka nothing, which is why you're not on the bottom of the ocean right now."

"How has she remained hidden?" Emma asked, still unable to believe that her mother was somehow alive. "Everyone in your organization knows what she looks like."

"Very true," Ivan said. "She lives a life of luxury on one of my estates—one that no one knows about. A little cosmetic surgery, a change of the hair... Surely, you of all people understand how someone can become another person."

Emma's head spun. How was all of this possible? Yet, despite the fact that she knew Ivan lied about most everything, on this one thing, she was certain he was telling the truth. Emma's father had been used by her mother and Ivan from day one. It didn't make him less than the murderer he was—and Emma was also sure that Coach Mayhern wasn't his only victim—but it made him slightly less awful than Ivan and her mother.

Her mother!

"My father requires an answer," Josef said. "There's a lot in it for you if you stick around."

He gave her a smile and rubbed his crotch.

A wave of nausea rolled over Emma, and every instinct that

yelled at her to play along was completely overridden by the disgust of imagining Josef's hands on her.

"I will never align with you," she said.

Josef's expression went hard and he grabbed her arm. "We'll see about that, won't we? I always get what I want. I found you. All I have to do is ask my father to give you to me as a reward for a job well done. I leased this boat for a week. Plenty of time to make you wish you'd made another choice, then rid my family of you and the trouble you caused forever."

"Let her go!"

Emma felt the blood drain from her face as her mother stepped out of the cabin and onto the deck. Even with the changes to her face and hair, Emma would have known her anywhere. But instead of the slightly bored and dissatisfied look she'd always worn, now Emma saw hardness and cunning.

"Helenka!" Ivan said, clearly as surprised as Emma at her mother's appearance. "What are you doing here?"

"Making sure things go as necessary," Helenka said and gave Josef a pointed look. "I said let her go."

Josef's face turned red. "I did your bidding for eight years. My father gave up, but because you asked, I kept going. Now you tell me to stop? After I did all the work? Took all the risks? You don't care about her, so why do you care if I have my fun?"

"Because she's your sister," Helenka said. "Why do you think I never wanted you to date?"

Ivan gasped, and Josef released Emma's arm as if she were on fire. Emma stared in shock. Was there anything about her life that had ever been the truth?

"My... She's my daughter?" Ivan asked, his disbelief so genuine that Emma realized she hadn't been the only one who'd been fooled by Helenka.

"You say that like it was never a possibility," Helenka said.

"But you got pregnant in the old country after you married Gustav," Ivan said. "I was already in the US."

"And you made a trip back to collect from those who still owed you," Helenka said.

Ivan's eyes widened. "Why didn't you tell me?"

"Because you married another woman," Helenka said.

"I killed my wife for you!" Ivan said.

"Almost thirty years too late," Helenka said.

"I needed her family," Ivan argued. "Her connections. You know this."

Helenka shrugged. "What I know is that I spent the best years of my life underneath an infertile lackey. Wearing leather when I should have been wearing furs. Vacationing to exotic locations once a year instead of living in them every day. Your wife had my life, and you cared more about the money than me. You could have gotten rid of her sooner if you'd wanted to."

"You've gone mad," Ivan said. "I won't tolerate this from you. You stand here and talk to me as if I'm your servant. Have you forgotten your place?"

Helenka pulled out a pistol and pointed it at Ivan. "I'm certain of my place. Are you?"

"Josef, shoot her!" Ivan said.

"*Or*, Josef, you could let me shoot your father and then you'd control everything," Helenka said. "I only ask for the home I live in and a monthly stipend for living expenses. I think I'm owed that much for all that I've given up. I care nothing about Ivan's empire. It would all be yours."

Josef looked between the two, clearly surprised by the turn this had taken. Then his jaw started to close, and his eyes narrowed as he looked at his father. And as an evil smirk crept onto his face, Emma knew that neither she nor Ivan would make it back to shore.

# CHAPTER TWENTY-NINE

MARK CLENCHED THE SIDE OF THE BOAT AS THEY POUNDED through the waves in the Gulf. They'd been en route twenty minutes now but still hadn't caught up to the yacht, and with every passing minute, Mark grew more afraid that Emma was going to be lost to him. Luke cut the throttle and grabbed the radio as he'd been doing every few minutes to get an updated position on the yacht. The starting and stopping made their progress slower, but going fast in the wrong direction wouldn't benefit anyone.

"Position?" Luke asked.

The marina manager gave the coordinates. "She's been stopped for a couple minutes now."

Luke glanced at Mark, his expression grim. As long as the boat was moving, that meant Josef was occupied, assuming he was alone, which is what they'd elected to go with. But short of engine trouble, there was no reason for the boat to stop, save one.

"How far?" Mark asked as Luke punched in the coordinates.

"Five minutes, maybe less."

Mark blew out a breath. In five minutes, everything might be over.

He strained to see something in the ever-increasing darkness, but the moon kept dipping behind storm clouds, limiting their vision to only what was right in front of them. In the seconds the moon broke free from the clouds, Mark scanned the water, looking for any sign of the boat.

He checked his watch—two minutes had passed since he'd gotten the five-minute estimate from Luke, but he still hadn't seen anything, not even the running lights from a passing boat. The wind had picked up and the gusts contained bursts of cooler air that always preceded rain. Mark prayed that the storm held off a little longer. The odds were already stacked against them, and a storm would just make matters twice as bad.

"There!" Luke shouted and Mark leaned forward.

Finally, he made out lights about a hundred yards in the distance. Luke grabbed the radio and verified the boat's coordinates.

"That's it," Luke said and pulled binoculars from a diver's bag and passed them to Mark before pulling out another pair.

Mark immediately zeroed in on the boat but could only make out the running lights. Then a door on the cabin of the boat opened and light flooded the deck. He sucked in a breath as he spotted Emma sitting on a back bench and Josef standing in front of her. Another man stood off to the side, and Mark recognized him from pictures as Ivan Danek. Oddly enough, a woman had come out of the cabin. Mark hadn't pegged Danek as the type who had women working for his organization, but maybe Josef was making things progressive.

"Josef and Ivan, I presume," Luke said. "Who's the woman?"

"No idea. Josef has a gun."

"I'm betting the others do as well."

The rain began to fall, first in spotted drops, then harder, and Mark knew the deluge was coming. He blew out a breath. "You can't get closer without them hearing the engine."

"I know." Luke opened a bench and pulled out fishing rods and rain slickers. "Stick this in that holder and secure it."

Mark immediately clued in. The rods were their cover. They were just two guys out fishing who got caught in the storm. Once they got the rods secured and they'd donned the slickers, Luke pulled out the distress flag and fixed it into place.

"Now I'll approach and we'll ask for help," Luke said. "Radio and GPS aren't working and we can't make our way back inland. We'll ask them to call for help or guide us back in. Pull your hood as low down as you can. Josef knew where to find Emma, so he probably knows what you look like."

Mark nodded and double-checked his weapon as Luke started inching forward. The rain was getting harder now and the clouds were so thick they'd completely blocked the moon. Only the lights from the yacht penetrated the darkness enough to guide them. As they inched closer, Mark lifted his binoculars, trying to make out something on the boat. The figures were still on the back deck, but they were all standing now. If they went back inside, it would be even harder to rescue Emma.

Either way, the odds weren't in their favor.

---

EMMA STARED AT JOSEF, seeing the shift in his expression as soon as it crossed his mind. Unbelievable! He was going to kill his own father. It shouldn't surprise her, but Emma just couldn't wrap her mind around the way these people thought.

"Let me do it," Josef said.

"You can't be serious!" Ivan yelled. "You're my son!"

"The son you refused to put in charge," Josef said. "The son you sent Marek to check up on. Marek—who isn't your blood and is a fool at best. But don't worry, that fool just checked up on me for the last time. As soon as I get back to California, I'll deal with Marek."

"You think my organization is just going to follow you?" Ivan asked. "What are you going to tell them when I don't return? My men know where I went. They'll know what you did. They won't follow someone they can't trust."

Josef smiled. "*My* men will hear that Katarina escaped and managed to get hold of a gun. That she shot you before I could take her out, but that I avenged your death."

"They won't believe you," Ivan said.

"But they'll believe me," Helenka said. "When I return from the dead and tell them how I assisted with my own daughter's death to keep the organization secure, they won't question things. Your attorneys know who cuts the checks and won't balk at shifting everything to Josef's name. Josef and I will report you as missing, and law enforcement will assume you've fled the country or that a rival has eliminated you. Either way, they won't work hard to find you."

Ivan, realizing that his longtime lover and son were actually conspiring to kill him, reached for the gun at his waist. But before he could pull the trigger, Helenka fired three times, hitting him squarely in the chest. He staggered backward, hand on his chest, and Emma could see the blood gushing between his fingers. As he neared the side of the boat, a huge wave tossed the entire vessel up, and Emma, Helenka, and Josef all fell onto the deck. When they jumped back up, Ivan was gone.

Helenka and Josef rushed to the side and peered over.

"No way he could survive that," Josef said.

"But someone might find the body," Helenka said. "I wanted him weighted down."

"No choice now," Josef said. "But we need to head farther out before we get rid of Katarina. We can't risk having both bodies found in the same location."

Emma had inched toward the opposite side of the boat as they'd discussed how to dispose of her body. The ropes around her wrists had loosened when she fell and she'd finally managed to twist her hands free. Her chances of surviving the water in the storm were already slim, but if they went even farther out to sea, her odds decreased with every inch. In the distance, she'd seen a flash of light—small, but visible. Then it had blinked away. But possibly it was another boat or even the shore. Jumping in was a horrible option, but it was the only one she had.

She inched up the back of the bench and said a quick prayer.

Then as the rain began to fall, she leaned back and fell into the stormy sea.

———

MARK JUMPED up from the back bench as the shots rang out and grabbed the console as the blood rushed from his face. The woman had shot Ivan and he'd gone overboard. Luke's idea to fool Josef as distressed fishermen was over, as they'd just witnessed a murder. Luke cursed and grabbed the radio, sending a mayday call for the coast guard. Mark clutched the console as Luke flipped the GPS back on then launched the boat forward. As they pounded through the surf, Mark prayed for a miracle.

The rain stung his face and he squinted, trying to protect

his eyes so he could lock in on the yacht. Suddenly, the moon peeked out from behind the clouds and the yacht appeared right in front of them. Mark watched in horror as Emma fell backward off the side of the boat. Even over the roar of the storm, he heard the thud when she hit the side of the boat as the waves tossed her about. Josef and the woman ran to the side of the boat and peered over, and Mark felt his stomach drop when Josef leaned over the side with his pistol.

Luke swung the Zodiac around to the side Emma had fallen from. "Get Emma! I'll cover you!"

Mark readied himself at the side of the boat as Luke drove right by where Emma had gone overboard. As soon as Mark could see the back deck of the yacht, he dived into the turbulent water. As soon as he surfaced, he heard gunfire behind him and knew Luke was trying to draw attention away from him. He'd said a prayer for all of them as he dived. Luke was a SEAL, but he was also outmanned and had no cover.

But Mark couldn't worry about Luke right now. He had to find Emma, or all of this was for nothing. Even though the Gulf was usually clear twenty or thirty feet down this far offshore, visibility required light, which was scarce, and the storm was impairing him even further. He could barely make out his arms as he swam.

*Think! If she is unconscious, how would she have drifted?*

He stopped swimming for a couple seconds and released all the air he'd been holding, allowing himself to drift with the current. Then he swam that direction. His chest ached and he forced himself into a calm state where his body wouldn't try to suck in that breath that it desperately wanted. All of his training with the Navy and every wave that had held him under during his surfing career rushed back into play.

He spread his arms and legs out as he swam, hoping to make contact with her. Another thirty seconds, maybe less, was all he had left and then he'd have to surface. His chest ached more every second that passed and finally, he knew he had to get a breath of air or he wouldn't make it. Silently cursing, he forced himself around and started up to the surface, but as he went, his leg brushed against something.

Frantic, he whirled around and reached out with his arms, trying to find what he'd touched. Maybe it had just been a fish or debris, but if there was any chance...

And then hair swirled around his hand. He grabbed it and pulled, and Emma's body appeared. He wrapped one arm under hers and swam as quickly as he could for the surface. He had to get the salt water out and air in before she drowned. Gasping for air, he broke the surface and clung to Emma in the tumultuous sea. He tried to check her pulse, but it was impossible while being tossed about. They desperately needed to get her out of the water.

He couldn't hear gunfire any longer, but that could mean a lot of things, and most of them, not good. He blinked several times trying to clear the salt water from his eyes so that he could see what the limited visibility offered. The odds had not been in Luke's favor any more than they'd been in his. And finding Emma was only the first miracle he needed. Now he prayed for several more. The blinding rain made it almost impossible to see anything, but off to the right, he barely made out a light.

Praying that Luke had won the battle with Josef and that the light was friend and not foe, he started swimming toward it. Then his hand struck something soft and he squinted as he tried to figure out what it was. At that moment, lightning ripped through the sky, and he gasped as he realized he was clutching the body of a very dead Ivan Danek.

Something hard bumped into his waist, and fear coursed through him as the shark fin surfaced on the other side of the body and grabbed the arm. He shoved as hard as he could against the body and swam in the opposite direction. A bloody body in the water was like ringing the dinner bell for ocean predators.

His arms and leg muscles burned with the strain of not only keeping them afloat but moving them against the storm and away from the body. Every few seconds, a wave crashed into them, tossing them back and flooding his eyes and mouth with salt water. Despite all his years of training and careers spent in the ocean, Mark knew he was about to lose this battle. It was the first time he'd ever felt despair start to creep in while he was in the water, but he could no longer keep reality from taking over his thoughts.

Suddenly, a light shone in his eyes and he closed them, blinded by the brightness. This was it. Josef had spotted them and all of this was for naught. A second later, he heard a shout.

Luke!

He opened his eyes and the light was gone, but he could barely make out Luke in the Zodiac just a couple feet away. A life preserver landed right next to him, and he clutched it with one arm and Emma with the other as Luke pulled them in. He hung from the side of the boat and helped Luke get Emma in, then pulled himself over and they started CPR on Emma.

They were silent as they worked, and Mark was beginning to lose hope when finally, Emma gasped and coughed up seawater, regaining some consciousness. But relief was short-lived because a second later, a bullet flew right past Mark's head and went into the boat's engine. The motor sputtered, then died. A second bullet whizzed by and tore through the side of the Zodiac, and Mark pulled his pistol and fired in response.

The boat wouldn't last long with that hole in the side, especially in the storm, and they were drifting right back into the ring of blood where sharks were already circling. A defensive position was certain death. They had to go on the offensive.

"Cover me," Mark yelled to Luke before he dived over the side of the boat.

He'd gotten a good idea of the position of the yacht before he entered the water and stayed just below the surface as he swam toward it. It was hard to estimate the distance covered in the storm so he'd have to rely on his instincts and all those years he'd spent in open water. Josef and the woman wouldn't be expecting an attack from the water. It was the only move they had left. If they were engaged with Luke in the raft then he could come at them from the other side.

His hand struck something hard and he grasped the anchor line, pulling himself toward the side of the boat. Then he slowly surfaced. He heard gunfire as soon as he broke the surface and prayed that neither Luke nor Emma had taken a hit as he stuck his pistol in his mouth and began to pull himself up the anchor rope. If Luke could just keep them engaged a little longer, he'd have his shot.

Or shots. Because he needed two deadly accurate ones.

By the sound of the gunshots, Mark could tell that Josef and the woman were both on the other side of the yacht. His arms were already strained from swimming in the storm and pulling Emma to the surface, but he knew he had to make one last huge effort because he had to take out both Josef and the woman before they could return fire. Summoning every ounce of strength he had left in his body, he pulled himself up the side of the yacht with one arm and leveled the gun at Josef and fired.

Direct hit!

The bullet caught Josef in the neck, and he dropped his gun and grabbed his throat. But before Mark could take another shot, a huge wave tossed the yacht and he lost his grip and fell back into the water. When he surfaced, he was staring down the barrel of a pistol held by the woman. A shot rang out and he braced himself for the impact that never came. Instead, the woman's eyes and mouth opened wide and she spun to face the back of the yacht as Emma crawled up the ladder and took another shot.

This one was fatal.

The gun fell from her hand onto the deck and she collapsed, still staring at Emma in shock. Mark tossed his pistol onto the yacht and swam for the ladder, where Emma had fallen when another wave tossed the boat. She was still hanging on to the ladder, but it took him only a second to realize that her left arm was wedged between the ladder and the boat. With every toss of the waves, she screamed in pain.

He pulled himself onto the swim deck and knelt in front of the ladder. He knew it was going to hurt her, but he had no choice, so he leaned over, grasped her under her arms and pulled as hard as he could. Her arm wrenched loose from the ladder and she slumped onto the swim deck with him.

"Luke?" Mark asked.

Emma shook her head. "The boat sank. He told me to dive but there were sharks nearby. I saw the fins."

Mark climbed onto the back deck of the yacht and grabbed a spotlight. He trained it on the water where the Zodiac had been. He and Emma yelled for Luke as he moved the light across the surface, but there was nothing.

He was starting to lose all hope when a voice sounded over a loudspeaker.

"US Coast Guard approaching!"

Suddenly, a giant beam of light lit up the entire back of the boat and they held their arms up to shade their eyes as the coast guard cutter pulled alongside. And the first thing they saw was the smiling face of Luke, looking down at them.

Mark turned around and gathered Emma in his arms and pulled her close, careful not to squeeze her left arm, then lowered his mouth to hers. Their lips were rough and the kiss was salty, but they were both alive.

Which made it absolutely perfect.

# CHAPTER THIRTY

EMMA CARRIED THE MARGARITAS OUT TO THE DECK AND sank onto the bench next to Mark. Their bruises, which had turned a brilliant purple in the last few days, were finally starting to fade a little, and her arm was aching less and less. The harder part to heal from had been the revelations that were made on the deck of the yacht and those fatal shots she'd delivered to the woman who was supposed to be her biggest champion but had turned out to be the enemy. Emma still had nightmares where she saw her mother's expression as the bullet tore through her, but Bea had gotten her set up with a counselor. And even though she'd only had one session, she was already processing things better.

As soon as she placed the drinks on the table in front of them, Mark gathered her in his arms and gave her a long, lingering kiss—an appetizer, so to speak, of what the night held. Lily was spending the night with Nelly and her husband and either being spoiled rotten or corrupted, likely both. She'd had a couple nights of restless sleep after Emma's rescue, but with a level of resilience that only children seemed to manage, was already letting the entire episode slip from her memory.

After the rescue, Mark and Emma had maintained their friendship status in front of Lily, but after a couple days, the clever girl had finally asked one night at bedtime if he would make Miss Emma his girlfriend so that Lily could have a mother again.

She'd found him out on the deck that night, crying, and had been alarmed at first, but then he'd told her about the exchange and they'd cried together. For Lily and for Beth. But they'd also promised to make the best life for the three of them, and the next day, they'd told Lily that they would start working on being a family.

And so they had.

"I love you so much," Mark said as he broke off the kiss. "I never thought this would happen for me again."

"I never thought it would happen for me at all," Emma said.

"Did you talk to Levi today?"

She nodded. "The FBI and the DA's office are busy dismantling Danek's empire. They've raided his private properties and found so much evidence they'll be unraveling it for months, but Levi is beside himself. He's officially a hero, which appears to embarrass him, but I know he's thrilled about how everything turned out. What about Luke?"

"He said his commander didn't even raise an eyebrow at the story he concocted about trying to plan for a drill and losing the boat, even though the man absolutely knew he was lying. Granted, they'll never find the Zodiac, so those bullet holes won't be giving him away, but he took a big risk. One I'll always appreciate."

"Me too. And I'm forever thankful that he's so valuable to the Navy that they're pretending nothing was amiss." She smiled and brushed her lips across his. "It's nice to be surrounded by heroes."

"You were pretty heroic yourself."

She kissed him again.

"Sounds like we're perfect for each other."

*I HOPE you enjoyed this visit to Tempest Island. If you want to know if Alayna's restaurant will open, about Bea's run for mayor, and if Izzy's budding romance moves forward, look for the next book in the series, coming in 2023.*

# UNDERTOW – COMING 2023

*When Jill Morgan left Tempest Island after high school, she didn't have a plan. Her parents had moved to New England to care for aging relatives and Jill had gone off to college, but with no idea of what she wanted to be when she grew up. Then an observant English professor pointed out her talent for creative writing and encouraged her to pursue it. Jill never expected to become a bestseller, but her books—written under the pseudonym Kate Coleson—had brought her millions of happy readers.*

*And a stalker.*

*When the police suggest she duck off radar until they locate the man threatening her, her first thought is returning to Tempest Island. After all, her real name has been carefully hidden from the public, so she ought to be safe in her hometown. Right?*

Made in the USA
Coppell, TX
05 November 2022